The Lady in Question

"He was trying to kill *me*," Elyse said.

"Tell me what happened."

Elyse nodded. "Campbell Sawyer. My friend. She had an accident. She borrowed my car yesterday, but I know it wasn't an accident. The man who was following me thought she was me. . . . If she dies, it's going to be all my fault." The tears began sliding down her face. I knew my cue and handed her a tissue.

"Who do you think this man is?"

"The man who killed Julio."

"Who is Julio?"

"My husband."

DEATH ON A CASUAL FRIDAY

A SCOTIA MacKinnon MYSTERY

SHARON DUNCAN

A SIGNET BOOK

SIGNET
Published by New American Library, a division of
Penguin Putnam Inc., 375 Hudson Street,
New York, New York 10014, U.S.A.
Penguin Books Ltd, 27 Wrights Lane,
London W8 5TZ, England
Penguin Books Australia Ltd, Ringwood,
Victoria, Australia
Penguin Books Canada Ltd, 10 Alcorn Avenue,
Toronto, Ontario, Canada M4V 3B2
Penguin Books (N.Z.) Ltd, 182–190 Wairau Road,
Auckland 10, New Zealand

Penguin Books Ltd, Registered Offices:
Harmondsworth, Middlesex, England

First published by Signet, an imprint of New American Library,
a division of Penguin Putnam Inc.

First Printing, August 2001
10 9 8 7 6 5 4 3 2 1

To the memory of my father, with love.

WITH SINCERE APPRECIATION . . .

To Michelle Kirsch, for editorial assistance on both sides of the Atlantic.

To Ed De Avila, Marion Duncan, Martin Garren, Jr., Joe Gores, Carolyn Hart, Nancy Hird, Cynthia Hubbard-Tripp, Monica Meeker, Portia Polner, Robert Stamm, Meridee Talbott, Louise Wells, and Rudi and Bill Weissinger, for moral support, astute reading, and editorial suggestions.

To LTC Philip Bauso, USAR, Ret.; Bill Cummins, San Juan County (Washington) Sheriff; Fay Faron, the Rat Dog Dick Detective Agency, San Francisco; Inspector Sergeant Holly Pera, San Francisco Police Department; *Redshift* skipper Michael Smith; and San Francisco attorney Joseph Tomsic, for sharing knowledge, experience, and procedures on private investigation, law enforcement, and firearms.

To Elaine and Bill Petrocelli and their extraordinary staff at The Book Passage, Corte Madera, California, for exposure to the best and the brightest.

To my agent, Meg Ruley, and my editor, Ellen Edwards, who believed in the book and made it a reality.

PART 1

Don't wait for the Last Judgment. It takes place every day.

—Albert Camus

1

It would be the perfect crime.
The crime with no evidence.
The murder with no motive.
Above "T" dock, to the east of the new Berkeley Harbor Master's office, a man with a dark drooping mustache zipped his yellow foul-weather jacket and studied the notices pinned to the kiosk.

Mussel quarantine warning.
Sailboat for sale. Coronado 26'. Two Spinnakers. $4,000.
Lost cat on Dock "S" Slip 19. Tortoiseshell. Reward.

Without moving, the man shifted his focus and gazed down at the security gate and beyond the gate to the moored boats. Beyond the breakwater, the summer afternoon winds were whitecapping the waters of San Francisco Bay.

There was no sign of the Camelot. He stared over his left shoulder. Behind him, beyond the marina parking lot, the long municipal fishing pier was thick with Berkeleyites, shoulders hunched in the cold July sun. He had seen them when he drove in: walkers, hikers, couples with small children, small groups of somber, dedicated fishermen. Sniffing the salt air, bracing themselves against the gusting wind and the dense curtain of fog billowing over the red towers of the Golden

Gate Bridge, they were oblivious to the drama about to unfold.

Along the path to the man's right, a lone cyclist in black-and-green spandex approached, helmeted head down, legs pumping like pistons. The man with the mustache leaned forward, intent on the ad for the sail-boat. One hand shielded his face.

The cyclist passed.

The man heard a mewling sound and looked down. A half-grown tortoiseshell cat wound itself around his ankles. He reached down and stroked it. The cat purred and arched its back, then strolled away in the direction of the Yacht Club, tail waving in the air. He watched it move away and wondered if Snowy was okay.

The man's head ached. He rubbed his right temple. Walking toward the dock with its locked mesh security gate at the foot of the ramp, he pulled a cell phone from his jacket pocket, lifted it to his ear, and leaned against the sturdy wooden and metal railing on the side of the ramp. The large coniferous tree behind him shad-owed his face. Phone to his ear, he reviewed the sce-nario. His lips moved silently, as if chanting.

Work alone.

Blend in.

Disappear immediately.

He continued watching, sweeping his gaze over the moored boats, and finally he spotted it. A sailboat with a dark-blue hull appeared at the end of the fairway. The headsail lay on the foredeck, the white mainsail was tied along the boom with faded blue sail ties. There were two men on board: the Jew and the Bean Picker. He watched the boat approaching. White cursive letters along the hull of the boat proclaimed it the Camelot.

The man jerked involuntarily. He scratched his mus-tache and watched the boat glide into the slip and come to a stop immediately below and to the right of where he was standing. The shorter, brown-skinned one in the Greek fisherman's cap stepped off first and tied the bow line around a large metal cleat on the dock, then caught the other docking line the Jew threw to him. He knotted the second line around another cleat and arranged the ends of both lines in precise, flat coils on the wooden dock.

"Aha, a Flemish coil. You're getting way too fancy for me, compadre." The words of the taller, bearded man in the white skipper's cap floated upward.

The brown-skinned man gave a quick thumbs-up. Joining his companion in the cockpit, he flung himself on the seat, his back to the heavy security gate, and pushed his longish, straight black hair under the cap. He leaned back against the lifelines. "Our timing, capitán, it was impeccable. Another thirty minutes and we wouldn't have gotten the spinnaker down." He spread his arms along the lifelines. "¡Qué día más increíble!"

The man with the mustache listened and clenched his jaw.

Effing spic.

Listening to the brown-skinned man roiled images of a long-ago autumn afternoon. The roar of the crowd when he intercepted the pass and headed for the end zone. The jolt when he was tackled and the sickening knife of pain when his knee met the shoe of the quarterback from Yakima. The effing bean picker from Yakima. One of the effing mud people.

A cold stream of hate coursed through the man's body. The headache was getting worse. He shivered and continued watching his quarry.

"Spinnaker, hell, we wouldn't even have found the Gate. That fog isn't exactly creeping in on little cat feet. How about some liquid refreshment? We'll do the sails later." The bearded skipper went belowdecks, returned with two aluminum cans, lowered his lanky body onto the seat, facing his companion. Twelve miles away on Point Bonita, a foghorn boomed.

"What do you suppose the poor people are doing today?" the skipper said. Both men smiled, popped the cans, and swigged appreciatively.

The man with the mustache narrowed his eyes, glanced back toward the parking lot, saw no one. He entered a set of numbers on his cell phone and checked his attire one more time: faded blue jeans with a ragged hole above the right knee, worn topsiders, gloves with the fingertips cut out, a yachting cap that said "East Bay Sailing Club." And as a finishing touch: the yellow foul-weather jacket that was perfect to cover the shoulder holster.

All the right stuff.

His throat was dry. He swallowed and adjusted the cap, eyes shaded with black wraparound sunglasses. He touched the comforting bulge of the shoulder holster. He smiled. It was time.

Time for payback.

Time for Christ's sword.

Time to deal in lead.

The foghorn boomed again, low and mournful. Farther out on "T" dock, two women in yellow foul-weather jackets strolled toward the locked gate. As they approached, the shorter woman with curly dark hair pulled a key out of her jacket. It dangled from a red-and-blue miniature plastic float, unsinkable if dropped in the murky harbor.

The man with the mustache gazed over his shoulder once again, glimpsed a small red foreign car turning into the far end of the parking lot. Damn.

His index finger pressed the Send button on the cell phone. He strode down the ramp toward the locked gate, a friendly smile on his face.

Now.

2

Early November

Character is destiny. Don't ever forget it, child.

I heard it often from my Grandmother Jessica, a sturdy and taciturn Scotswoman whose ancestors had sailed from the rocky Western Isles. She might have added that geography is also destiny, especially for an island dweller.

Whether it was character or geography or negative karma that lured me into the Montenegro case, I'll never know. If I'd had even a glimmer of the convoluted machinations that would be set in motion that windy, overcast morning in early November, I swear I would've cast off *DragonSpray*'s lines and sailed away for ports unknown.

But I didn't.

Instead, I closed the padlock on the *DragonSpray*'s hatch cover and stepped down onto the dock. The air was damp with autumn, the wind out of the southeast with a tang of salt and a serious promise of early storms from the Gulf of Alaska. Rounding the flashing marker on Reid Rock, the green-and-white Washington State auto ferry pushed a bow wave through the deep, current-infested waters of San Juan Channel. To the west of the marina, the village of Friday Harbor climbed up the rocky hillside with picture-postcard perfection. One of the ten best places to retire in the U.S., a major East Coast daily described it. A place where nothing wicked ever comes. A real estate agent's dream.

I'm not a real estate agent. I'm a private investigator on San Juan Island, a thirteen thousand-year-old pile of rock in the San Juan Archipelago that lies between mainland Washington State and Vancouver Island in British Columbia. I live aboard *DragonSpray*, a thirty-eight-foot replica of the sailing yacht the intrepid Captain Joshua Slocum sailed around the world in the last years of the nineteenth century. Most of my day-to-day work consists of research and investigation for attorneys and insurance brokers and occasional private clients on San Juan, Orcas and Lopez Islands.

The November day was sunny; my mood was cheery and lighthearted. Last week I'd closed the missing diamonds case over on Orcas; the Petrovsky estate matter was on hold pending the appearance of a missing heir; I had a nine-o'clock appointment with a new client; and Nick and I were going to take *'Spray* up to Ganges on Saltspring Island for the weekend. Nick is Nicholas Anastazi, my lover and significant other, a maritime attorney with an office in Seattle overlooking Elliott Bay and a house here on the island overlooking Haro Strait and the Discovery Islands. Life was almost as good as it gets.

"Morning, Scotia." My nearest marina neighbor, a recently divorced, clinically depressed mortgage broker, moseyed onto the deck of *Pumpkin Seed*, his thirty-foot white plastic motor yacht. Coffee cup in hand, he yawned and ran his hand over the gray bristle on his chin.

"Morning, Henry." I closed the lifelines, stepped back, and caught one foot in a loop of the yellow shore power cord Henry had run along *my* side of the dock because it was too short to reach from *his* boat to the power post. And not only was the electrical cord too short, it was old and frayed and the wires were showing through, and it wasn't the first time I had tripped over it. I grabbed at *DragonSpray*'s toe rail for support and glared at Henry.

"I know, I know," he said. "I'm going over to Anacortes next week. I'll get a new cord."

"Great idea, Henry," I said with frost in my voice. "That's thirty amps lying naked there. And while you're at it, why not get a longer one so you can run it along *your* side of the dock. Might save one of us from electrocution or hypothermia." Without waiting for an answer, I turned my back, closed the lifelines, and gave *'Spray* a visual once-over. The indigo mainsail cover I'd splurged on when the check came in from the De Angelo arson case was my pride and joy. But I noticed one of the mooring lines would soon need replacement, and I was going to need a canvas cover for the newly varnished hatch boards or the bright work wouldn't survive the winter storms. Always something.

I simultaneously regretted and rejoiced that I no longer used *'Spray* as my office. A home office is fine, but on a sailboat, space belowdecks is intimate. Intimacy is not something I encourage with my clients. After a spine-chilling visit from an estranged wife with multiple personalities, I rented a one-room second-floor office in the Olde Gazette Building on Guard Street.

I bade adieu to Henry, who was now accompanied by a sleep-tousled young woman at least twenty years his junior with feathery dark hair. Last week's sleep-over had been a redhead. I headed up "G" dock, wondering what next week's trolling at the pub would net him.

The tide was out and the main ramp that connected the floating docks with terra firma was canted steeply. I spied Matt Petersen, looking like a bearded Norseman, stomping down the other side of the wide ramp, red toolbox in hand. His face was set and closed. I raised a hand in greeting, but he ignored me. Matt, one of Friday Harbor's commercial fishermen and the husband of my best friend, Angela, appeared to be off to a bad start for the day.

I shrugged and trudged uphill, past the Port building, the Spinnaker Restaurant and the movie theater. At the bakery, I stood in line behind a tall man with curly brown hair and a cap that said "Seattle Huskies," paid the bored young woman in oversize denim overalls for my sticky bun and orange juice and dropped two quarters in the vending machine for this morning's edition of *U.S.A. Today*.

Scanning the feature article that focused on the declining polar bear population, I nearly collided in the doorway with a blonde woman I'd never seen before. She glared at me and continued berating her companion, a handsome man with skin the color of rich latte. "I told you, Art, I have to be back in Redmond tomorrow. Just make it happen." Her voice was snappish. She wore neatly pressed designer jeans and a red North Face jacket.

"Hey, don't get on my case. This was your idea, remember. You *had* to ride the cute ferry, *had* to explore the quaint little village, *had* to see the killer whales." The man nodded at me and followed her inside.

I hated it when couples quarreled in public, and these two were destroying my optimistic, all's-right-with-the-world mood. I let the door slam behind me and headed for the office.

The two-story, brown-shingled Olde Gazette Building on Guard Street—I call it the OGB—had housed the *Friday Gazette* since its inception in 1926. Several years ago the *Gazette* moved to new quarters on Blair Street and the owner sold the building to a California couple. The OGB is located in one of the town's historical areas, which seemed to provide an excuse for not updating the building. Since it hasn't been improved anytime in the recent past, my rent is more reasonable than in non-historical buildings. There were two cars parked outside the OGB this morning: a dusty tan Morris Minor and equally dusty red Karmann-Ghia.

The main floor of the OGB enjoys an open-space plan, most of which is occupied by Zelda Jones, proprietress of New Millennium Communications, and her canine consort, a black Labrador named Dakota. Zelda is a graphic artist and computer consultant whose primary source of income derives from creating elegant brochures and provocative web sites for her island clients. New Millennium serves as communications clearinghouse and reception area for myself and Soraya, the naturopath from Lopez Island who rents the downstairs office and comes to Friday Harbor two days a week.

Zelda does research for me when my information needs exceed my modest computer skills—which is fairly often—or when I have a sufficient number of clients to afford her, which is less frequent. However, in the past year, the number of clients has increased. I don't know if the increase is due to my growing reputation, or is directly related to a proliferation in the number of items published in the Sheriff's Log of the *Gazette*.

New Millennium was fragrant with freshly brewed coffee and resounding with opera music. I poured a cup of Starbucks breakfast roast, retrieved two pink message slips from my mail cubby and greeted Zelda. Her ensemble consisted of a black-watch plaid kilt, white sweater, black-and-white argyles, and clogs. Her long, straight, below-the-shoulder hair was a deep henna red today, the top styled to resemble stalactites. Or maybe they're stalagmites. I can never remember which point up and which point down. Her eye shadow matched her hair.

One of my messages was from the judge's wife, requesting an appointment. The other was from Nick. He was back on the island, would call later about dinner tonight. Glancing toward the nearest quadraphonic speaker, I inquired as to the operatic artist. It's an arrangement we've refined since I moved my office from the boat. While I don't have any great interest in opera, Zelda lives and breathes it. Among many other lessons life has taught me is that investing a few seconds' interest in one's neighbor's passions can produce significant returns.

"Julius Caesar," she responded without looking away from her large-size monitor. "Beverly Sills as Cleopatra lamenting her love life."

"Nice." I nodded and moved toward the narrow stairway. A lamentable love life is a state Zelda is intimately acquainted with.

"The Snow Queen is upstairs."

I looked back. "Excuse me?"

"Your new client," Zelda offered with a wave toward the open stairway that led to my second-floor cubicle. "She didn't want to wait down here with the peasants."

Much of my investigative work is done over the phone or by e-mail. It is quite common to spend weeks or even months on a case and never meet the client. When someone does request to see me, it is usually a local who wants to check me out. I looked up the stairway.

She was tall and boyishly slender, and she stood beside the dirty window outside my office, staring down at the untended vacant lot on Jensen's Alley. She wore faded blue jeans and a denim barn jacket that was too big for her and had a dark smear on one sleeve. Her brown stable boots were dusty, the kind my daughter Melissa wore for a year when she was eleven and horse-crazy and just before she discovered boys. And despite her attire, she didn't look like a local.

She turned as I came up the stairs, which had a wonderful historical creak in every step.

"Good morning." I extended my hand. "I'm Scotia MacKinnon." She was blonde and thirty-something with a peaches-and-cream complexion and eyes as clear and blue-green as the waters off Green Turtle Key.

"Good morning." She neither offered her name nor responded to my outstretched hand, simply stood beside me while I juggled the coffee cup, bakery bag, newspaper and message slips, fumbled for my key and unlocked the heavy wooden door that said "S. J. MacKinnon, Research and Investigations." I switched on the old art deco lamp on the desk and motioned her inside.

She hesitated in the doorway, looked around the room, took in the scarred oak desk I inherited from the previous tenant, the two white wicker chairs with dark-green cushions from Pier One, the tall healthy ficus in the corner by the window. Her face brightened. Somewhat. As if it was better than she expected. For no good reason, I was glad I'd tidied up the stack of files last night and piled them on the credenza behind the desk.

"It's . . . nice," she said.

"Thank you."

She sat in the wicker chair farthest from the desk, put a big leather handbag on the floor, and shrugged out of her jacket. She was pretty, like a finely molded porcelain figurine is pretty. Pale blonde hair fell to her shoulders. I looked at her eyes again. Aquamarine eyes that expressed no emotion whatever. Perfectly groomed brows and pale lashes lightly tipped with brown mascara. A strong, rectangular face with a straight nose, prominent cheekbones and a determined chin. Her pale pink mouth turned up at the corners despite the emptiness of her eyes. A pearl eardrop decorated the exact center of each earlobe. Her beauty was effortless, and I felt the inevitable pang of envy that a woman of ordinary looks feels when confronted with such perfection. She crossed one faded denim knee over the other and looked expectantly at me without smiling.

I looked expectantly back, thinking for the umpteenth time that my clients—the ones who visited me in person—often behaved as if they'd been summoned to my office. As if I'd invited them and would tell them how to repair their lives.

"How can I help you, Ms.—?"

I let the interrogation hang in the silence. There was no response.

"Coffee?"

She shook her head, frowning. Feeling like a damn therapist or a divorce attorney, I reached in my bottom desk drawer for an audiocassette tape, inserted it in the player on the side of my desk, turned the volume low. The hollow notes of Larkin's bamboo flute filled the quiet room. I leaned back in my chair and looked at her. The music seemed to have unlocked something. Tears were falling silently down her smooth cheeks, and I resisted an unprofessional burst of compassion and the inclination to get up and hold her. Instead, I proffered a tissue, which she took and silently mopped away the tears. She began to speak in a husky voice that hinted of an East Coast education.

"My name is . . . my name is Elyse Montenegro. I haven't lived here very long. I moved up here after . . . after Julio . . ." She hesitated and took a deep breath, as if the imparting of this small bit of information depleted her energy bank.

Reaching for a yellow lined pad, I nodded encouragement.

"What is your address, Ms. Montenegro?"

"I'm living with Campbell Sawyer, my friend, out on Five Fingers Lake Road. I don't know the number." Five Fingers Lake Road was a single-lane country road bordered with tall overgrown grasses and blackberry bushes that meandered through an area of nontraditional houses about five miles from town.

"Phone number?"

She provided it.

"Do you work on the island?"

"I'm working at the Percheron Ranch. I'm,— I'm . . ." She swallowed and continued. "Campbell works there, too." She paused and took two deep breaths.

San Juan Percheron Ranch is owned by Rebecca Underwood, who inherited it from her father. She's also an awesome sailor and racer. I met her when

I got roped into serving on the Memorial Day race committee for the Griffin Bay Yacht Club. Rebecca breeds and trains gigantic black draft horses called Percherons.

"How can I help you?" I said.

She inhaled another deep breath. "I think a man is following me. Stalking me. He drives a black Cherokee."

"Do you have any idea who this person is?" I've learned that men don't have a monopoly on stalking.

She shook her head. "Campbell thinks I'm paranoid."

"How long have you known Campbell?"

"A long time. Since we were little. We lived next door to each other. And she was my roommate at college."

"How long has the person been following you?"

"Almost a week. He's been following me around town, but I don't think he knows where I live. I always drive around, you know, and come into town and try to lose him, before I go home."

If Elyse Montenegro was indeed being stalked, I doubted her ploy was very successful. It's unusual to meet more than one or two cars in a ten-mile drive across the island; keeping another car in sight doesn't require a great deal of cleverness. It would be difficult for either the stalker or the stalked to hide. On the other hand, if someone was following her on a remote part of the island, which is most of it, there would be no witness to anything that happened.

I frowned. There are a number of clients I don't take on. These include those that don't pass the Circle Test. Or perhaps I should call it Dante's Circle Test. Anyone falling below the Fifth Circle of Hell is going to be too much trouble. That includes serious criminals and psychopaths or anyone whose life may be in danger from the above. All that belongs to the past I left in San Diego.

"Ms. Montenegro, this sounds like a matter for the sheriff's office. I do investigations, research things for people, help find people. I'm not a policewoman or a bodyguard. I can't protect you."

She shook her head and groped in her handbag.

"No, please, they wouldn't, I . . . I just can't. It's too dangerous." She laid a scrap of yellow paper on my desk. "This is the license number of the Cherokee. The man that's been following me. Money isn't a problem, I can pay you." She stood up and stared at me. "Please help me. Before it's too late."

I looked down at the piece of paper with its three numerals and three letters. I shook my head and frowned.

"Ms. Montenegro, I can't—" I looked up and stared at the closing door.

The Snow Queen was gone.

3

An alleged stalker.

A six-character alphanumeric on a scrap of yellow paper.

A disappearing client.

I didn't need it. I had to write the report on the jewel theft case for Property Casualty, and I was having dinner with Nick tonight. I considered deep-sixing the scrap of yellow paper, but didn't.

I carried it downstairs and stood beside Zelda's desk.

"So what's with the Snow Queen?" she asked, eyes on the monitor.

I didn't think Elyse Montenegro was the icy maiden Zelda made her out to be, but the tears might or might not have been real.

"Let me guess," she said, staring at the e-mail message she was composing. "Some guy is giving her a hard time."

She swiveled around to face me, raised her eyebrows and attempted to fluff the red stalactites. "Probably somebody she picked up at George's."

Without success, I tried to visualize Elyse Montenegro perched on a bar stool, surrounded by clouds of nicotine and pitchers of suds, at the old saloon on Spring Street. The image didn't play.

"She's working for Rebecca Underwood."

Rebecca and Zelda were the founding members of the Corona Club, a group of self-styled "uppity Island women" who assembled on Wednesday nights for a movie followed by libations at George's.

"Yeah, Rebecca's trainer got pregnant. She was really in a bind. But I never saw this Montenegro chick before. Must keep to herself."

If Zelda hadn't seen her, Elyse Montenegro was indeed reclusive. I placed the yellow paper on Zelda's desk. She glanced at it, her fingers flying over the keys.

"A plate number. I'll see what I can dig up. I have to send this message to Hans and then do the brochure for the Chamber Musicfest."

"Hans? What happened to the highlands laird? I was planning to visit you at Cairngorm Castle."

She scowled. "The laird forgot to mention a mite of information."

"Oh?"

"The lady of Cairngorm Castle."

"A mere trifle. It's probably a big castle, you'd never run into her."

"I also found out he doesn't own the castle anymore. The government does, and they give tours every Sunday, which would be worse than hordes of tourists gawking at the Orcas at Lime Kiln." Her tone of voice told me the laird was history. She glanced at the yellow paper again. "I'll take the license number apart and see what I can find."

Zelda's computer talents were honed by a number of years at Microsoft followed by a stint at a Seattle firm that provides information security, computer forensics and business recovery services.

In my early days at the San Diego Police Department, I had reluctantly crawled up to speed on an Apple Two Plus. After I married Albert and moved to San Francisco, I switched to Big Blue and for a while managed to hold my own with Windows, hard drives, and modems. But the Internet, JavaScript, viruses and increasingly more convoluted technology had ultimately dampened my enthusiasm.

The investigative firm I went to work for in San Francisco after Albert died subscribed to the best of the professional database providers, which supplied civil and criminal court records, Department of Motor Vehicle records, real property ownership, birth/marriage/divorce/death records, and a lot of other information most people assume is personal and private. When I moved to Friday Harbor, my budget dictated that I settle for a smaller provider that allowed "spot buys," or sold information a la carte, so to speak.

Once installed in the Olde Gazette Building, I'd realized in less than a week that having Zelda run my low-profile research was more efficient than my own bumbling around, whether on CD-ROMS and their updates or directly on the information superhighway. While computerized investigation had caused no end of whining among the Luddites of the P.I. community, the truth was that good investigation required fast access to public records across the country, or, at times, across the world or the universe.

Most of the time I didn't know whether Zelda was the craziest woman I'd ever met, or the smartest. It scared me to think she might be both. Her forays into cyberspatial investigation were breathtaking. Not only did she unearth names, addresses, phone numbers, marriages, divorces, and DMV records, she also ferreted out medical histories, phone-number traces and lists of a suspect's associates and contacts. In one instance, she provided a transcript of comments made in a chat room and e-mail messages sent and received. Big Sister Zelda would scare the bejeesus out of Orwell.

Zelda's passion for computer research, however, was not limited to S. J. MacKinnon Investigations. Her number-one goal was to find a life partner. Having exhausted the considerable pool of bachelors on the island, Netscape had become her magic portal to intergalactic singledom, uncovering such gems as the oil-tanker pilot whose hobby was crocheting and a New Orleans shrimper searching for a Cajun cook. And most recently, the highlands laird.

"Who is Hans?"

"A philosophy professor in Berlin. He says *Guten Morgen.*"

"To me?!"

"Yeah, I told him all about you. He thinks spooks are cool." She clicked the Send button and picked up the yellow paper. "The mail's in. I didn't get time to sort it out yet. Busy morning, you know."

Cyber-romance is labor intensive.

I riffled through the untidy stack of mail on the table near the door, extracted two window envelopes whose green contents said "Payable to," and deposited nine catalogs for worldly goods I didn't fancy into the "Paper for Recycling" container. Clutching the two window envelopes, I climbed the stairs and pondered Hans's dubious compliment. A spook. The moniker made me feel slightly tarnished, and conscientiously I reviewed my most recent cases.

There was the five-year-old who had been kidnapped by her mother from her fisherman father in Newport, Oregon, and hidden in a tent on Waldron Island. Before that, it was the live-aboard at the shipyard who'd set fire to his trawler rather than split half the sale proceeds with his ex-wife, who had run off with the Griffin Bay Yacht Club manager. He probably would have gotten away scot-free if he hadn't been so indiscreet as to brag about it to Sheldon Wainwright, one of Zelda's admirers.

The case I had to write up now for Property Casualty involved the theft of more than a million dollars' worth of diamonds, emeralds and bearer bonds from a Hollywood actor. It was a caper that made me unwontedly intimate with Seattle pawnshops. Two hours into the report, the phone rang. It was Angela Petersen.

"Wanna do lunch?"

"Another hour and I'll be done."

"Churchill's at one?"

"See you there."

I wrote the concluding paragraph of my report, spell-checked it, saved the file, clicked on the print icon, then opened my e-mail. I read the one new message, from my daughter, Melissa, a junior in political science at St. Mary's College in California.

Her advisor was a dork; she was dating a hot guy from Brazil who was in her math class; she hated economics and would probably flunk it. Her favorite classes were Spanish and bowling. Overall, the tone of the message was positive, considering she had wanted to transfer to U.C. Berkeley this year, a choice vehemently opposed by her left-wing maternal grandmother because the university had dropped its racial quota program.

> *Mom, Gilberto asked me to the homecoming*
> *dance. I need a new dress, something sexy.*
> *I'm the only student here without a credit card.*
> *Please send me one on your account. I*
> *promise to send you all the receipts.*
> *Love, Melissa*

I clicked on Reply to Sender and pleaded that I'd cut up all my credit cards and gone on a cash system, inquired as to what had happened to the sizable checking account she'd started the semester with, assured her I loved her, and signed off just as my ancient wall clock produced one off-key chime.

Time for lunch with Angela at Churchill's. Maybe I could find out what Matt Petersen had been in a snit about this morning.

4

Churchill's Cafe occupies a renovated brown-shingled building perched above the ferry landing. It was a hideaway, a place to recharge with a mocha and an old travel magazine, a refuge I'd been deprived of all summer and early fall during the Invasion of the Touristic Hordes. All very nice people, from Moses Lake and Helena and Detroit, who traveled hundreds or thousands of miles to adore the whales . . . but hordes nonetheless. There was one glimmer of hope in the war between the residents and the tourists, albeit in a dim sort of way: Given the slow decimation of the resident orca pods—whether from a decline of their food supply, environmental pollution, or harassment from the boaters—the decline of the tourists was sure to follow.

Now, a week after Halloween, Friday Harbor was on its way to becoming a ghost town until the next major holiday. The only customers in the cafe were two women with their heads together over bowls of chowder. No sign of Angela. Thin rays of sun illuminated the round table in the bay window overlooking the harbor. I staked out the table by throwing my jacket on the blue-and-pink flowered vinyl tablecloth and approached the minuscule cubbyhole that serves as order-taking counter and deli case. I studied the list of specials on the wall.

"If you're eyeing that Old San Juan baked French toast with custard sauce, I assure you it contains a full day's allotment of calories."

Among the things I hate being accused of is contemplating a sin I am, indeed, about to commit. It leaves me with no choice except to vehemently deny the accusation, even if it comes from my best friend, which it did.

I gave Angela a quick hug and denied any intent whatever. "In fact, given the newest BMI brouhaha, which I don't necessarily agree with, I'm having the fruit salad."

BMI stands for body mass index, a table of numbers that the feds came out with. Overnight, BMI turned fifty-five percent of the U.S. population into a nation of fatties. As far as I can determine, nobody except the anorexic personal trainer at the health club agrees with it. At five feet five inches and one hundred fifty-five pounds, I, who had been previously "healthy," was now "overweight."

Angela, small-boned, slender and perfectly proportioned, has never gained an extra ounce of avoirdupois in the fifteen years I've known her. She duplicated my order, and we settled ourselves at the round table and watched the line of departing cars snaking its way into the gaping mouth of the inter-island ferry.

Angela was unusually silent. I studied her oval face with its high cheekbones, the softly curling dark lashes, and the wonderful, short dark curly hair with a few threads of gray. Angela's father, a young medical doctor in Havana when Fidel Castro and his troops came down from the Sierra Maestra, emigrated with his wife and young daughter to Miami. Angela followed in her father's professional footsteps. I met her back when I was working the San Diego Harbor Patrol, in between husband number two and marriage number three. She was the new SDPD Medical Examiner, and single like me. Neither of us fit into Southern California urban culture, so we hung out together, talked about men and sex and politics, saw a lot of movies and shared after-work drinks at odd hours. I marveled at the few traces the years had left on her face and body. I also continually marveled at the improbability of a marriage between a sophisticated doctor and an island-born, island-reared commercial fisherman.

"Matt had a tantrum this morning. Ranted and raved and said I was a lousy housekeeper and left without his breakfast."

Matt Petersen was Old Island Family, descendant of a long line of Norwegian commercial fishermen whose annual take of silvers and cohos from southeastern Alaska had produced hundreds of thousands of dollars. When his father died, Matt had taken over the *Fairweather Princess* and continued a way of life that had begun in the late nineteenth century. The first spring after their elopement, Angela had accompanied him to Alaska in April. They returned in September, and the following year her time in Alaska was limited to two weeks at the end of the season. She never told me why, and last summer she took the dispatcher's job in the sheriff's office. Which would be strange anywhere but in the San Juans. Here, we have a retired cardiologist who grows organic vegetables and a former Wall Street trader painting houses.

"I saw him down at the Port this morning," I said. "He ignored me. Any particular reason for the tantrum?" I contemplated the remaining chunks of cantaloupe, six green grapes, and a minuscule wedge of pale watermelon. If Angela hadn't been there, I would have ordered the meat loaf with gravy and mashed potatoes, BMI be damned.

"Ostensibly, it's about my working."

"As in, he doesn't want you to?"

She nodded. "Tutoring Spanish at the high school was okay, but working as the sheriff's dispatcher isn't." She made a face.

Angela did the laundry, cleaned the house, kept up the gardening, and cooked breakfast, lunch and dinner during the fall and winter months when Matt was not in Alaska. It was a lifestyle far removed from her previous privileged existence, which had included a gardener and a weekly cleaning lady. A far remove, but apparently, from Angela's view, a fair exchange. A one-way ticket out of the mean streets of Los Angeles.

"He's okay with my not going to Alaska with him. Not many wives do. But when he's here, he wants me one hundred fifty percent of the time." She played with the wedge of watermelon and pushed a grape around her plate.

I wondered if she was having regrets, and I couldn't think of anything appropriate to say. She finished the cantaloupe and continued. "He worries a lot about the fishing. Whether the ocean will be warm or whether it'll be cold, whether the spawning grounds will be damaged by farming and logging." She frowned. "And I think he views my going to work as a failure on his part. God knows, I'm not doing it for the money I'm making, but if I don't have something to do all those months he's away, I'll go stark raving mad."

"So how are you going to appease him?" I stared at my empty plate, knowing I'd never make it through the afternoon without a snack, and decided to eat a piece of cantaloupe.

"I don't know." She flashed an impish smile. "Maybe just buy some new red underwear." Angela had confided that Matt was a spectacular lover. They'd met at a Yacht Club wedding when Angela was visiting me right after I moved to the island. Matt was the tall, dashing, bearded blond-haired giant who monopolized every dance, kept her out all night, and then followed her back to San Diego. After a whirlwind courtship, she tendered her resignation and flew to Puerto Vallarta to marry him in a tiny chapel overlooking Bahia de las Banderas. And, I assumed, had never looked back.

She sighed. "Sorry. Don't mean to whine." She finished the salad, wiped her mouth, repaired her lipstick. "Tell me what's going on with you. Finished with the theft of the family jewels?"

"Just finished the final report. Turns out it was the live-in boyfriend." I swallowed the last bite of cantaloupe and stared out the window, watching two slen-

der blonde-haired women walk up the hill from the
ferry landing. One of the women was Elyse Montenegro. She was accompanied by a woman in blue jeans,
a worn brown leather jacket, and red baseball cap who
was carrying a large brown paper package tied with
string. They stopped in front of Remainders, the used-
book store, appeared to confer, then crossed the street
and came into Churchill's.

Elyse paused inside the door, scanned the room,
noticed me, and nodded without smiling. I watched
them approach the order counter.

"Do you know either of them?" I asked Angela.

She nodded, looking out the window.

"The one in the baseball cap is Campbell Sawyer.
She gives art classes at the middle school. Lots of
talent, but I think she has a hard time keeping body
and soul together. Worked as night dispatcher for the
sheriff for a while, then quit. Worked at the Spinnaker
last summer, but that only lasted till Labor Day. I
don't know what she's doing now."

I watched the two young women walk into the back
dining room and take a seat next to the aquarium
filled with tropical fish on the back wall. Campbell put
her package on an empty chair and removed her cap.
A cascade of blonde hair, one shade darker than
Elyse's pale tresses, fell to her shoulders. Except for
the difference in hair color, their profiles were amaz-
ingly similar. As if they belonged to a generation in
which all the females were New American Barbies.

"Any interesting new cases?" Angela finished off
the last bite of cantaloupe.

"There was a woman in my office this morning.
Thinks some guy is following her. Got pretty hysterical
about it. Has the sheriff had any complaints about
stalkers?"

She shook her head. "Not that I know of, but I'll
keep my eyes and ears open." She stood up.

"Going back to the office?" I asked.

Another impish smile. "Yeah, after I get a naughty
new nightgown."

5

Naughty lingerie was not something I'd ever had an abundance of, I thought with some chagrin, zigzagging my way around the construction on Nichols Street. My sturdy, albeit well-muscled French-Scottish physique wasn't designed to be tarted up in red satin Miracle Bras or black lace teddies. Besides, they take too much time to get out of. And the truth is, twenty years of law enforcement and private investigation, plus three marriages, plus ten years of single parenting equals one pragmatic female with zero time for Red Door Days at Elizabeth Arden or ruffled poets' shirts, thank you very much.

However, I must admit that after meeting Nick, who in my prejudiced eyes is one gorgeous hunk of man, I did a quick self-appraisal of bare skin and superfluous padding. The appraisal resulted in a new regime of exercise that was as simple as getting out of the old Volvo wagon and walking. While I'm still not the Miracle Bra type, I've recently added some lacy camisoles to my wardrobe, and I don't look bad in leggings.

The sky was darkening and the chill damp wind blowing up from the harbor buffeted me as I stood on the corner of Spring Street and Blair Avenue waiting for the traffic to clear. I huddled in my wool jacket and found myself scanning the streets and sidewalks in all directions, acknowledging the thought that had been nagging the back of my mind since Elyse Montenegro had fled from my office: If this woman was being stalked for some reason, her stalker might have followed her to my office. Without thinking about it, my level of alertness had climbed from white to yellow.

Law enforcement personnel and others who managed to stay alive by developing and maintaining an innate sense for danger—private investigators, security guards, FBI and CIA operatives, Green Beret types—had a color hierarchy of alertness levels. The alerts went from white, signifying no danger, through yellow and orange to red. A red alert was a perception of a situation that was, or would immediately become, life-threatening. It had been a long time since I'd had to worry about spotting a tail or wondering if I should have a remote ignition for my car in case somebody had planted a bomb.

I hurried into the post office, acknowledging a greeting from Allison Fisher, the suntanned newcomer to Friday Harbor from Santa Cruz. Allison, who sells real estate, is Angela's bridge partner. She was chatting up Jared Saperstein, the *Gazette* publisher. Jared turned, smiled and waved. Jared likes me a lot. I hold that thought in the back of my mind like an emotional insurance policy and pull it out on days or nights when I'm feeling insecure about Nick.

I was back at the office by two-thirty. The building was redolent of sandalwood and filled with Japanese flute music. I paused at Zelda's desk. She tucked a wad of chewing gum into a corner of her mouth, tossed her hair over her shoulder, and waved a sheaf of papers at me.

"Snow Queen has found herself a pretty interesting admirer," she said, reaching for the chirping phone. "New Millennium, please hold."

I riffled through the papers.

"The first page is what I got from the rental car agent," she said. "You'll never believe what I had to promise him."

"I'd rather not know."

"The rest I found on my own. Mostly. He looks squeaky clean for the first few pages," she said. "Oh, by the way, Nick called again. His message is in your box. Sounds like hot and sweaty sex tonight." She grinned wickedly and went back to her incoming call.

Nick's message was short. I read it walking up the stairs and felt that funny electrical charge somewhere in my solar plexus that any communication from the tall, dark-haired Hungarian always created. *Dinner at my place. Come before sunset. Miss you.* I would make every effort to arrive before sunset.

My office was cold. I flipped the switch on the small electric wall heater, turned on the art deco lamp and began reading Zelda's report.

Report on License Tag 224 PUGET

Automobile: Jeep Cherokee, current year model
Owned by: Puget Sound Rentals, Seattle, Washington
Rented by: George Simms, 442 Santana Avenue, Mill Creek, California
   Phone number 415 339-0076, on November 3, at SEATAC airport
   California DL 998765, no outstanding warrants or accidents
   Rental charged to MasterCard
   Term of rental: November 3–November 10
   Contact in Friday Harbor: Seven Swans B & B

On page two of Zelda's report, I learned that Simms had stayed at the Seven Swans on Argyle Avenue for two nights. According to innkeeper Norm O'Shaunnessy, Simms was a little over six feet tall, forty-something, had a "gorgeous body, curly light-brown hair, dazzling blue eyes and a mustache." Simms wore glasses for reading. He had asked for maps and spent a lot of time exploring the island. He checked out yesterday and said he was going to Orcas Island.

Page three included a list of recent charges to the MasterCard, the number of which I assumed Zelda

had wrested from either Norm O'Shaunnessy or the
hapless clerk at the rental agency. The total of
$1,340.13 included charges at Puget Sound Auto Rent-
als; REI, Seattle's upscale outdoor sportswear empo-
rium; the Spinnaker Restaurant; George's Tavern; the
Seven Swans B & B; and the Topsail Inn.

A typical autumn vacation in the Pacific Northwest.

Page four was titled "Phone Calls" in Zelda's large,
sprawling backhand, with a notation that Simms had
made a number of long-distance calls from the Seven
Swans to a Boise, Idaho, phone number which, my
tenacious assistant had discovered, was an Internet
provider. I wondered why someone from Mill Creek,
California, wherever that was, would use an Idaho Internet provider.

The fragrance of buttered popcorn had replaced the
scent of sandalwood. I sniffed and turned to page five,
which told me a zip-code directory showed no zip code
for any place called Mill Creek. The phone number
belonged to Loretta's Beauty Salon in San Francisco.
So the guy was a hairdresser. Then I noted that Zelda,
never one to leave a stone unturned, had called Loretta's on California Street, and learned that they had
never heard of George Simms.

The last page included a note that Norm, the Seven
Swans innkeeper, had spied his former guest entering
the Topsail Inn. Wondering why Simms had lied about
his destination, Norm had called the Topsail, ostensibly to pass on a message for Mr. Simms, where the
owner of the Topsail had confirmed that a man match-
ing Simm's description and driving a black Jeep Cherokee had registered on Sunday, *but under the name
of Jason Simmons.* Zelda had found zip on Jason
Simmons.

I tapped the papers into a neat stack and followed
the fragrance of popcorn downstairs.

I helped myself to a plastic container from the coffee cupboard, filled it with the buttery morsels from
the green ceramic bowl, and sat in the chair beside
Zelda's desk. Dakota uncurled his sleek black body

from the rug in the corner and came to stand beside
me, his brown eyes following each handful of kernels
to my mouth. Dakota is Zelda's constant bodyguard,
a reject from a canine drug-training academy. I listened to Zelda's conversation with the chairperson of
the Chamber Music Festival, who apparently wanted
Zelda to design a festival T-shirt. She promised a
sketch by next week and terminated the call.

"Pretty interesting, huh?" she said, scooping a
handful out of my bowl.

"A T-shirt?"

"No, the Snow Queen's admirer. You read the
report?"

I nodded. "Is Simmons still registered at the
Topsail?"

"Checked out this morning. Headed back home to
San Francisco."

I chewed, swallowed and began thinking out loud.
"It is possible that George Simms is legit. It is possible
that the clerk at the rental car company made a mistake in recording the San Francisco phone number or
didn't copy down the right address. It's been known
to happen." I paused and grabbed another handful
of popcorn.

"It's also possible he had a logical reason for checking out of the Seven Swans and going over to the
Topsail." Zelda continued my train of thought. "I
heard Norm's had problems with the breakfast cook.
I also know Norm can be, shall we say, somewhat
predatory at times. Maybe Simms just wanted to
escape."

"It's a little harder to account for the change of
names when he registered at the Topsail."

"Unless he's a spy like you."

I frowned, thinking of the aliases and disguises I
had used in the line of duty and confidentiality. But
she was right; Simms could be a private investigator
who had a legit reason for following Elyse Montenegro. It wouldn't be the first time a client had turned
out to be less than lily-white.

"Are you going to share this with the Snow Queen?" Zelda pulled Dakota's leash out of her bottomless bag under the desk.

I nodded, went back upstairs, pulled out my tattered San Juan Islands phone book, and dialed the number for San Juan Percheron Ranch.

A man with a friendly voice answered. Elyse Montenegro was out in the stables, he said. Did I want to leave a message? I left both office phone and cell phone numbers for Elyse, and realized it was almost four o'clock. I glanced at my alpaca sweater and faded blue jeans. Sunset comes early to the San Juans in November, but I still had time to run back to the boat and change into something more appropriate for dinner with a handsome Seattle attorney.

6

People migrated to remote islands for a great variety of reasons, I mused as I turned off San Juan Valley Road onto Douglas Road. Some made the move for the novelty of it. Some to escape the painful shards of shattered illusions that littered their daily path. Others arrived in search of privacy and seclusion, a simpler life in a small seaside hamlet. And for perhaps more people than would ever admit it, it was the last hope at the end of a long, hard road, the most northwesterly point in the lower forty-eight states.

It was a quirk of fate—my pursuit of a divorced parent badly in arrears on child-support payments—that introduced me to this sky-washed, fifteen-by-eighteen-mile pile of rock bordering on Haro Strait that was surrounded on all horizons and in all seasons by snow-covered mountain peaks. The serenity of mossy green hillsides and towering Douglas firs had lingered with me long after I returned to San Francisco. Lingered after Albert's sudden demise, and even after my meeting with Nick.

I met Nicholas Anastazi in San Francisco when my employer, H & W Security, was retained by Nick's previous law firm to investigate allegations of arson on a mega-yacht that burned at South Beach Marina. The attraction between us was instantaneous, mutual, and explosive. But Nick was married and I wasn't interested in becoming a part-time lover. After the arsonist was arrested, I didn't see Nick again for several years.

When Melissa departed for St. Mary's College, a small liberal-arts school tucked away in the bucolic Rheem Valley east of Berkeley, I decided a lifestyle change was in order. I had accumulated enough hours for my own investigator's license, and San Juan Island seemed a good place to lick my wounds. So I had a huge garage sale, loaded up the old Volvo wagon, and headed North on Interstate 5.

It wasn't a particularly rational decision, but the wounds healed, Nick divorced his wife of twenty-five years, left San Francisco, and now had a growing maritime law practice in Seattle, which allowed him occasional escapes to the island. Escapes, from my point of view, that were all too infrequent.

I abandoned my reminiscences and concentrated on avoiding the nomadic herds of wild turkeys and itinerant, suicidal deer that lurk alongside nearly every island road, seemingly poised to leap in front of unwary motorists. And when the kamikazes are not turkeys or deer, then they're little bunny rabbits or their predators, slinky red foxes. I've heard that some seventy-five percent of auto accidents in San Juan County are blamed on wild animals, although I have a theory that the much-maligned deer are scapegoats for many an inebriated miscalculation.

Rounding the bend where Bailer Hill Road becomes West Side Road above Haro Strait, I experienced the dramatic, wide, wide expanse of water lying milky pink beneath a magenta sky. Following the curve below Hannah Heights, I was suddenly aware of a vehicle close behind me and saw a flashing red light in my rearview mirror.

The sheriff's white Blazer.

I glanced at the speedometer with guilt. Thirty-five in a twenty-mile zone. *Merde!* A moving violation and I'd be late getting to Nick's. I sighed and was about to pull the Volvo to the side of the road when I realized the flashing light wasn't for me. The white Blazer passed and continued around the bend. I speeded up, adrenaline starting to pump, then heard a siren behind me. Somewhere up ahead, there was a heart-attack victim or a car accident or some other medical emergency. I pulled into a driveway and the Emergency Medical Services van passed. The sound of the siren led me past the state park and up West Side Road to Mt. Dallas.

The EMS vehicle had slowed heading up the mountain, but I hadn't caught up with it. At the intersection with Starflower Lane, I parked behind the van and the white Blazer, on the edge of the rocky hillside that fell steeply to a small lagoon on the bottom of the canyon called Walden's Pond. Two men with a stretcher appeared through the brambles, followed by the deputy. They climbed up the crest of the hill and disappeared behind the van. I approached as they slid the stretcher inside.

"Who is it?" I asked, as if I had the right to know, nodding at the motionless body on the stretcher disappearing into the van. I had caught a glimpse of blood on a white shirt, but the face of the victim was hidden behind the large body of the deputy.

The taller of the men looked at me. "Can't give out any information 'til we notify next of kin. You next of kin, ma'am?"

Resisting an impulse to answer affirmatively—or to remind him that if I didn't know who it was, I wouldn't know if I was next of kin—I shook my head. The two men got into the van, made a wide U-turn, and headed back to town. I moved toward the sheriff's car. The deputy saluted me, started the engine, and followed the van. So much for local camaraderie.

I peered down the steep cliff, started to pick my way across the hillside, and then glanced at the sexy sandals I had donned in honor of my rendezvous with Nick. The trail was rocky and a sprained ankle or broken leg would ill serve my hot date. Besides, the accident didn't have anything to do with me. I started to turn away, then caught a glimpse of something red below. I moved to the right, stared through the underbrush, and saw a small upside-down red car resting against a large boulder. The car would have rolled over a hundred feet down the stony hillside, maybe more, from the road. This area of Mt. Dallas is wooded and secluded, with no houses in sight. There were no other cars around.

Who would have called in the accident? Why did the car look familiar? Who did I know on the island that drove an old red Karmann-Ghia?

1

The crumpled little red car bothered me all the way up the hill. A mile and a half above Starflower Lane, I turned off Mt. Dallas Road and followed Crows' Nest Drive for half a mile. Nick's house was the first one on the right, a weathered, gray-shingled, single-story residence that sprawled along the side of the mountain hillside and commanded a take-your-breath-away unobstructed view of water and Olympic Mountains and the city of Victoria. Marmalade, the ancient yellow cat that came with the house, was optimistically trying to find some warmth in the last rays of afternoon sun on the corner of the deck. He acknowledged my arrival by raising his head and flipping his tail twice on the grayed wood.

"Scotty, nice to see you." Nick was leaning against one side of the doorway, his six-foot-four, one-hundred-ninety-three-pound body clad in a blue oxford-cloth shirt open at the neck, slightly wrinkled khakis, and the fleece-lined moccasins I'd given him last Christmas. The deep creases at the corners of his brown eyes bespoke a recent lack of sleep. He smiled and moved toward me as I came across the deck, and I stood on tiptoe to return the bear hug and the anything-but-chaste kiss that erased all thoughts of an inverted red car.

Inside, standing in front of the wall of windows, I absorbed the sunset hovering in the mist over Vancouver Island, sighed and lowered myself into the well-worn leather chair facing the corner fireplace, where orange flames were dancing.

"Chardonnay?"

"Please." I watched Nick move behind the waist-high room divider that also served as a small bar. Scientists have recently identified a number of chemical substances, cousins of amphetamines, that are secreted by the brain when we meet a special person. Chemicals that produce the euphoria of falling in love. Dopamine, norepinephrine, phenylethylamine. Whether or not our meeting had been directed by karmic forces, there was never any doubt about the mutual chemistry. And these fizzy chemicals cared not a whit for the fact that at the time of our meeting Nick was a devout Catholic and married with children.

"Here you are, my lady." Nick handed me the crystal glass and raised his own in a toast. He smiled at me. "So, madame investigator, what villains are you pursuing this week? Is the missing heir still lost at sea?"

The missing heir was Harrison Petrovsky, son of the recently deceased San Juan Island resident, Anastasia Petrovsky. Harrison, one of four beneficiaries to Anastasia's considerable estate, was last seen a year ago, sailing out of the Strait of Juan de Fuca in a gaff-rigged cutter bound for the west coast of Mexico and the Marquesas.

"Harrison's last e-mail to his sister said he met a Tongan woman who was his long-lost soul mate and they were headed for New Zealand. That was just before Typhoon Mario took out four cruising boats in the Tasman Sea. It was a dead end for me, so Zelda found a Kiwi P.I. to help us."

"Any new clients lurking in the shadows?"

I thought about my meeting with Elyse Montenegro and sat up with a gasp, remembering where I'd seen the small red car.

"Oh, my God, I have to make a phone call."

I pawed through my big canvas carryall for the cell phone. Nothing on my voice mail. I dialed what I thought was the number for San Juan Percherons. This time Rebecca Underwood answered. I asked for Elyse.

"She left with Gregg about five minutes ago," she said. "Is anything wrong, Scotia?"

I exhaled. If they had just left five minutes earlier, then it couldn't have been Elyse in the red Karmann-Ghia that was upside down on Mt. Dallas.

"Just ask Elyse to call me tomorrow, Rebecca. She's got the number."

We exchanged sailing pleasantries. She said her son, Gregg, was going to move back to the island while she went to New Zealand with her boyfriend, Lars.

I sank back into the cushions. My sigh of relief was audible.

"Elyse?" Nick raised his eyebrows. "New client?"

I shrugged. "I'm not sure she's a client." I described her visit to my office, the alleged stalker, the small red car in the accident. "If she left the ranch five minutes ago, it couldn't have been her. Must be two red Karmann-Ghias on the island."

I didn't mention Zelda's report on the stalker. Nick and I provided mutual sounding boards, but neither of us invaded the details of the other's business life.

"The car probably hit a deer," he said. "The island's getting overrun. I'm beginning to think Matt Petersen's right, the deer-hunting season should be longer." Nick moved toward the kitchen area. "Come talk to me while I finish up this gourmet repast I've been slaving over all afternoon."

The sunset had diminished to a pink glow on the southwestern horizon. I followed Nick into the galley kitchen and leaned against the counter. "What's for supper?"

"Tomato spinach soup," he said with a flourish, "followed by the biggest, juiciest New York steak I could find, roasted red peppers and portobello mushrooms on toasted sourdough and a Gorgonzola walnut salad."

"What, no dessert?"

He leered. "You're looking at it."

I leered back, savored the fine wine, and watched him assemble our meal on two trays.

"What can I do?"

"Nothing. Just stand around and look beautiful." He leaned over and gave me a soft kiss and I felt the warmth in my face. "By the way, I like that outfit. Nice color on you."

I glanced down at the white shirt and long scarlet jersey jumper and was glad I'd taken time to change. I watched him tear the romaine lettuce into bite-sized pieces. Nick is nothing if not self-sufficient. He does his own cooking, washes the dishes, does the laundry. He certainly doesn't keep me around to take care of him.

I'm not into astrology, but as I watched Nick fix our supper, I thought of the computerized horoscope Zelda had produced on him.

Strong attachment to family, food, and home life. Ruled by the Moon. Emotional, sentimental, artistic. Interested in heredity and ancestors. Meticulous in attire.

Nick's parents were born in Budapest and immigrated to Toronto during the 1956 Hungarian uprising. Nick was born in Toronto, and later the family moved to San Francisco, where his father worked on the docks. From what I've pieced together, Nick's mother taught piano lessons so he could attend parochial school. Nick often fantasized about getting a grand piano for the house here.

"What's happening in your office?" I asked.

"A new case." He crumbled blue-veined cheese over the greens and sprinkled whole walnuts on top. "Plaintiff is a Philippine seaman, employed on a ship of Panamanian flag and registry, owned by a Japanese corporation."

"Sounds like a nice, straightforward case. What's his complaint?"

"The fellow signed on in Manila, and was injured when the ship was docked in Seattle." He ladled the fragrant steaming soup into white bowls and gingerly removed a foil-wrapped loaf from the oven. "He filed suit in Seattle and is claiming damages under the Jones Act and general maritime law for unseaworthiness and negligence against his Japanese employer and a Washington corporation that acted as its husbanding agent in Seattle."

"Good grief!"

Maritime law fascinated me, though a lot of the legal maritime jargon sounded like a foreign language. Admiralty law, maritime torts, black-letter laws, and the horrific problems of jurisdiction when the parties involved had diverse citizenship were way over my head. And I'd forgotten what the Jones Act was.

"Scotty." He put his arm around me. "I'm really sorry, but I have to leave early tomorrow. There's a preliminary hearing on the case at nine o'clock and Tony and I have a meeting at eleven to talk about a big new client." He paused, avoiding my eyes. "And Nicole needs to talk to me about something tomorrow night. Could you pop down to Seattle for the weekend? I could arrange a flight on the floatplane to Lake Union."

I tried to swallow my disappointment along with the wine, which had suddenly turned bitter. I was only partially successful. Nicole is Nick's twenty-two-year-old daughter who's recently moved to Seattle to look for work. Something appropriate to her degree in art history.

"I thought you were going to spend the rest of the week on the island." I kept my voice even, wondering if the problem was really Nicole, or if he just didn't want to "camp out" on *DragonSpray* anymore—his words a month ago when we got drenched in an early fall storm at Prevost Harbor on Stuart Island.

"I was, and I know you cleared your calender so we could go up to Ganges. And I regret it as much as you do." He looked at me, frowned, and ran one hand through his curly, salt-and-pepper hair. His eyes were serious and there was silence between us. Two weeks ago we had canceled a cruise on *'Spray* because of Nick's work. I moved away from his encircling arm.

"Scotty, I know you love to sail, and I know we want to spend more time together." He stared at his empty martini glass. "Finding time to come up here is getting harder and harder. The price of success, I guess. Lately, I've been wondering why I even have this house." He moved over to the stove, checked the broiler, and slid the huge steak under the flame. "Have you ever considered living in Seattle? Maybe we'd be able to see each other more often."

I blinked and felt an icy chill along my spine. Seattle was wet and cold and the traffic was a nightmare.

"Why don't you think about it?" he said.

I nodded. "When do you have to leave?"

"Andy says six-thirty. However, until tomorrow at five-thirty a.m., I am totally yours."

Andy was Andrew Cooper, Nick's partner in Anastazi Cooper Nakano. Nick, Andy, and Tony Nakano had all been associates back in San Francisco. All three had simultaneously decided to chuck the Bay Area rat race. Tony had grown up in Seattle, had good family contacts, and after passing the Washington Bar exam, the three opened an office in an old Victorian on Queen Anne Hill. A year later, Andy had inherited his family's old summer home here on the island, bought a little Piper Arrow, and began doing weekend commutes with his wife between Seattle's Boeing field and the private airfield at Roche Harbor. Nick had started tagging along, and had bought this place three years ago in a divorce sale.

"Then I guess we have to make use of what time we have," I said, trying not to think what it would mean to me if Nick didn't have the house here.

He kissed me hard on the mouth, unfastened the top button of my white shirt, under which I was wearing nothing but a lacy white camisole, and planted a strategic kiss. "I love buxom women. And that's a deposit, the balance to be collected after supper." He picked up a tray and headed for the dining alcove.

"By the way," he added over his shoulder, "the hot tub is functional and hot."

So, I hoped, was he.

8

Wednesday morning dawned cold and damp. I dropped Nick at the Roche Harbor landing strip at six-thirty and struggled with the wrenching separation that comes from parting after a night of skin-to-skin warmth. I fervently wished it weren't so windy. Andy had the Arrow warmed up when we arrived. I watched them taxi down the narrow strip in the middle of the field, turn around and take off unsteadily over the trees into the brightening sky.

With immense reluctance, I tugged my thoughts away from my lover and headed the Volvo east on Roche Harbor Road, through pockets of lingering ground fog, and into town. I reviewed my list of things to do and wondered if I could finish up everything by Thursday and grab the floatplane down to Lake Union as Nick had suggested.

I left the Volvo in the permit parking lot above the Port and got my OJ, a latte, and a maple bar from the bakery, which at this hour of the morning was full of locals, mostly men hunched over their coffee cups, trading gossip and watching the girls behind the counter.

"Morning, Scotia."

It was Rebecca Underwood of San Juan Percherons, tall and raven-haired, dressed in dirty blue jeans, an old red wool sweater, and muddy work boots. She was adding sugar to her coffee, and she looked grim.

"Hi, Rebecca. How's life on the ranch?" I fitted a

plastic cover tightly over the top of the paper coffee container and tried to figure out how I could carry it without scalding my fingers.

"Well, for starters, Elyse is so upset about Campbell she could barely work this morning. Two of the yearlings got out last night and got tangled up in my neighbor's barbed-wire fence. One of the mares we wanted to show in Denver in January is lame. And it's only seven-thirty."

"What's wrong with Campbell?"

"Didn't you hear? She had an accident last night with Elyse's car."

I flashed on the crumpled little Ghia I'd seen on Mt. Dallas. "Is she okay?"

Rebecca shrugged, "She was medivacced over to Bellingham. We have our fingers crossed." Her cell phone beeped, and she pulled the tiny black device from her shirt pocket. "This'll be the vet," she said. "I'll talk to you later. Oh, I told Elyse to call you."

I asked the counter girl for another cup to put under the scalding one she had given me, put the OJ and maple bar in my carryall. I left Rebecca frowning and murmuring into her cell phone and headed uphill, wondering why Campbell Sawyer was driving my client's car. And also wondering if Elyse Montenegro was still my client.

It was seven-fifty when I got to the office. Soraya's car was parked in the street and the front door was unlocked. Zelda's work space was dark and silent, but two pairs of Birkenstocks rested companionably on the coco mat outside Islands Naturopathic.

Pink message slips in hand, I dribbled coffee up the threadbare stair carpet. I switched on the computer, turned on the heater and the desk light, and spread the two slightly damp pink slips on my desk. One was from Zelda saying she would be late this morning because she had to take Dakota to the vet; the other one was from Petra Von Schnitzenhoff inquiring as to news on her missing brother, Harrison.

Nothing from Elyse Montenegro. I shrugged. Okay by me if she didn't want to return my calls.

I stared at the Von Schnitzenhoff message. *Call as soon as possible*. I wished I'd never taken the case. As I'd told Nick, Harrison had sailed off for the Marquesas a year ago, and from the moment she'd gotten the news of her mother's death, Petra had been relentlessly "helping" me find her brother, since the will specified that no distribution could be made until all the heirs were located.

After tracing Harrison as far as Tonga and learning of his intended stops in Australia and New Zealand, I had contacted all the marinas in and around the Port of Sydney. I'd sent Harrison my own e-mail messages. I'd notified the Sydney police. And two weeks ago, at the behest of La Von Schnitzenhoff, who had suggested perhaps we should have Harrison declared dead, we'd found a P.I. in New Zealand by the name of Brian MacGregor. There was no point in calling Petra back until I had some info from Brian.

Windows was up and colorfully awaiting my command. On the Eudora mail window I was about to click on the New Message icon when my phone rang.

It was Elyse Montenegro. I settled back in my chair and listened to her voice, which was more tremulous than yesterday. Before I could ask about the red Karmann-Ghia, she said she needed to see me right away. I told her to come over.

While I waited, I queried the Kiwi P.I. at *down under.net* and read two more incoming messages—an announcement from the Joshua Slocum Society about a holiday get-together in Seattle and a message from daughter Melissa. Economics was too hard, and she wanted to change her major to dance. Grandma thought it was okay. I gritted my teeth and typed back, *Sorry you're having a hard time with economics. I did too. Hang in there and we'll discuss it at Thanksgiving*.

Over my dead body was my daughter going to change her major to dance. One Isadora Duncan wannabe in the family, namely, my bohemian mother, Jewel Moon, was sufficient.

I heard the downstairs door open, swiveled around and peered through the window. A dusty Ford pickup with a "San Juan Percherons" decal on the door was backing into the street. There was a dark-haired man at the wheel. The pickup turned right on Blair and disappeared. I heard a door slam and quick steps on the stairs, then Elyse Montenegro stood in the doorway.

Her pale lashes were devoid of mascara today, and the turquoise eyes were reddened. She wore a brown leather flight jacket over a man's wrinkled white shirt, many sizes too large for her, and faded blue jeans. Her pale hair was twisted into an untidy knot at the back of her head. And yet, despite her dishevelment and obvious anxiety, she was probably still the most elegant woman in San Juan County. I motioned to the wicker chair, and today she chose the one closer to the desk.

"Campbell was in an accident yesterday, but it wasn't an accident." Her words tumbled out. "He was trying to kill *me*."

"Tell me what happened." I reached for a yellow lined pad.

She nodded. "Campbell Sawyer. My friend. She had an accident. She borrowed my car yesterday, but I know it wasn't an accident. She's a really good driver. The man who was following me thought she was me."

"The red Karmann-Ghia that was in the accident on Mt. Dallas is yours?"

She nodded and spoke rapidly. "She had to deliver a commission on Mt. Dallas. She borrowed my car and—"

I interrupted her. "A commission for what?"

"Campbell is an artist. A sculptor. A couple that live up on Mt. Dallas commissioned a sculpture of an eagle."

"Why did she borrow *your* car? Doesn't *she* have a car?"

"She forgot and left her lights on when she came home the night before and her car had a dead battery. She was getting it charged, so I told her she could use mine. She promised to be back to pick me up at five-thirty. She didn't come back. If she dies, it's all my fault." Tears began sliding down her face. I knew my cue and handed her a tissue.

I felt as if I had come into this drama in act two. I had to find out what happened in act one. I took a deep breath and refrained from reminding her I'd suggested notifying the sheriff yesterday. "Where is your friend now?"

"At St. Patrick's Hospital in Bellingham."

"Have you spoken with her?"

She shook her head. "She's still unconscious."

I frowned. "Does she have any family?"

"No. I mean, yes. Her mother lives in Boston. But she doesn't talk to Campbell."

"Why not?"

"She thinks Campbell's stupid for wanting to be a sculptor. She wanted her to be a teacher. She's a total control freak."

I swallowed, thinking of my recent message to Melissa, and reached for the manila folder with the six pages Zelda had assembled yesterday. I told Elyse what we had learned based on the license tag number she'd given me. Neither the name George Simms nor Jason Simmons meant anything to her. No, she couldn't describe the driver. He always wore dark glasses and a cap. Was she sure it was a man? She wasn't.

"Elyse, have you been dating anyone on the island?"

She shook her head, then hesitated. "Well, I've been hanging out with Gregg."

"Rebecca's son?"

She nodded.

"Talked to anyone in a bar?"

Another negative. "I don't drink."

I looked at her, remembered her evasiveness yesterday.

"Who do you think this man is?"

"The man who killed Julio."

9

"Who is Julio?" I asked.

"My husband."

"When was he killed?"

"July thirteenth." She said it without inflection, as if the date was etched on her brain cells for an eternity.

"Where did this happen?"

"In Berkeley."

"Do you want to tell me about it?"

Twisting the tendrils of fair hair that were escaping from the blue elastic, she chewed on her right thumbnail and began her recitation.

It was a Friday afternoon, she said, and Julio Montenegro and his colleague Peter Aaron had taken the afternoon off and gone for a sail on San Francisco Bay on Peter's boat, *Camelot*. Elyse and Peter's wife, Carmela, were supposed to have gone shopping in the city that morning, but there was a big accident on the Bay Bridge. They didn't want to get caught in the Friday-afternoon rush-hour traffic, so they had changed their plans and spent the afternoon at the stables instead.

"What stables?"

"Tilden Ridge Stables. In Berkeley. I . . . I used to work there before I got pregnant." She paused, her eyes narrowed, then she continued with determination. "Carmela was pregnant, too. Anyway, we had lunch and spent a couple of hours at the stables and then we came down to the marina. We were going to

surprise Julio and Peter and take them to dinner at
Force Five instead of cooking at home."

She took a deep breath and shook her head as if to
clear it. When they got to the marina, Elyse had
headed down to the dock while Carmela went to the
rest room. Elyse didn't blink when she told me that
on arriving at the boat, she'd found that both Julio
and Peter had just been shot.

"There was blood everywhere, and when I climbed
into the cockpit, I slipped and I fell down in the cockpit and I . . . I hurt so bad and Julio didn't move. I
screamed and screamed and then the police came and
an ambulance. I had a miscarriage after we got to
the hospital."

"What happened to Peter? You said he was shot,
too."

"Just his shoulder. He was down in the cabin and
started to come up when he saw Julio fall, and he
got hit."

Julio had been hit from behind, she said, and he
was dead on arrival at the hospital. The police thought
she must have passed her husband's murderer coming
out as she went through the security gate on the dock.
She said she had only the foggiest recollection of a
man in a dark cap she saw on the ramp. She'd looked
at photos the detective put together, but was unable
to make a positive identification of anyone.

I wondered if Julio and Peter had been victims of
a random rampage, of some sicko who didn't like sailors or didn't like the way the wind was blowing that
day.

"What was Julio's work?"

"He was an attorney. He was working at LAUD."

"What is loud?"

"L-A-U-D. Latin American Union for Defense. It's
kind of a Legal Aid Society for Spanish speakers.
They represent Latin Americans who have immigration problems or get in trouble with the law, or when
there are discrimination cases. Labor relations. That
kind of stuff."

"How long did Julio work for LAUD?"

"He started working there three years ago, when he was still studying at Hastings. Then when he passed the Bar, he became a legislative staff attorney."

"And before law school?"

She recited their move from the East Coast to San Francisco, Julio's work with the international division at Bank of America in the city, his switch to Pacific Financial, a small financial consulting firm on Union Street. Then Hastings Law and the stint at the public defender's office in the city.

"Then we moved over to Berkeley so he could work with Peter."

"Who, exactly, is Peter?"

"Peter Aaron. He was Julio's roommate at Yale. He's the director at LAUD."

"Was Julio born in the U.S.?"

She shook her head. "He grew up in Mexico. And in Europe. His father was a commercial attaché to France and later to Portugal."

The scent of freshly brewed coffee wafted up from below and Elyse sniffed. I went downstairs, greeted Zelda, and brought back cups for both of us. Elyse sipped the steaming brew and regarded me over the rim of the cobalt-blue cup.

"After Julio was killed," she said, "I started noticing a van following me when I left work. Not every day, just a couple of times a week. I never knew for sure, and it never got close enough for me to get a license number."

"Where did you work?"

"I was a social worker for Alameda County and I taught English classes for immigrants at the high school."

"Did you report the van you thought was following you to the Berkeley police?"

She shrugged. "Sure."

"And?"

"They needed a license number or a description, or something. He never got that close."

"Do you know for sure it was a man?"

She didn't.

"Did anyone ever threaten you? Any phone calls? E-mail?"

She shook her head. "Carmela, Peter's wife, said it was my imagination." She shrugged. "My parents wanted me to go and stay with them, but I couldn't."

"Where do your parents live?"

"In San Francisco. Sea Cliff."

Sea Cliff was a manicured enclave of the affluent stretching along San Francisco Bay on the northwest side of the city between the Presidio and Land's End. It sounded like a good place to recuperate from her travails in Berkeley.

"Why didn't you want to go there?"

She hesitated before answering. "My father wanted me to marry his partner's son. He had my whole life planned out for me. I didn't want him reminding me that if I had followed his advice, I wouldn't be a widow." She twisted her hands in her lap.

I looked at her, remembering similar times when I had messed up my own life and didn't want to give Jewel Moon a chance to say, "I told you so."

"So the police made no arrests?"

She shook her head. "Nobody to arrest." She paused, sipped her coffee. "I couldn't concentrate on my work, so I took a leave and came up to visit Campbell. She needed help with her rent and it was nice here, so I just stayed." She hesitated, then added, "The Bay Area has too many sad memories."

I could relate to that.

She drained the cup and I looked back over the notes I'd made on her previous visit. "You said you knew Campbell from college?"

"Actually, she grew up next door to me in Connect-icut. And we roomed together at Sarah Lawrence."

Sarah Lawrence College was an elite liberal-arts school half an hour by train from New York City. It encouraged individualism and self-expression, and I had wanted desperately to spend four years there, studying philosophy and languages in its old English Tudor mansions. My mother, however, had just discovered San Francisco, and had far different plans for me.

I'd known women who attended Sarah Lawrence, and while Elyse Montenegro certainly looked as if she would have had the money for the tuition, somehow she didn't fit my image of the vocal, self-sufficient, independent individuals that the college often turned out.

"After Campbell graduated," Elyse continued, "she worked as curator in a museum in Boston, but she was always fighting with her mother. She came here because she met a guy who was a chef at Roche Harbor. They separated last year and he left, but she decided to stay. Even though she has a hard time making money here. That's why she's working for Rebecca at the ranch."

"Where is Campbell's father?"

"He divorced her mother when Campbell was little. I think he lives in London."

The drama that Elyse outlined had an intriguing cast of characters, but as far as the murder was concerned, the case was very cold.

"What do you want me to do for you?"

"Find out who killed Julio. Find out who tried to kill Campbell."

I shook my head. "That's a job for the police."

"They don't have any leads."

The Berkeley Police Department is highly organized. Their detectives are thorough. If there had been no arrests after four months, Elyse was probably right, there were no suspects. Whoever had killed Julio had done a clean job. I stared at Elyse for a long minute, reached for the phone, dialed the sheriff's office, asked to speak to Nigel Bishop.

"Sheriff Bishop."

I identified myself.

"Oh, yes, the lady investigator. What can I do for

you, ma'am?" The words were courteous; the tone was insolent.

I hesitated. For ten years prior to the last election, San Juan Island had enjoyed the services of a reasonable, intelligent sheriff, well educated in law enforcement. But after a family crisis two years ago, he had decided not to run for reelection, and Nigel Bishop, former logger and dyed-in-the-wool conservative, had taken over the office. I had clashed with Nigel on a case involving the battered wife of one of Nigel's cronies at the Hunting Club. It wasn't likely he'd forgotten.

"Sheriff, the owner of the car that was involved in the accident on Mt. Dallas yesterday is a client of mine. Ms. Montenegro suspects there may have been foul play involved in the accident." I suggested that he talk with her.

"Foul play? I don't think so. This is San Juan Island, Miz MacKinnon, not San Francisco or Cabot Cove."

"Ms. Montenegro believes she's been followed this past week. She thinks the stalker may have thought she was in the car at the time of the accident."

There was a belly laugh on the other end of the line. "Well, ma'am, with all due respect to Miz Monte Negro's colorful imagination, that accident was either caused by some critter wandering into the road just as the lady took the curve, or she was driving too fast to make the corner. Or maybe she'd had an early cocktail. I believe she's known for that. But we don't have stalkers on San Juan Island. Now, if you'll excuse me, ma'am, I've got a Little League meeting to attend."

The line went dead. I replaced the phone and stared at Elyse. "Does your friend have an alcohol problem?"

"She's been going to AA." She frowned. "But they're not supposed to talk about that stuff outside the meetings. How did he know?"

"There are no secrets in Friday Harbor."

Elyse stared at me and I stared back. If Nigel had

been willing to talk to Elyse, I could have walked away from her problem with a clear conscience. But he wasn't. Someone needed to follow up. I quoted my fee to her, adding twenty-five percent, expecting that would end the matter.

She reached into her bag, pulled out a checkbook. Her name was engraved on the black cover. She wrote out a check, signed it and slid it across the desk. As she did, I noticed the bracelet she wore. It was made of gold links and looked old, and the charms appeared to be medals of some sort.

The check was for ten thousand dollars, drawn on an assets-management account at a major San Francisco brokerage firm. It looked real. I wondered where she got the money.

I stared at the check, a dozen uses for it running through my mind.

The new electric windlass for *DragonSpray*.

A dance dress for Melissa.

A new computer that would handle the demands of the database I wanted to buy.

I contemplated the intricacies of a case that had already involved one murder, a miscarriage, and perhaps an attempted murder on this very island. If I didn't take the case, would there be more deaths?

I picked up the check and put it in the top desk drawer.

"I will try to help you, Elyse. To do that, I need you to tell me everything that you can remember about Julio and his associates and any cases he might have worked on. About your friends. About any possible enemies." I swung around to my computer and opened a new document file.

She nodded, moved closer to the desk, and began to fill in the details of her life with Julio Montenegro, deceased.

10

One half of my brain was still processing Elyse Montenegro's tale; the other was responding to my stomach's need for nourishment.

I stared at the Wednesday lunch specials on the menu board at the Madrona Landing. Still in a funk over Nick's leaving and the change in weekend plans, and now burdened with the Montenegro case, I definitely wasn't going to be motivated to prepare an elaborate dinner for one tonight. I passed up the shepherd's pie and settled on the New Mexico chili, salad with ginger tamari dressing, and fresh-baked corn bread.

Seated at the small table in the window alcove, I stared at the courthouse across the street and thought about Elyse's story. It had begun as the perfect equation for a fairytale romance. Take one lovely blonde heroine, Elyse Christine Muehler, adored only child of wealthy East Coast parents, raised in Connecticut on the Sound and educated at Miss Abigail's and Sarah Lawrence. Add one charismatic Latin hero, Julio Montenegro, eldest son of wealthy Mexican parents who traveled in international diplomatic circles and sent their son to study finance at Yale. The sum should be happily ever after. But something unexpected had been added to or subtracted from the equation.

People get killed every day. Excluding the random shootings in the workplace, acts of terrorism, or fatal encounters resulting from so-called road rage, most homicides are related one way or another to something abusive, illegal, or immoral.

Drugs. Infidelity. Alcohol. Theft. Smuggling. Greed and cupidity. Larcenies and felonies.

None of these had been mentioned in Elyse's narration. Julio sounded like an intelligent, well-educated young attorney who wanted to right the wrongs of the world.

Was it possible her husband wasn't as pure as Elyse painted him?

Or was Julio's friend Peter the target, and Julio happened to be in the wrong place at the wrong time? If Julio was the intended victim, then Elyse didn't know everything that was going on in her husband's life or she was holding something back.

Homicides are often committed by someone close to the victim. Was there an irate spouse or lover in the equation somewhere?

The logical place to start the investigation was with the Berkeley PD. If I were still in law enforcement, getting a report on the crime would be easy. But I wasn't and I knew that a cold call to the BPD would produce a big zero. I might as well read back issues of the *Berkeley Gazette* or the *Daily Californian*. I started on the chili. It was spicier than the order-taker had led me to believe. I wished I had a cold beer to wash it down.

"Well, well, Jessica Fletcher in the flesh."

It was Angela. She slid into the narrow space between the table and the wall with much more grace than I had, balancing a plate of spinach pie and a glass of water.

"What do you mean?"

"That's what Nigel's been calling you since you asked him to talk to your client."

I muttered an expletive. "Do you have a report on the accident?"

The chili was getting spicier the nearer I got to the bottom of the bowl.

She nodded. "I'll see what I can find when Nigel goes to lunch. Anyway, aren't you and that handsome Hungarian hunk about to take off for some R and R on *DragonSpray*?"

"Trip's off. Nick had a hearing early this morning on a new case. But I'm trying to get out of here and fly down to Seattle tomorrow." I finished the chili and changed the subject. "How's Matt? Did the red night-gown do the trick?"

"Yes, *ma'am*. The party of the second part hasn't had a word to say about the party of the first part's employment." She ate a mouthful of the spinach pie. "However, the newest *cause célèbre* is guns."

"Guns?"

"And gun control laws. He's furious that the feds might have a file on him. Outraged that there's a wait-ing period to buy a gun. Thinks it's an abridgement of his constitutional rights. Hates the press. Hates aca-demics. He's even muttering about starting a vigilante group. I don't know what's gotten into him. As long as I've known him, he's never even fired a gun."

I knew that a large percentage of the fishermen and boaters around the county were carrying guns. "Did you tell him about your firsthand experiences with the results of Saturday night specials? Or cite any of the statistics regarding the number of felons that would otherwise have guns without a waiting period?"

Angela laughed. "I wouldn't think of it. He's got his own statistics that show more guns mean less crime. He wouldn't hear a word of what I might say. There are only two ways of doing things in this world. Matt's way and the wrong way. Far be it from me to trample on his constitutional rights. Besides, it keeps his mind off my job."

I looked at Angela and wondered if I should be taking notes. This was her first marriage and she seemed to know something about maintaining domes-tic bliss that I, after three marriages, had never learned. For just a nanosecond, I wished I could be like her. That I could live with a man whose politics and moral philosophy diverged a hundred and eighty degrees from mine. Was integrity less important than I thought? Could I learn to use sex to sugarcoat philosophical differences? Should I?

She caught my questioning look. "Yes?"

"Just marveling at your ability to live with a redneck."

I didn't have the right to say it and she should have taken offense. She didn't, but her face grew serious.

"There are lots of Matt's ideas I don't agree with," she said in a quiet voice. "But he's a package deal. Challenging him will only start World War Three."

She ate the last of her lunch. "And then where would I be?" she asked without looking up.

11

I was back at the office by one fifty-five. New Millennium Communications welcomed me with Puccini and rays of afternoon sunlight splaying over the red geraniums behind Zelda's desk. Her Royal Highness was on the phone. I checked my mail slot, picked up the single pink slip, and was headed for the stairway when my assistant's dulcet tones stopped me.

"So he returned the Cherokee last night? Any scratches on it?" She paused. "Was it serious?" Another pause. "Howie, could you be a sweetie and find out if there was any paint on that grille?" Zelda's voice took on a cooing quality. "Oh, Howie, that's so nice of you. And Howie? The next time I'm in Seattle I'd *love* to meet you. Would you have time for a drink? You do? Terrif! My treat. See you then, sweetie."

I rolled my eyes and Zelda replaced the phone in the cradle and smirked at me. "Damaged front grille. No big deal since Mr. Simms had full coverage. But Howie is going to find out if there was any red paint on the grille and call me."

"I do hope you and Howie have a lovely drinky-poo." I started for the stairs again.

"Uh, boss?"

"Yeah?"

"I'm going to have a visitor for the weekend."

"Anyone I know?"

"Michael. A yacht broker from Seattle. He's got a

prospective listing here, and he's coming up Friday afternoon. So if you don't have anything rush, I'll probably disappear after lunch."

I didn't ask about Hans. A Seattle beau seemed eminently more practical than one based in Berlin.

"Where's he staying?"

"With me."

To this old-fashioned Cape Bretoner, such an arrangement seemed intimate for a first date. I flung a short verbal caution over my shoulder.

"No problem," she said. "Dakota will be there. And the Roberts' house has five bedrooms." Zelda, unwilling or unable to mortgage the rest of her life for four walls and a roof, was a professional house sitter. She was currently caretaking a huge house at Davidson Head on the northwest side of the island for a family that was wintering in the south of France. She lifted a color printout from her Canon 610 and reached for a folder. Her haute couture theme for the day was Hispanic. Or was it Basque? Embroidered white blouse, flowing multicolored skirt, and blue espadrilles with two-inch cork soles. The henna-colored stalactites were gone, replaced by a strawberry-blonde French braid. A miniature red plastic pepper dangled from each earlobe, moving in time to the music as Zelda lip-synched along with the soprano. "Lucia de Lammermoor in the mad scene," she said to my unspoken query.

How appropriate.

I glanced around the office. "Where's Dakota? Not sick, is he?"

"Nope. He got a booster rabies shot today and went to spend the afternoon with Rebecca and Big Boy."

"Do I know Big Boy?"

"Rebecca's Bernese mountain dog."

Upstairs I mulled over the info on the Cherokee while I hung my jacket behind the door. If the driver of the Cherokee was the one stalking Elyse, and the Cherokee was returned to the rental agency last night, then she was probably safe for the time being. The damage to the front grille might well be connected with Campbell's accident. Might also be coincidental. I opened the Montenegro file and reread the notes from my last conversation with Elyse. Time to get some hard information on the case. Time to call Ben Carey.

I flipped through my messy Rolodex, wishing I'd been more diplomatic when I'd dumped Ben for Nick. Ben was a homicide detective with the Berkeley PD. He and I had a short romance following his breakup with his wife and Albert's death. I knew I had wounded Ben's ego when I'd stopped being available without explanation. The night I'd run into him at the Italian place on Green Street and introduced him to Nick, his acknowledgment had been curt. I heard later he was romancing a divorcée in the mayor's office. Mary Louise something. I hoped they were still together, which was unlikely. Cops aren't known for the longevity of their romances.

I stared at his card on the Rolodex, shrugged and dialed his direct line.

"Homicide, Carey."

"Hi, Ben. Scotia MacKinnon."

An indrawn breath, then a half laugh. "Well, well, the beautiful Scotia MacKinnon. Nice to hear your voice," he drawled. "And where on God's green earth might you be calling from? I heard you closed up shop here."

I decided to play it light. "From Friday Harbor, Washington, Sergeant. Nice to hear your voice, too."

"Lieutenant, now, my dear."

I congratulated him and after five minutes of kibitzing and trading gossip, I learned that Mary Louise had become history when she'd hocked his mother's silver tea service to finance her cocaine habit. I commiserated and then zeroed in on the purpose of my call.

"Ben, I need some info on a homicide in Berkeley. Back in July of this year. July thirteenth, to be exact. Julio Montenegro. The widow is a client of mine. Apparently, no ID was ever made. Now she thinks she's being stalked."

He was silent. I could hear him tapping the pencil on the desktop, a habit that used to drive me crazy. "The Mexican civil rights attorney with LAUD. Sergeant Wineheart has that case. Let me see what I can do for you."

We exchanged e-mail addresses and I sidestepped a broad hint that he was due for vacation and weren't the San Juans just a day or so's drive from the city? He didn't ask about Nick. I hung up the phone and sat for a minute. I checked my appearance in the tiny mirror behind my desk. I didn't feel beautiful. There were new vertical lines beside my mouth, I had been too sleepy to put on mascara this morning before I left Nick's place, and my lipstick was history. I would never have walked around San Francisco like this.

I went back to reading the Montenegro file and speculated about the little red car. I wanted to see the Ghia and I wanted to check out the scene of the accident. I swiveled around to the computer and composed a message to Angela.

A: Sorry about the redneck comment at lunch. Unnecessary and uncalled for. RE the Montenegro auto in Tuesday's accident, do you know the extent of damage and current location of car?

The message went off and three new messages came in. The first was from the Kiwi P.I.

RE Harrison Petrovsky, S/V Ocean Dancer is anchored outside the port of Russell, N.Z. No one on board. Skipper and Tongan crew were last seen at The Duke of Marlborough, they told bartender they intended to head for the Red Rock. Estimated return: late November. Shall I continue the investigation?

I advised Brian to submit his fee for time and expenses, and to keep an eye on *Ocean Dancer*. Then I dialed Petra Petrovsky Von Schnitzenhoff, advised her that Harrison et al had survived the typhoon, and we'd have to wait until he could be notified in person of his inheritance. She wasn't happy. "I'd think that by now, Ms. MacKinnon, given all that we've been paying you, you'd have some *real* information." Before I could think of a pithy retort, she hung up without farewell. I e-mailed the pertinent information to Carolyn Smith, the attorney for the Petrovsky estate.

I was about to succumb to the afternoon lure of popcorn when a new message came in from Ben Carey.

> *Sergeant Wineheart says there was a similar incident in Denver in September. A Puerto Rican civil rights attorney shot. He's working on it with VICAP. Details later.*

I stared at it, swallowed, then read the message again. VICAP, the Violent Criminal Apprehension Program, is the data collection unit of the FBI that deals with violent criminals. What had I gotten myself into? Tucking the implications of Ben's message into the back of my mind, I went downstairs. The fax in my message box was from Angela: the report on Campbell Sawyer's accident.

> *Single-vehicle accident. Cause of accident: excessive speed. Driver unconscious, lacerations and contusions. Driver medivacced to Bellingham. Vehicle insured with F. & F. McGillicutty Insurance.*

I hoped the sheriff hadn't seen Angela faxing the report to me or Matt wouldn't have to worry about an employed wife. I helped myself to a bowl of popcorn and stood beside Zelda's desk.

"What?" she said without looking up. Her voice was crisp. I have a lot of conversations with the back of Zelda's head.

"The McGillicuttys are listed as the insurance agent

on the wrecked Karmann-Ghia. I want to see the car."

"Fran McGillicutty's a Corona. I'll see her tonight. The Coronas are going to see a rerun of *Titanic*. I'll talk to her about the Ghia."

I gobbled up half a bowl of popcorn and turned to head back upstairs.

"By the way, change of plans for the weekend," Zelda said over her shoulder. "Michael can't come, so I'm going down to Seattle."

"How nice. You can buy Howie that drink you promised him."

"Yeah, sure. By the way, boss, would you have a scarf or a jacket or something I could borrow to jazz up the little black dress I found at the thrift shop today?"

I stared at her. *A little black dress? Zelda?* "What are you two doing in Seattle?"

"Michael's taking me to dinner at the Sorrento. I hear it's kind of . . . uh, elegant."

The Sorrento Hotel is a favorite of mine. Several months ago when Nick's work schedule was crazy and his condo was being repainted, we spent a memorable weekend there. Zelda was right about the elegance, and I couldn't imagine her dining in the hotel's Hunt Room in her flowing Mexican skirt.

"Sure, come on down tonight and I'll see what I can dig out that's citified. I'm not sure what's left. I gave a lot of stuff to Second Time Around when I moved onto *DragonSpray*."

The check Elyse had given me was still in the top drawer of my desk. I opened the drawer and stared at it. I thought about Ben's message, about the possibility of a serial killer, about the FBI being involved. I could call Elyse, tell her the case was too big for me, and return her check. I continued staring at the rectangular blue piece of paper, read Ben's message one more time, then picked up the check and endorsed it "for deposit only."

About to shut down the computer, I realized I hadn't read the last message. When I did, I wished I hadn't.

I don't think I'm going to pass econ. And I think my major is my decision. Can we go to Mendocino for Thanksgiving? Last year you didn't have time. Melissa.

I put the Montenegro file and Elyse's check in my battered briefcase and locked up, idly wondering how much it would cost to bribe Melissa to study something practical. Like business. I also wondered if I was a controlling mother.

Downstairs Zelda and Soraya were discussing homeopathic remedies for insomnia. I bade them farewell and contemplated all the way to the bank Melissa's request that we go to Mendocino to visit her grandmother for Thanksgiving.

12

The line at the bank was unusually long for Wednesday afternoon, and I had ample time to enumerate all the reasons I did not want to spend Thanksgiving in Mendocino with my mother.

One, I did not want to spend several days listening to the artistic pontifications of Jewel Moon's significant other, a painter of dubious talents named Giovanni.

Two, I did not want to listen to Jewel Moon's sympathetic ministrations on my widowhood, since Albert's heart attack while he and his brother were cruising in the Pacific on his sailboat, two days east of the Marquesas, however unexpected, had saved me the trouble of a divorce. God does move in mysterious ways.

And finally, I didn't want Jewel Moon exerting any more of her free-spirited influence on Melissa.

As the queue inched toward the single teller, I wondered what had inspired Jewel Moon, *née* Barbara Baskin, to drop out of Middlebury College long before there was such a thing as the Flower Child generation, and trek off to St. Ann's Bay, Cape Breton Island, Nova Scotia, to study Gaelic dance. But trek she did, and immediately met my father, the handsome son of a Grand Banks fisherman. A whirlwind courtship followed and after the wedding, Jewel Moon MacKinnon settled into what she imagined would be a roman-

tic life on a mountainous island surrounded by wild
seas.

"Wool gathering, Scotia?"

I turned and smiled at the balding, bespectacled
man behind me.

"Hello, Jared. Just dreaming up an excuse to get
out of Thanksgiving at my mother's."

"You have my sympathies. How about a drink at
George's when we get out of here?"

"Best offer I've had all day." Jared was the owner
and publisher of the *Friday Gazette*. He had taken
over the newspaper after retiring as an international
freelance journalist. Rumor had it he'd covered both
the Vietnam and the Persian Gulf Wars and had
garnered a number of journalism prizes for his coverage of African tribal conflicts. We had met when he
did the feature story on my Waldron Island child-
kidnapping case.

I usually had a drink or a coffee with Jared once a
week. I knew, the way a woman knows, that Jared
was very fond of me, and that I only had to say the
word to create more than a friendship. With Nick
around, I'd never been motivated.

In response to the slightly impatient "Next, please,"
I moved up to the window and handed over Elyse's
check. I maintained a blank face when the teller gave
me a quick look of surprise at the amount. My normal
deposits are far more modest.

She produced a receipt for me, I waited for Jared
to complete his transaction, and then we sauntered
over to George's, which was surprisingly quiet for
five p.m.

"I hear you have a new client."

I nodded, took a long sip of the dry vermouth and
soda, and resisted asking how he knew.

"Too bad about Campbell," he said. "Nice lady.
You think there was foul play involved?"

"Why do you ask?" I contemplated my pale face in

the beveled mirror behind the bar and wished I'd put on some lipstick before I left the office.

"My editor's son has been cleaning stables out at the Percheron ranch. He says Elyse thinks Campbell's accident was intentional."

What the hell. I shrugged, established that our conversation was off the record, and told Jared about Julio Montenegro's murder and his wife's theory that her stalker was the murderer. I also mentioned the Denver incident involving the Puerto Rican attorney.

"Sounds like you might have a serial murderer on your hands. A serial murderer with interesting politics." He pulled a pipe from his pocket and began to fill it.

"Interesting how?"

"The victims were both Hispanic, weren't they?" Jared sipped his Guinness stout and looked at me thoughtfully. "A journalist friend of mine did a lot of research a couple of years ago and wrote a book on the white separatist movement. Traveled all over far-right America, interviewed everybody from Klansmen to militiamen to loggers and farmers."

"What did he find out?"

"What *she* found out was an eye-opener. She discovered there's an astonishing number of very disillusioned citizens in this country who feel their voices don't count. Who feel life has become too fast, too technical, too expensive and too regulated." He lit a match and touched it to the aromatic tobacco.

"And, pray tell, Dr. Watson, what does that have to do with two Hispanic attorneys being shot?"

"In connection with your new client and her deceased husband, who I understand was a Mexican national, a lot of people are convinced that the country is being invaded and taken over by foreigners, all of whom speak some awful language they can't understand. And they see these people everywhere. At the movies, at the supermarket, at McDonald's."

"You're suggesting that my client's husband might

have been killed by some weirdo who doesn't like foreigners."

"Think about it. And consider the fact that the murderer may be only beginning his career."

"Well, now, that's an uplifting thought."

Jared scribbled something on a white napkin and handed it to me. "This is the book my friend wrote. You might find it illuminating."

I looked at the scribbles on the napkin and tucked it into my jacket pocket.

"What's your next step in unmasking the murderer most foul?" Jared took a long swallow of his Guinness. "Are you going down to the Bay Area?"

"As soon as I check out the Karmann-Ghia and the accident scene and see if I can figure out any connection to what happened in Berkeley in July. It would be a big help if Campbell regained consciousness."

"Ah, the process of detection." He stared at his pipe, which appeared to have gone out. "Always a backward process, isn't it? Reasoning from an effect to the cause."

I nodded and watched him fumble in his jacket pocket for another match. Jared is a mystery buff. He collects first editions of Arthur Conan Doyle and Edgar Allan Poe and was fond of quoting odd philosophical bits and pieces of crime detection.

"Well, my dear, according to Holmes's theory of deduction and analysis, the perfect murder is not one that's unsolvable, it's the one that most rigorously tests your mettle." He held the lighted match over the bowl of the pipe and drew on it. "You have a cold case. No suspects after four months. Possibly a serial killer. It would appear your mettle's going to be tested."

Unlike Sherlock Holmes, I preferred cases that were quick and simple, not unsolvable. And I wondered how I would juggle an unsolvable crime and still fly down to Seattle to meet Nick tomorrow. I checked my watch. Six o'clock. I suddenly remembered Nick was going to call right after work. I finished the vermouth and soda and slid down from the bar stool.

"I'm sorry, Jared, I have to run. I'm expecting a phone call. Thanks for the drink and the advice."

He looked surprised and helped me into my jacket. "Good luck with the investigation. Don't forget the law of progressive homicide. Call me if you need me."

The theory that once one murder occurs, subsequent murders will be committed to cover up the first one.

I left him staring through the pipe smoke at the mirror behind the bar. All that was lacking was a deerstalker cap.

13

A surprisingly frigid gust of wind struck me as I came out of the corner grocery with the *Seattle Times* and a piroshki from the deli and headed for the Port. I wished I'd dressed more warmly this morning. Then I remembered that when I left for Nick's yesterday, it was warmer. Yesterday seemed eons ago.

Standing on the corner of First and Spring Streets waiting for the traffic to clear, I thought about Jared's, or more likely Dr. Watson's, theory of progressive homicide.

Did that mean Elyse was correct in her suspicion that her stalker mistakenly caused Campbell's accident, thinking that Elyse was driving the car? If so, then the murderer must have believed that Elyse could identify him. The young woman I'd seen with Elyse yesterday at Churchill's could easily be mistaken for Elyse at a distance. And was the connection between Julio Montenegro's death and the shooting of the Hispanic attorney in Denver one of race, as Jared had suggested? I'd know a lot more when I talked to Sergeant Wineheart at the Berkeley PD. Practically speaking, I should go down to Berkeley as soon as possible. Maybe I could leave from Seattle after I saw Nick on Thursday. Which was tomorrow.

While I was using the rest room below the Port office, the wind kicked up a few more knots. Head tucked into my jacket collar, I hurried toward "G" dock, which used to be for transients only. Along with everything else on the island, the number of live-aboards had increased after the marina expansion last year. Henry the mortgage broker was trotting up the dock, headed for his diurnal libation at the pub. He saluted me. "Calico's been fed. Don't let her bamboozle you."

Calico the cat had come to live on "G" dock in the spring. I had religiously resisted her wiles for several weeks until one rainy night when I found her curled under the canvas binnacle cover trying to stay dry, and I'd taken her in and fed her Chicken of the Sea. The following morning, rather than have me take her to the animal shelter, Henry suggested that we become joint foster parents. It seemed to work; when one of us was away, the other made sure she had a dry cushion to sleep on.

The bell on the Turn Island Light clanged its melancholy warning and choppy waves were piling up beyond the breakwater. Back on Slip number 73, I checked *DragonSpray*'s mooring lines and unlocked the hatch cover. Below, I turned on the heat, pulled on a heavy hooded sweatshirt and made a cup of Red Zinger tea. The new instant hot-water dispenser I'd gifted myself with made life a lot easier. A search through the locker in the galley produced a small, unopened sack of corn chips. Minutes later, the diesel heater kicked over to warm air.

I emptied my briefcase, put the Montenegro file on the table, sorted halfheartedly through the last two days' mail.

A reminder from the Port that I was late paying the November moorage fees.

The October bank statement.

P.I. Magazine.

A postcard from Jewel Moon, the front of which displayed the picturesque village of Mendocino, California, cloaked in Pacific mist. I turned it over.

> *Looking forward to seeing you for Thanksgiving. Giovanni is going to Phoenix to see*

*his granddaughter. It will be just us girls. Love,
J. M.*

A sudden gust hit *DragonSpray* and she rolled
against her mooring lines. The silence in the cabin was
loud. I slid a Luther Vandross CD into the player and
glanced around the boat. *DragonSpray* was, above all,
a vessel designed for heavy weather, sturdy and sea-
worthy. I'd bought her from a couple who had cruised
and lived aboard for fourteen years. She was custom-
built of fiberglass. Belowdecks, the main cabin and
staterooms were appointed with brass grab rails, the
bulkheads faced with honeysuckle and mahogany. The
doors over the bookshelves were leaded glass, and ma-
roon velvet covered the settees in the main salon, elegant but not always practical. Although the former
owners had cruised mostly in the tropics, the floors
were overlaid with cork, a real plus in the rainy
Northwest.

I warmed the piroshki in the microwave and wondered when Nick would call. The portable phone was
in the master stateroom, buried under a blanket, its
message signal buzzing. *Merde!* I checked messages
and didn't like what I heard.

"Scotty, Nick here. I guess you're working late or
something. I'm sorry, but Thursday isn't going to work
out. The hearing went well this morning, but the new
client needs a lot of my attention. A millionaire who
hunts offshore sunken treasure. This could be a big
one, sweetheart. I'm taking Nicole to dinner tonight,
and this weekend I have to help her find an apartment.
I'll try you later. And, Scotty"—there was a pause—
"thanks for last night."

Merde encore! I felt childishly disappointed and last
night seemed a thousand light-years ago.

I listened to the message again, heard the excite-
ment and then the tenderness in his voice, hated myself for wishing he hadn't gotten the new client, for
selfishly wishing that the firm of Anastazi Cooper Nakano hadn't become so successful.

Since the beginning of my relationship with Nick, there had been a long line of obstacles. The divorce proceedings dragged on for three years. The property settlement was signed only six months ago. The divorce had taken a toll on Nick and a heavier toll on his children, Stephan, nineteen, and Nicole, twenty-two. Nicole, especially, was still furious with her father for ending the fairytale life on Belvedere Island. She had recently deigned to talk to him, but my presence was intolerable to her. Even though she didn't know Nick and I had met before her parents divorced, I was the Home Wrecker, the Other Woman, the Harlot. And far be it from me to suggest it was time for Nicole to grow up and face the reality that Mummy and Daddy weren't going to get back together.

"Permission to come aboard?"

I opened the companionway hatch boards. A burst of cold wind followed Zelda below. I replaced the hatch covers and offered hot tea.

"Is that all you have?"

I pointed to the reefer. "Help yourself. How was the movie?"

"Outrageously wonderful. But the Coronas are turning into a bunch of fuddy-duddies. No one wanted to go to George's for a beer." She pulled out a Full Sail ale and twisted off the cap.

"Did you have a full contingent tonight?"

She shook her head. "Just me and Rebecca and Abby and Sheldon."

Abby was Abigail Leedle, a septuagenarian wildlife photographer, widow of a former Friday Harbor high school superintendent.

"Sheldon? When did the Coronas become coed?"

"Sheldon's an honorary member."

Sheldon Wainwright was a ship's pilot and a long-time Zelda admirer. Two weeks a month he worked out of Port Angeles, over on the Olympic Peninsula, guiding megafreighters in and out of the Strait of Juan de Fuca. The other two weeks he spent with his aunt at Cape San Juan, which was where the two had met when Zelda was house-sitting out there. Sheldon was patently smitten by Zelda's outrageousness and she found him as exciting as Milquetoast, even though she was intrigued by his job. I also suspected the fact that Sheldon made beaucoup bucks didn't hurt. How Sheldon fit into Zelda's life and her ongoing quest for love, I neither knew nor wanted to know.

"Everyone's really depressed about Campbell's accident. If it was." She took a long swallow of the ale. "What have you got that'll spice up the black dress and impress my yacht broker?"

I motioned her into the stateroom, pulled out a wooden box from the locker over my bunk and dumped the contents. "I'm afraid my accessories are limited. You have three choices in scarves: a wine-colored silk with fringe, this black paisley number, or, my favorite, this big green wool challis print."

"I love the silk, and the black is super elegant, but I think the green will brighten it up." She draped the green challis around her shoulders mantilla-fashion. "Whadya think?"

"The green is great with your hair." It was still strawberry blonde. I wondered what color it might be by Friday.

"Can you believe it, Scotia? Me, in a simple little black dress?"

I reached into a small drawer and pulled out my jewelry box. "I think the scarf would be lonely without these." I handed her a small white box. She opened it and held up a pair of pale-green stained-glass earrings I hadn't worn in a long time.

"Cool. You know, this is important. He says he likes classy women. I really want him to like me."

I gave her a quick hug. "Be careful what you wish for."

We put the scarf and the little white box in a bag.

"By the by," she said, flinging herself onto the settee and picking up the half-eaten bag of corn chips. "Fran McGillicutty says the Ghia was totaled. It's

parked behind their office, ready to get hauled off-
island. Better check it out tomorrow if you want to
see it." She lifted three chips out of the sack, crunched
them, took another gulp of ale. "Any new leads on
George Simms alias Jason Simmons alias God knows
who?"

I shook my head, not ready for public dissemination
of the Denver shooting incident. With Zelda, there
was no such thing as off the record; all incoming information was instantly processed as "For Immediate
Distribution."

"I'm waiting to hear from my Berkeley contact," I
said. "Maybe tomorrow."

"I've been thinking." She drained the bottle of Full
Sail, leaned back on the cushions, and put her feet up
on the settee. She rubbed her wrist and frowned.

"Sore wrist?"

She nodded. "Carpal tunnel syndrome. I need a
break from that computer. I'm thinking of starting a
catering business. Maybe the dude she thinks was
stalking her wasn't really a stalker. Maybe he was a
legit private eye the murderer hired to find her, like
she was a missing person, so he can finish her off.
Does that ever happen?"

Reeling from Zelda's lightning switch from carpal
tunnel syndrome to new careers to my new client, I
nodded. A similar nasty thought had occurred to me.
"It could, though if he was a P.I., then that would
mean Campbell's accident was really an accident.
Legit private eyes aren't usually contract killers."

She nodded. "But if it was an accident because
Campbell had too much to drink, with no malice
aforethought or whatever, and the guy in the black
Cherokee was hired to find the Snow Queen, he'll
report to his client that he found her, then the bad
guy will be arriving on the island any day now. Or, if
it wasn't an accident, and the schmuck did intend to
do away with her, sooner or later he's going to find
out he made a mistake, and he'll be back." She took
a deep breath, unfolded herself from the settee, and

stood up. "Either way, boss, looks like you got your work cut out for you."

Yeah.

"Gotta run. I'm leaving on the red-eye tomorrow. Have to stop at the mall and get some classy boots to go with the dress."

"Dakota going with you?"

"Rebecca's keeping him at the ranch for the weekend. See ya Monday." I opened the sliding hatch, she climbed the companionway and was gone.

I closed the hatch, nagged by something Zelda had said about the Montenegro case.

The file lay open on the table. I made another cup of tea and sorted through the pages of notes and reviewed the names my client had given me.

Elyse's parents: Alice and Wilhelm Muehler.

Julio's colleagues: Peter Aaron, director of the Latin American Union for Defense; LAUD staff attorneys Felipe De los Santos and Judith Karamazov.

Peter's wife, Carmela Aaron.

No close friends except the Aarons.

I found the comments on Julio's work for LAUD. He had been working on three cases just before the murder. The big one had involved the Coalition for English Only, some kind of grass-roots group that opposed bilingual education. Elyse didn't know what the other two cases were. I frowned, staring at my notes. Julio had run unsuccessfully for Berkeley City Council, and had traveled to Mexico several times as an emissary for a peace and justice group in Berkeley. Julio Montenegro had a penchant for political activism. I thought about what Jared had said about following an effect back to its cause. I might not have to follow it very far. But, if that were true, then the Berkeley PD would already have found the murderer. I organized the pages, closed the file, and considered the more immediate problem of Elyse's stalker. Zelda's analysis was right on. There was a good possibility he would return to the island. I wondered what Ben Carey had found out.

I kept a laptop computer on the boat for days when I didn't have any appointments. There was one new e-mail message, from the Berkeley PD. I opened it and the phone rang.

"Scotia MacKinnon."

"Scotty, Nick." His voice was breathless. "Glad I caught you. We just got back from dinner."

"Have a good time?" I asked, beginning to read Ben's message.

> *Sergeant Wineheart reviewed the Montene-*
> *gro file with me. Only possible witnesses*
> *were victim's wife and colleague and two*
> *women on the docks. No positive IDs.*
> *Sandy Silver, our Public Information Officer,*
> *will . . .*

I read to the bottom of the screen and tried to concentrate on what Nick was saying.

". . . a good talk and then we stopped by Pete's for a cappuccino. I think she's starting to forgive me."

"What does she have to forgive you for?" The words slipped out before I could bite my tongue.

There was a short silence. "Nicole is still very young, Scotia," Nick said. "The divorce was hard on her. It takes time. We've discussed all this before." I heard a door open and close in the background and Nick's voice changed. "How's your new case going?"

"Slowly. And not nearly as interesting as your new client," I lied. "A treasure hunter, yet?"

"A treasure hunter. He actually heads up an exclusive investment group specializing in deepwater salvage. Current project is Manila galleons off the west coast of Mexico. Hold on." I heard a petulant female voice in the background.

Nick sighed and lowered his voice. "Anyway, I apologize for the change in plans. I'll make it up to you soon."

I kept my voice even. "I'll look forward to it, Nick.

Have a nice visit with Nicole. Good luck with the Manila galleons."

"Yeah, sure. I'll call you next week." The line went dead.

"Night, Nick." I stared at the phone. It was ridiculous for an adult woman to feel jealous of her lover's daughter, but I did. Disassociating myself from the unsatisfactory conversation, I replaced the receiver in the cradle and returned my attention to the computer screen. I scrolled down and read the rest of Ben's message.

> . . . *send you details on the Denver case*
> *tomorrow. Meanwhile, be careful! See you*
> *soon? B.C.*

I took a deep breath and closed down the computer. Teeth brushed and face washed, I put on my blue plaid flannel pajamas, turned off the heat and crawled under the white comforter. The boat was rocking gently. Just before sleep overtook me, I thought again about Jared's theory of progressive homicide. Or was it Dr. Watson's?

And if Dr. Watson was right, who would be the next victim?

14

I arrived at the office slightly before nine on Thursday morning, a late arrival for me. I'd run into Jared in front of the movie theater and allowed him to talk me into a cafe mocha and a cinnamon roll. Now, I felt like a sugary toad. An afternoon walk was unavoidable.

There was no sign of Soraya, and Zelda was conspicuous in her absence. No aroma of freshly brewed coffee. No Puccini or Vivaldi. No infectious smile or lewd comment. Upstairs, I turned on the wall heater and switched on the computer. I was eager to see the info on the Denver shooting. I connected to the Internet server and waited impatiently for my messages to download, which seemed to take forever. I wondered if I'd acquired a new virus. While I waited, I checked my calendar. I had a nine-thirty appointment with Wilma Winterbottom, the judge's wife. I had been amused by her secretive demeanor on the phone last week and wondered what she wanted.

I glanced back at the computer screen. One new message had downloaded. It was from Officer Silver, Berkeley PD.

Roberto Alarcon, an attorney for the Rocky Mountain Center for Legal Defense in Denver, was shot and fatally wounded as he was leaving the Municipal Courthouse at 2:30 p.m. on September 6. Alarcon's assistant told

*police two shots were fired as Alarcon was
about to get into his car.*

*No one saw the attacker, who apparently fled
into a group of anti-abortion protestors pa-
rading in front of the courthouse. Alarcon suffered two bullet wounds to the shoulder and
chest and died on September 10. Alarcon was
at the Municipal Court to attend a hearing
involving a client of his who was suing her
employer for gender and racial
discrimination.*

I was pondering the similarities between the Montenegro shooting and the Denver shooting—both Hispanic attorneys, both victims of an attacker who
disappeared immediately after the shooting—when I
heard firm steps on the stairs. The partly closed door
opened and the plump, well-dressed figure of Wilma
Winterbottom marched into the room.

She glanced over her shoulder as if she were being
followed, and closed the door firmly. She returned my
greeting, sighed, sat in the chair next to my desk, and
patted her artfully arranged blonde hair.

"I know you must be wondering why I wanted to
see you," she said in a throaty, conspiratorial voice,
sliding her gray tweed coat off her shoulders. "I'm
only coming to you as a last resort." She arranged her
mauve suit jacket over the top of her mid-thigh skirt.

"How can I help you, Mrs. Winterbottom?"

"Please, call me Wilma."

I nodded, wanting to get back to the e-mail. She
twisted the handles of her tapestry handbag and
frowned at her lilac fingernails. "Well, you see, it's . . .
it's so embarrassing. But I may just as well spit it out.
I think the judge is having an affair."

"An affair? The judge?" I sat up straight, trying to
repress a smile. It was common knowledge among
Matt Petersen's cronies that Wilma had been making
clandestine visits to the captain of the *Alaskan Queen*
whenever the seiner was in port for the past ten years.

Although I couldn't imagine the dignified, wintry figure of the Honorable Julius Winterbottom in a compromising position, I wondered if the worm had turned.

"I'm positive of it," she said. "He started dieting and last week he went and bought a new suit. Besides that, he's worked late for the last two weeks."

I nodded, and said, "Hmmm."

"I know it must be a shock to you, Scotia, and I know you will keep this confidential, but I simply won't stand for it. I must know who the woman is."

I said, "Hmmm" again, and wondered how I could get out of this one.

"I want you to collect evidence, for the divorce, you see."

"Divorce?" Did she plan to take her share of the judge's not inconsequential assets and move aboard the *Alaskan Queen*?

"Yes, of course. I will not be made a laughingstock. But before I get a lawyer, I need evidence."

"Evidence?" I parroted, feeling like a grade-B detective on a late-night rerun of *Dragnet*.

"Yes, you know," she said irritably. "Photos, recordings of his phone conversations, a bug or something. I'm sure you do it all the time. Just tell me what your fee is and I'll give you a retainer." She reached for her purse.

Marveling at the growing number of clients with deep pockets, I maintained a serious demeanor, avoiding the image of my skulking around the judge's chambers with my Nikon and a state-of-the-art listening device.

"Actually, Mrs. Winterbottom, Wilma, most of my work involves insurance matters. I seldom get involved with domestic cases of this sort." I reached for my appointment book, riffled through the pages, closed it and laid it down. "The truth is, I'm up to my eyebrows in work and I have some extensive travel coming up. I don't think I could do justice to your problem. But

I'd be happy to refer you to a colleague of mine in Mt. Vernon."

"Well, really." She pulled the tweed coat over her shoulders and stood up, lips pursed. "I wouldn't think of hiring someone off-island." She pursed her lips again. "I suppose I'll just go directly to my lawyer in Seattle and have him collect the evidence. Thank you for your time." She marched to the door, closed it firmly and was gone.

Thank God.

I stared at the closed door for a minute, collected my thoughts, then reread the account of the Denver shooting. Two Hispanic civil rights attorneys, two months apart, the first in the San Francisco Bay area, the second in Colorado. Pattern or coincidence? Random acts or carefully planned executions?

I opened the second new message. It was from Angela.

Campbell Sawyer died early this morning at St. Patrick's Hospital in Bellingham without regaining consciousness. Since her blood alcohol level was .18 when she was admitted, the sheriff considers the case closed.

The phone rang. It was Elyse. Without preamble, and in a high thin voice barely controlled, she repeated what Angela had told me. "Ms. MacKinnon, she's dead. Please find out who killed her! Please find out who killed Julio!"

"Elyse, I am so sorry about your friend. And yes, I'm going to try to find out who killed Julio."

"And Campbell, Ms. MacKinnon!" Her voice was full of tears and on the edge of hysteria. "Don't forget Campbell!"

I nodded, as if she could see me. "I'm leaving tomorrow for San Francisco." I told her that if she thought of any new information, she was to call my cell phone.

"Take care of yourself," I said. "And stay out of sight."

All physical events occur in a cause-and-effect progression. Murder is no exception. I needed to find out more about causes and a lot more about the character of Julio Montenegro.

It was time to visit the scene of the crime.

PART II

Dime con quién andas y te diré quién eres.
(Tell me who you hang out with and I'll tell you who you are.)

—Miguel de Cervantes Saavedra

15

The large white cat crouched on one side of the desk and stared out the window overlooking the lake. Winter had come early to the mountains. A thin covering of icy snow lay on the old wooden dock. The white cat turned from the window and with clear green eyes watched the man power up the computer and log on. The San Juan Island web site appeared. The man clicked on the link for the Friday Gazette. *Ignoring the throbbing behind his eyes, he stroked the cat's silky fur and waited. The blue and green graphics filled the screen. The man read the digitized headline and smiled.*

San Juan Island woman in fatal auto accident.

Finally. The witness was gone!
Still smiling, he clicked on the purple text and read the full story.

A single-fatality, single-car accident on November 7 shocked and saddened the island community. Campbell Marie Sawyer, a talented island artist, suffered numerous contusions and lacerations and was unconscious when transported by helicopter to St. Patrick's Hospital in Bellingham Tuesday afternoon. Ms. Sawyer failed to regain consciousness and died shortly after 4:00 a.m. today.

Sawyer?!

The man's face contorted in anger. He slammed his hand down on the desk. The white cat leaped to the floor. The Montenegro bitch had escaped. What the hell happened? Shit. He'd trailed her for three days. Knew her schedule. Knew what car she drove. Knew where she lived. He'd been waiting down the road from the ranch when she left work early on Tuesday. She'd been wearing a hat, but he'd recognized the long blonde hair and she'd gotten into the Ghia with a big brown package. He'd followed her all the way to the top of Mt. Dallas, waited until she came out of the house and started back down the hill. How could he have made a mistake? He frowned, massaged his right temple, and continued reading.

The accident occurred at the intersection of Mt. Dallas Road and Starflower Lane. Apparently Ms. Sawyer failed to make the hairpin curve, and a preliminary investigation suggests that excessive speed may have been involved. The car, which is owned by Ms. Sawyer's friend, Elyse Montenegro, left the roadway, rolled several times down the rocky hillside and came to rest against a boulder. The San Juan County Sheriff's Department is investigating the accident. Anyone having information regarding the accident is asked to call this newspaper or the sheriff's department.

The man narrowed his eyes. He'd missed his target. Damn! He hit the desk again with his fist. The one witness from the Berkeley Marina was still alive. He'd have to go back. Shit! If she had been where she was supposed to be that Friday back in July, he'd be clear. But she wasn't, and she had almost knocked him down when she came through that security gate.

And he had promised there would be no witnesses. He swiveled around in the chair and stared out at the lake, gray and choppy under the dark sky. Thick aspen leaves, partly covered by last night's snowfall, lay along the path that led out to the dock. Even in summer, the lake held only bad memories. Memories of the summer his father had insisted he learn how to swim and had repeatedly pushed him off the dock. He remembered the shame of the tears, of running away, of hiding far back in the woods.

And he had never learned to swim.

He wished he could have moved somewhere else, but taking over the house and building on the addition to live in when the old man died and his mother moved into town had been perfect. The house was at the end of the road and nobody ever knew about the paint and body jobs he did for the brotherhood. Thank God he'd never gotten involved personally. All those bank heists in Seattle and the armored car thefts in California. Who did they think they were fooling? And taking out that talk-show host in Denver was the stupidest move of all. Half the guys were either dead now or in a federal pen somewhere.

There was a knock on the door.

He reached for the weapon in the desk drawer, the little Harrington and Richardson .25 caliber automatic that had become his favorite, and spun around to face the door. There was another knock. He frowned. No one ever came out here unless he ordered something. He held the weapon behind his hip as he approached the door on stockinged feet. Through the partially curtained window he spied a brown UPS van parked in the driveway. He remembered, then, and smiled. He tucked the weapon into the back of his fatigues and opened the door. The big white cat came to stand beside him.

"Hi, there, Georgina. Got a surprise for me today?" He smiled at the woman in the brown uniform.

"Looks like it, Jamie. Just sign right here on the pad." She knelt down and patted the white cat. "How's Snowy?"

"Oh, he's sulking around because of the cold weather."

He scribbled a signature on the computerized pad, bade her farewell, and eyed her shapely bottom in the brown pants as she climbed into the van. Georgina was the daughter of the local UPS franchisees. He'd gone to school with her older brother, Doug, who'd been his best friend. He still remembered the day Doug had left for his basic training for 'Nam, while he, Jamie, stayed behind.

Rejected because of the knee injury.

He carried the package inside and glanced at the return address. It was the new books he'd ordered online. He loved ordering online. Loved the privacy and not having to go into a bookstore and be stared at if he ordered something the owner thought was strange. He opened the cardboard mailer and smiled. How to Design a Wildcat Cartridge *and* The World's Handguns.

It was the next step in his plan.

He opened the first book and read the table of contents.

How to Convert a Cartridge Case.

How to Design a Wildcat Cartridge.

Necking Cartridge Cases.

Choosing Shoulder Angles and Case Tapers.

Damn, but he'd rather stay here instead of going back to that hick island with its cutesy hotels. And that limp-wristed innkeeper. God!

But there was no way out of it. He had to finish the job. It was time to move on.

The phone rang and he tensed, waiting for the answering machine to pick up. He heard the soft, tired voice, heard her hang up, saw the red light on the machine begin to blink.

It was his mother. She called every day now since he blew up at her a week ago. When he'd told her, no, he wasn't taking his effing meds anymore, she'd wanted him to go and see some new shrink at "the clinic." Only it wasn't a clinic; it was an institution, and he would never, ever let her put him there again. He shivered and wished his head didn't ache so much. The headaches started a long time ago, before he went into the state hospital. It was right after the old man got laid off at the mine and his mother went to work at the truck stop over in Spokane and he had the big row with the mongrel from Yakima who had ruined his life. And then there was the fight at the Silver Ass in Wallace, and the trial, and his lawyer had gotten him off by entering a plea of diminished capacity and agreeing for him to go to the mental hospital. Even the judge couldn't have known the state would reduce the funds and he'd be outside in six months.

He turned back to the computer, stared at the web site for the Western Minority Defense Fund, waited impatiently for the orange and red and yellow graphics. The digitized headline brought another smile.

Another one down next week!

He walked to the closet, unlocked the door, and stared at the contents, shelf by shelf. He stroked the hair on the dark wig and moved it beside the dark mustache. He loved disguises, loved being someone else. The Drama Club in high school had been the most important thing in his life. He would never forget the day Mr. Drew, the drama teacher, told him he was eligible for the scholarship to study theater. All he had to do was to get his parents to fill out the financial part of the application. His old man had refused. "It's nobody's damn business how much money I make," he'd screamed. And when he'd tried to explain how important it was to him, Pa had flown into one of his rages. "We're not having any fairies in this family!" He had underscored the refusal with his fists.

He pulled one of the caps off the lower shelf and read the logo on it. "Los Angeles Earthquakes." He smiled. Always the right stuff. And so easy to get. Nothing you couldn't buy on the Internet now. Absolutely nothing.

He continued the visual inventory, surveyed the weapons and the ammo, knowing that the decision to

*go to the militia training camp at Timberline had been
one of the best decisions of his life.*

*He closed and locked the closet door with a feeling
of responsibility and purpose, a sense of following
God's plan for the Chosen People.*

16

The eleven-thirty Harbor Airlines flight to SEA-TAC airport was on time. As a draft of frigid air blew through the open rear door of the eight-seater Grand Caravan I fastened my seat belt and shivered and thought about all the other things I'd rather be doing on a cold Sunday morning. The station agent finished loading the carry-ons, locked the rear door, and a pilot I didn't know climbed into the cockpit, introduced himself, gave us the two-minute briefing special on exit windows, fire extinguishers and inflatable life vests, and we were taxiing our way down the runway in the intermittent rain and gusty winds. Flying off the island in winter is an iffy proposition. As the plane fish-tailed in the crosswind, I wished I had driven down to Seattle, even if it had meant taking the six a.m. ferry. The red-eye, as the locals called it.

The runway and fields on the outskirts of town fell away below us, the plane banked steeply, and we were out over Griffin Bay, then San Juan Channel. The wooded community of Cape San Juan passed below, and a minute later I looked down on the boiling green waters of Cattle Pass, the narrow, rocky channel that separates San Juan from Lopez.

Not for the first time, I mused that San Juan Island bore a distinct resemblance to the physical shape of North America: Cape San Juan was geographically equivalent to Mexico's Yucatán Peninsula, tucked away on a point of land at the end of Griffin Bay.

The flight became distinctly bumpy over Iceberg Point, and I turned my thoughts to the events of the past three days and the purpose of my trip—which was to find out who, if anyone, was stalking my client, and what, if anything, he had to do with the death of her husband and Campbell Sawyer. The messages from Ben Carey and Officer Silver had been unsettling, to say the least. If Julio Montenegro was killed by the same person who killed the Denver civil rights attorney in September, the case was out of my league.

After a bumpy landing on the narrow runway at the Oak Harbor Airport on Whidbey Island, we off-loaded one passenger and on-loaded another, and were off again, out across the whitecapped open waters of the Strait of Juan de Fuca. To take my mind off the fragility of the little plane in the ever-stronger gusts out of the southeast and the iciness of the water three hundred feet below, I reviewed what few facts I knew regarding the Montenegro case.

I knew Julio Montenegro was shot at close range by an unknown assailant in July of this year. Subsequent to the murder, Elyse thought someone was following her in Berkeley.

In September, a Puerto Rican attorney had been killed in Denver by an unidentified gunman.

A month ago Elyse came to Friday Harbor to live with Campbell Sawyer, a family and college friend.

Five days ago, while Campbell was driving Elyse's car, and after having consumed enough alcohol to raise her blood alcohol level well beyond the legal limit, Campbell was involved in a fatal, single-vehicle accident.

Elyse believed the man who was stalking her caused Campbell's accident.

On Friday I'd contacted Elyse again, gotten a key to her house in Oakland, and asked her to call Julio's colleague, Peter Aaron, at LAUD. I'd also gone over to the lot behind the offices of McGillicutty Insurance and checked out the ill-fated little Ghia. It looked like someone had taken a sledgehammer to it, but Ghias 'were not designed in an era of test-car dummies. Fran McGillicutty said that after it was hauled to the mainland, the brakes would be checked for any indications of tampering. She'd promised to call Zelda with the report.

Yesterday, I'd gone out to Nick's house, replenished Marmalade's food and water, and revisited the scene of the accident on Starflower Lane. There were long skid marks in the dirt where the Ghia would have left the road. A significant portion of a blackberry patch had been torn out as the car skidded and rolled down the hillside and came to rest against a huge boulder which, eons ago, before the glaciers began moving, probably lived a thousand or more miles northwest of San Juan Island. Without that boulder, the little red car and its unfortunate driver would have ended up in Walden's Pond, two hundred feet below. I found no clues on the ground, no traces of anything other than the tracks of the runaway Ghia and the EMS van.

In final preparation for my visit to the scene of a crime possibly committed by a racist serial murderer, I had gone by Remainders bookstore and found a used copy of *White Tempest*, the book Jared's friend had written on the incipient white revolution.

The early-afternoon flight to San Francisco was uneventful, highlighted only by my observations of the young family seated across the aisle and in the row ahead of me. It was a thirty-something couple traveling with three children, two pretty girls between the ages of two and four, and a handsome, slightly older boy wearing a yarmulke. After takeoff, the young mother, with jet-black eyes, shiny hair, and porcelain skin, and who seemed the epitome of calmness, removed a children's book from an embroidered denim rucksack. Somewhere above Mt. Shasta, the father, handsome, pale, attentive and harassed, gave up his attempts to read the *New York Times* and began to read Bambi to the toddler beside him with the angelic, exotic face of her mother.

Their daily life—an intact family with both parents sharing the child rearing—was as alien to me as that of a family of Martians. When Melissa was three, her father went off to the Seychelles on a dive expedition from which he never returned. After infrequent postcards for a year, he wrote that he had found true love with the innkeeper at the Seychelles Beach Hotel, and was going to work as a dive instructor. Would I please do a divorce and send him the final decree? It didn't please me, but I did.

Melissa was ten when I remarried, this time to Pete Santana, a Mexican-American narcotics detective I met when I was doing Harbor Patrol in San Diego. Whether or not that marriage would have survived quickly became moot when Pete perished in the cross fire between a first-level cocaine dealer in San Diego and his Tijuana *patrón*.

By the time I met Albert, a San Francisco stockbroker who collected antique cars and liked to race fast sailing yachts, Melissa was a difficult thirteen, and I'd had enough of trying to improve society. While significantly lacking in husbandly qualities, Albert did provide a few years of parental supervision and left a small trust fund for Melissa, a house in St. Francis Wood, and three antique cars for me.

On the ground at SFO, I picked up the rental car, a late-model Oldsmobile Intrigue, and wished I'd flown directly into the East Bay, where most of my investigation would be focused. The only people I wanted to talk to in San Francisco were Elyse's parents, Alice and Wilhelm Muehler. They probably wouldn't appreciate an unscheduled visit.

I joined the Sunday-afternoon eastbound gridlock on the approach to the Bay Bridge and tried to forget that but for Nick's new client and mine, we'd be snugly anchored in a cove up on Saltspring Island, sipping cocktails in the romantic light of *'Spray*'s antique trawler lamp. *C'est la vie.*

*   *   *

Darkness was enveloping the Bay when I checked in at the Water's Edge Lodge at the Berkeley Marina. The hotel, previously managed by a major chain, was under new ownership, and had recently been renovated. My room was in the new wing on the northeast corner. I opened the drapes and could just make out the Berkeley Yacht Club directly across the choppy waters. I'd sent Ben an e-mail on Friday, asking to talk to Sergeant Wineheart. My stomach was requesting sustenance, but I wanted to get started early Monday, so I called East Bay information and got Ben's home number. He was living in Albany, a bedroom community of modest single-family homes in the Berkeley foothills. He answered on the second ring.

"Glad to hear you made it. Where are you? Can I buy you a drink?"

"I've been traveling all day and I'll take a rain check. Did you get my e-mail?"

"I did. And I talked to Sandy Silver, our public information officer. She's trying to get you an appointment with Wineheart tomorrow. Check in with her tonight, if you like." He gave me her phone number.

"Terrific. I'll start with Wineheart and then track down the victim's colleagues. I'll call you when I get a break and I'll buy *you* a drink."

"Deal. I'll look forward to it." There was a pause. "Talk to Wineheart about the Denver shooting. And for God's sake, be careful."

I called Sandy Silver next and learned I had an appointment with Wineheart at nine-thirty on Monday. She asked if I had seen Ben and suggested I come to her office first. Something in her tone suggested a more than collegial relationship between the public information officer and the lieutenant.

All was darkness beyond my window. A walk would have to wait for morning. I closed the curtains, changed into my flannel pj's and called room service, which promised to send up a pastrami sandwich and coffee in fifteen minutes.

My voice mail had one message, from Melissa. She

wanted to see me while I was in the Bay area, but
she had a paper due on Friday. No message from
Nick, which was disappointing but not unexpected. I
revisited the intimacies of last Tuesday, which now
had the qualities of a distant dream. I wondered where
he was and what he was doing.

My dinner order arrived while I was watching the
local TV news, after which I climbed into bed with
White Tempest and fell asleep somewhere in the midst
of an FBI siege of a safe house on Whidbey Island.

17

The Monday-morning East Bay commute into the city had always been fierce and time had not improved it. From the top of the Highway 80 overpass, I stared down at the lines of cars, moving at a snail's pace, four and five lanes deep, extending for miles on the approach to the San Francisco–Oakland Bay Bridge. I sped east in the rental car up University Avenue to McKinley, and arrived at the Berkeley PD promptly at nine twenty-five. The young Asian woman in the glassed-in enclosure on the second floor advised Officer Silver of her visitor, and she came out to greet me with a hesitant smile and a small frown. She was a tall, slender redhead with freckles on her nose and a body that looked like it had regular workouts. A wholesome type. Maybe Ben had learned a lesson from the Mary Louise episode.

I followed Officer Silver down the hall. She walked with the easy, graceful stride of a model, and on her, man-tailored pants and a crisp white shirt looked like designer gear. After a brief introduction to Sergeant Detective Wineheart, she excused herself. "Come down to my office when you're finished."

I nodded and directed my attention to the unsmiling homicide detective seated behind the gray metal desk. His skin was a rich brown-black and he was dressed in a long-sleeved blue oxford-cloth shirt with a navy blue–striped tie and a black leather shoulder holster. Two framed photos sat on the credenza behind his desk, one of a stunningly beautiful woman with short, curly dark hair, the second of a thin boy of five or six standing behind the wheel of a sailboat. A large photo of a ketch under sail decorated the wall above the credenza.

"Your boat?"

He nodded. "*Was* my boat. We sold it when my son Billy took up soccer and my wife decided to go to law school. How can I help you?"

I thought back to my five years in the detective bureau at San Diego PD. I knew Detective Wineheart had better things to do than discuss a cold case with a private citizen. Which is all a P.I. is.

"Sergeant, I appreciate your making time for me. I have no pretensions I can do a better job than you've done. I've agreed to represent Elyse Montenegro, who thinks she's being stalked by her husband's murderer. Since my schedule is not nearly as jammed up as yours—" I shrugged. "Who knows?"

His shoulders relaxed a fraction of an inch. "Ben told me your background. I'm happy to share what we know, which is not much." He stared at the manila file on his desk blotter. The tab said "Montenegro" in neat, black, handwritten script. He opened the folder and began reading from the pages in a stilted fashion. "An unarmed man was shot at the municipal marina. The victim was shot from behind. We recovered three .32 caliber bullets. The M.E. found one bullet lodged in his spine, one passed through his heart. The third bullet ricocheted off the bulkhead beside the companionway and struck Aaron in the shoulder. The attacker escaped without being identified. Probably used a silencer, since nobody remembered hearing the shots."

If he used a silencer, the gun was probably an automatic. "Did you recover the ejected cases?"

He nodded. "We sent a diver down. He recovered all three of them."

"And the weapon?"

"Must have taken it with him when he fled the

scene. Based on the rifling marks on the bullets and the action marks on the cases, we think it was a Beretta automatic."

A serious weapon, not a Saturday night special. I have a carry permit for a Beretta .380 myself. I've had it for years and I like it because it has a tip-up barrel that lets me load the chamber without racking the slide. I'd rather not carry a gun at all, and twenty years of law enforcement and investigation have instilled a strong dislike for weapons of destruction. But the life of a private investigator is unpredictable and the mere presence of the weapon probably saved my life the night I came up against the sentry on the Chinese sailboat that was smuggling illegal aliens.

"What was the ammo?" I asked.

"Winchester 60-grain Silvertip hollow points. A nasty load. This guy wanted to make sure the victim died. A very careful murderer."

I stared at the detective and he stared back. I had to agree that whoever killed my client's husband was very careful indeed. No fingerprints, no fibers, no DNA. Only the casings and the rifling on the bullets.

Rifling is a term that describes the series of grooves that are cut into the barrel of a gun by the manufacturer to improve the accuracy of the bullet's trajectory. These grooves are unique to each batch of firearms, or may even be microscopically unique to each barrel in a batch, and a good firearms person can usually determine what make, model and caliber of weapon the bullet was fired from.

"I can't imagine what your client expects you to find that we haven't found," Wineheart said. His diction was educated, his sentences precise. He folded well-manicured hands over the open manila file and looked at me somberly. "As far as witnesses go, we had only the sketchiest of descriptions. Five eleven or six-feet tall, probably male, wearing a yellow foul-weather jacket, sailing cap, blue jeans, sunglasses and mustache."

I nodded. "Nobody saw him on the docks?"

"Two women may have passed the attacker when he came into the marina. Mr. Aaron got a glimpse of his back. All Mrs. Montenegro could remember was that she passed a man wearing a yellow jacket and sunglasses. We did a computerized composite, but nobody was able to match it with any known criminals. So we don't know who the perp is, what he or she really looks like, or even what the motive was." He hesitated, then added, "Though, God knows, Julio Montenegro had his fingers in enough political pies."

"Such as?" I wondered if his list would match Elyse's.

He shrugged and shuffled a couple of pages.

"Bank of America, International Division. Public Defender in the city. Then LAUD. He ran for Berkeley City Council last year. Pro bono work for a Chicano labor group down in Salinas. The EZLN in Chiapas."

EZLN? Chiapas? What was that? I decided not to reveal my political naiveté. I would ask Melissa.

He shuffled a few more pages, chewed on the inside of his mouth, closed the file and stared at me with wide eyes.

"What about the car that followed Elyse right after the murder?" I asked.

"What about it? Mrs. Montenegro reported it, but she never got a license tag. She wasn't sure what color it was. Or if it really was following her."

Wineheart's phone rang. "Wineheart, Homicide." He listened and stood up. "Be right there."

I knew the look on his face. Somewhere in the precinct there was a body. By this time tomorrow there would be a new file on the detective's desk. Better him than me. At the time I resigned from SDPD, I thought it was for Melissa and Albert. Now I know it was for me. I've never been one for fighting losing battles.

"Ben mentioned you've been working with VICAP on this case. That there might be similarities with a shooting in Denver."

"I gave them what I had," he said. "They're trying to cross-reference it with the Denver attack. Same MO as this one." He reached for his jacket on the back of the chair, settled it over his blue shirt and leather shoulder holster.

I reached to shake his hand. "Thank you for your time, Detective."

A muscle clenched in his jaw. "I'd really like to be of more help, Ms. MacKinnon. My intuition tells me there's far more to this case than meets the eye. But I've got two boxes of unsolved cases over there."

I glanced at the documents storage boxes stacked next to the bookcase and followed him into the hallway.

"Officer Silver's office is the second one on the right. And if you find out anything new, I know you'll share it with us."

Across the corridor a door opened. A small, slender Hispanic woman in a well-tailored maroon-colored suit came out. Wineheart nodded to her and they hurried down the stairs.

Sandy Silver was on the phone, but terminated the conversation when I came in. She stood up with a forced smile. "So, was Wineheart any help?"

I nodded, not letting on I'd been hoping for more. "He had to leave."

She was standing, looking me over. Her face still wore a small frown. "Have you, uh, known Ben long?" she asked.

I needed more information from the Montenegro file, and had no current interest in Ben Carey, so I tried to set her mind at rest.

"We're strictly friends, Sandy. A long time ago Ben was working on a case where a teenager disappeared after her mother was arrested. The stepfather hired me to find the girl. Oh, yeah, and I think Ben's daughter and mine were in the same computer camp or something. I haven't seen Ben in years. Fortunately, I still had his card on my Rolodex when Ms. Montenegro turned up."

I didn't mention that our two daughters, both the same age, both spoiled only children raised by a single parent, hated each other on sight.

The frown lines disappeared from between her eyes. "Have a chair," she said, motioning me to the standard institution-issue metal chair with a gray upholstered seat. "Coffee?"

I nodded. She disappeared down the hall, returning shortly with two unmatched, not terribly clean mugs of steaming liquid.

Having established that I had no prior claim on the object of her affections, she confided that she'd met Ben in a U.C. Berkeley extension class on parenting. I listened to the affection in her voice whenever she mentioned his name and hoped maybe Benjamin might be ready to settle down. I emptied my cup, glanced at my watch and stood up. "I won't take any more of your time."

"Please let me know if I can be of any help," she said with a smile that reached her blue eyes.

I hesitated, then mentioned the Denver shooting. "There might be something from VICAP that could help." I handed her my business card. "The number for the Water's Edge Lodge is on the back. I'll be there at least through tomorrow night."

"I'll see what I can do. A friend of Ben's is a friend of mine."

As a woman, I knew she didn't mean it.

18

From a pay telephone on the corner of University and McKinley, I called Peter Aaron at the Latin American Union for Defense. The phone booth had no door and I pulled my raincoat closer against the chill wind blowing up off the Bay. It wasn't as cold as Friday Harbor, but almost. A woman's voice with a trace of Hispanic intonation transferred me. Peter Aaron's brisk, no-nonsense voice identified New York as his origin. Yes, he would be glad to see me. He had an opening at three o'clock this afternoon. He gave me crisp directions to the office on Delaware Street. "Dark red, a three-story house with a gable, big bay window upstairs, stained glass in the front door. No parking lot, but hopefully you won't have to walk too far."

It was only eleven-thirty. As good a time as any for a cursory visit to the scene of the crime. Making my way past a large woman in what looked like African tribal dress who was pushing a supermarket shopping cart filled with all her worldly possessions, I returned to the rental car, where an overtime parking citation on the windshield was whipping merrily in the breeze. I was glad that Elyse was picking up all the expenses. At least I hadn't chosen a tow-away zone.

University Avenue is the main east-west artery for the city of Berkeley. Beginning at the edge of the well-manicured U.C. Berkeley campus, it runs some three miles across town and over Highway 80, terminating

at the Berkeley municipal pier on the edge of San
Francisco Bay. Traffic was heavy in all lanes and I
inched my way across San Pablo Avenue and the freeway overpass. At the intersection of University and
West Frontage Road, I stopped for traffic and made
a left turn.

The fruit-stand-cum-convenience-store on the southwest corner of the intersection was still in business,
and I chose a Granny Smith from the pile of shiny
apples on the outside fruit display. Inside, I waited my
turn at the deli counter beside an impatient fast-track
woman in a charcoal-gray pinstripe suit. A tall, griz-
zled man with a white goatee, attired in black leather
motorcycle regalia and a Willie Nelson red bandana,
came to stand behind me. He looked over the suit and
looked me over and we smiled at each other.

Ten minutes later, pastrami and cheese on marbled
rye in plastic wrap, bottle of diet soda and apple in
hand, I queued up at the checkout counter. There
were two men ahead of me, both in casual clothes.
One tall, one short, both blond, both wearing caps
that said Cal Sailing Club, one wearing a yellow foul-
weather jacket. Behind me, two Asian women chatted
in a Chinese dialect. In Berkeley, nobody stood out.
If Julio's killer were standing beside me, right now,
I'd never know it. Nor would Emerson Wineheart. It
was anybody's guess what sort of face had been hiding
beneath the killer's sailing cap and dark glasses.

A mile west of the Highway 80 overpass, the road
divided, the right fork becoming Marina Boulevard,
the left continuing as University and passing by the
municipal marina until it dead-ended at Seawall Drive.
I took the left fork and turned right into the parking
lot across the road from the old municipal fishing pier.
I parked diagonally above the marina, probably very
close to where Elyse and Carmela parked the little
red Karmann-Ghia that fateful day after their aborted
shopping trip.

The marina was laid out in a series of piers, usually
called docks. Each dock had a finger pier where the

boats were tied in slips or berths. I could see "T" dock at the end of the nearest ramp in front of me. To the north of the parking lot were the Yacht Club and the public restrooms.

While the type of boats berthed in a marina will vary by region—those at Berkeley included a preponderance of sailboats—the activities that took place were pretty much the same. On a weekday, the people you'd encounter were employees of the marina or outside workers whose livelihoods involved working on boats: divers, mechanics, riggers. Also endemic to the weekday marina were those unemployed or retired individuals, mostly men, who were mucking about with their nautical toys. Repairing an alternator, refinishing the brightwork, replacing a halyard or a chafed line. On Saturday and Sunday, the regularly employed arrived, some to muck about, some to remove the mainsail cover, uncoil the lines, and head out to challenge themselves in the dependable fifteen-to-twenty-five-knot winds that slotted predictably through the Golden Gate. I finished the sandwich, emptied the can of cola and decided to confirm my theory of how the killer got into the locked marina.

Immediately in front of my car was an overflowing Dumpster, only partly concealed by a wooden housing. To the left of the Dumpster was a kiosk with a number of notices tacked to it. I climbed out of the car, green apple in hand, and sauntered over to peruse the notices.

A mussel quarantine warning.
A house in the Berkeley hills to share.
A Coronado 26 for sale.

Far over to the west of "T" dock I heard a car door close. I moved away from the kiosk and saw a fifty-something man in an oil-stained gray sweatshirt approaching. He carried a blue duffle bag and was talking into a cell phone. I strolled in the direction of the ramp, chomping on the Granny Smith, arriving at the

"T" dock gate just as he did. He pocketed the phone and produced a key from his pocket as he approached the foot of the ramp. I fumbled with my car keys, then gave him a smile as he held the gate for me. I wished the gentleman a pleasant afternoon. He ambled off to the left, toward the white Harbor Patrol boat tied up below the Yacht Club. I wondered where the patrol boat had been on July 13. I let the security gate close with a click, then turned the knob and the gate opened. Another bit of information.

Elyse hadn't known what kind of boat Peter owned, but I had no trouble finding it. The *Camelot* was moored a few slips down from the locked gate, almost underneath the ramp. An older Sabre, thirty-two or thirty-four feet, I guessed, with dark-blue fiberglass topsides and faded blue sail cover. She rocked gently and serenely on her lines, giving forth no information on the grisly scene she had witnessed. The Sabre is a performance cruiser and built with fine craftsmanship. When I was married to Albert, our neighbors in Sausalito had a Sabre 36. I noted the oversize self-tailing winches and the large steering wheel and wondered how a public advocacy lawyer got the money for such a toy.

I stared at the cockpit and tried to visually reconstruct the crime. As I understood it, Julio was shot twice from behind. One bullet had gone directly to his heart. A third shot had bounced off the companionway and hit Peter Aaron. I wondered if either Julio or Peter had seen the perp approach, or if the silenced shots had come out of the blue while they sipped their cold brew and reconstructed the afternoon sail. The image of the scene brought a sense of evil to me, a terrible invasion of leisure and privacy. There is something incongruous about peering over one's shoulder while on a sailboat.

The varnished hatch boards covering the companionway were padlocked and all the portholes covered by white curtains from within. The decals affixed to the right of the companionway illustrated the significance of the various signal flags that race-committee boats used to communicate with racers. I felt a small rush of adrenaline, a nostalgia for windy afternoons on choppy blue water.

The cockpit was clean and well scrubbed. Given the killer's MO, I was beginning to understand why Sergeant Wineheart had had so little success in his investigation. The killer had appeared from nowhere, fired three times, and disappeared, leaving nothing behind except the three Silvertip hollow-point bullets and the ejected cartridge cases.

I walked slowly back to the security gate and let myself out of the marina. Perhaps Peter Aaron could shed some illumination.

19

The gentrified area below San Pablo and north of University Avenue is known as the Berkeley Flatlands, and was even more prosperous now than when I'd left the Bay Area. Upscale restaurants and bars, shops flaunting the latest in landscape gardening tools, home furnishing shops, electronics, natural fiber clothing. A consumerism bridge between the Yuppies and Generation X.

At one forty-five, afternoon traffic was thickening. I turned off University onto Tenth, then right onto Delaware, and started looking for the number Peter had given me. A red house with a triangular gable, he'd said. I found it easily. A small, professional sign in the front yard said Latin American Union for Defense. An ancient VW bug and a dusty sports utility vehicle were parked in front of the attached two-car garage. Across the street I spied a well-polished black Alfa Romeo sedan. The nearest on-street parking space was three blocks away. On the corner of Delaware and Franklin, I squeezed the rental car into a semi-legal space and walked back to the red house. It looked as if the once-residential neighborhood was being commercialized; LAUD's immediate neighbors included an insurance broker to the west and a janitorial service to the east. The entrance door was darkly varnished wood inset with stained glass.

As the door closed behind me, a thirty-something

Hispanic woman looked up from her computer. Her red sweater was a bright spot of color in the room.

"May I help you?" Her smile was welcoming.

"Scotia MacKinnon to see Peter Aaron."

She pressed a button on her phone, announced my presence.

"Peter will be right out. Please have a seat." She nodded to the two chairs beside her desk, then answered the ringing phone.

I scanned the room, took in the battered walnut reception desk, the gray walls begging for repainting, the cork bulletin board across from the reception desk. I moved toward it, read the notices. Grant awards, job openings, political cartoons. Not exactly an upscale law firm.

"Ms. MacKinnon?"

I turned. A tall, thin man with a neatly trimmed dark beard and a receding hairline, dressed in a white-and-red–striped shirt open at the neck, khakis and running shoes was bearing down on me. I extended my hand, which he grasped in a firm handshake.

"I'm Scotia MacKinnon. Thank you for meeting with me."

"Peter Aaron." His voice was crisp, his eyes dark brown and direct. "My office is down the hall." He motioned to the corridor behind the receptionist's desk. "Rafaela, please hold all my calls."

I followed Aaron down the narrow, dim hallway, trying to keep up with his long-legged stride.

"As you can see, we don't have fancy digs." He opened the door of a small crowded cubicle on the left of the corridor. "This was Julio's office." The room had the requisite furnishings: a metal desk, a computer workstation, a chair, a credenza that looked like it came from a garage sale. Stacks of files were piled on the desk. Several document storage boxes filled an adjacent table. The metal mini-blinds were closed.

"We have a new attorney moving in next month, but for now we're just three." He indicated the closed door next to Julio's office. "This is Judith Karamazov's office. She's in San Jose today. And the one over there belongs to Felipe De los Santos." I glanced through the partly open door on the opposite side of the corridor. A dark-haired man in an expensive-looking gray suit stood behind his desk. He was in the middle of a phone conversation and turned to face the window behind the desk as we passed.

Aaron entered the office at the end of the hall, motioned me to the chair in front of his desk. The room was larger than the others, lined with bookcases filled with law books, furnished with a large walnut desk. Four wooden folding chairs surrounded an oval conference table. On the credenza behind his desk, a pewter frame enclosed a color photograph of a smiling dark-haired young woman holding an infant.

"Your family?" I nodded at the photograph.

"My wife, Carmela," he said with pride, "and our son, Emilio." I thought of the child Elyse had miscarried.

I pulled one of the folding chairs close to his desk and sat. "As I mentioned on the phone, Mr. Aaron, I'm representing Elyse Montenegro." I shrugged out of my coat and pulled a notebook from my canvas bag.

"I know," he said. "She called last Saturday and told us about her friend's accident. She sounded awful." He leaned forward and clasped both hands in front of him on the desk. "She left Berkeley right after Emilio was born, but she's never been out of my mind. I know the police are overworked, but for Christ's sake, a man was shot in broad daylight. There must have been witnesses, some evidence." He took a deep breath. "How can I help?"

"Tell me about Julio. How you knew him, what he was working on, who he was hanging out with." I pulled out the tape recorder. "Okay if I record this?"

Aaron nodded, leaned forward, picked up a pencil, and began to doodle on a yellow lined tablet.

"I met Julio in my third year at Yale. I was in prelaw. He was in international finance. We'd had some classes together, seemed to hit it off, got in the habit of having a couple of beers on Fridays. When my roommate got married two months into my junior year and left me with a lease, Julio moved in. We lived together for a year and a half." The pencil paused over the tablet, and he was silent, lost in thought. "We had some good times, though he was in a kind of, well, I guess you could call it a transition."

"In what way?"

"Julio's father was highly connected in Mexican politics, ambassador to both France and Portugal, I think. So Julio and his brother Fernando were mostly educated in Europe. Till he came to New Haven, Julio accepted his father's view of the world. The family agenda in sending him to the U.S. was for him to get a first-class education in finance and then return to a high-level job in Mexico. But one day Julio got a glimpse of a different reality and went into total rebellion against Papa, the Mexican government, and what he saw as the whole rotten financial and political quagmire of his native country."

"Did you know his family?"

"Somewhat. When Julio decided not to return home, his father came to New Haven. Actually, a very nice man. Cultured, polite. He seemed genuinely puzzled by the change in Julio, as if he couldn't figure out what had gone wrong."

"How could Julio just 'decide not to return home'? Wasn't he a Mexican national?"

Aaron smiled and was silent for a minute. "I'm not saying that Julio wasn't crazy about Elyse. Besotted would probably be more accurate. But, of course, once married to a U.S. citizen, his own residency was easy. He and Elyse got married and ran off to Martha's Vineyard a week after graduation. I didn't see much of Julio for a while after that. He got involved with a group of radical political dissidents at MIT. Then I heard he was writing a column for some kind of watchdog of a periodical. *Covert* something or other." He shrugged.

The description rang a bell. I looked up from my notes, remembering the term paper Melissa had done last year on U.S. interventionism in the developing world.

Aaron was silent for a minute, then continued. "Elyse is a very classy lady. She had the best clothes, the best schools, the best horses. Elyse is, shall we say, *crazy* over horses. She told Carmela she started riding when she was five or something. And she was keeping a horse stabled near New Haven when she met Julio. After they got married, she couldn't afford the horse. Or her father sold it, or something."

"How did her parents feel about her marrying Julio?"

"I think they were probably surprised by the elopement, but as far as I know, they were always gracious. I had the impression she was glad to be out from under her father's thumb." He paused. "Her mother came to New Haven once. A pretty, fragile woman who tried to please everyone. Elyse was glad to see her, but I don't think there was a close relationship between the two. Julio said he wasn't quite what her father had planned." He chuckled. "I remember him mentioning something about her father wanting to marry her off to his partner's son."

"Would you say Julio and Elyse made a good match?"

He considered the question. "The chemistry between the two of them was dazzling."

I thought about my own experiments in male-female chemistry. Such connections were usually good for five to seven years. Max.

"What brought all of you to the Bay Area?"

He swiveled his chair to look out the window, turned back to face me, folded his arms across his chest and leaned back. "I got involved in civil rights issues in New Haven. Did a law degree at Stanford and then got a job with a big firm in the city. I actually tried to do conventional stuff like trusts and wills and corporate law." He smiled. "And martini lunches and eighty-hour weeks and fancy women. I bought a Beamer and a sailboat and a house in Tiburón. I got married and then I got divorced, and I lost the house and the car and lived on the boat for a while and chased women. Not very original." He grimaced. "I knew something was drastically wrong with my life, but I didn't figure it out until I met Carmela. And I couldn't have her and work eighty hours a week. So I went to work for a small firm in the city doing immigration stuff, then one day I met the man who started this little office. LAUD had just received a substantial donation from one of San Francisco's philanthropists. He talked me into taking over as director and a year later he died."

"And Julio? He followed you?"

"Julio worked at an investment banking firm while he was getting his master's. He could've continued there after he finished, but he hated New York. When he got an offer from Bank of America International in San Francisco, he grabbed it." He paused. "Julio was not cut out for the megacorporation. He became disenchanted, went to work for a financial consultant in the city. Isabel something Del Valle. Whether it was Julio's expertise or just coincidence, her clients survived the fiasco of '94 when half of Wall Street lost its shirt in Mexican investments."

"And Elyse?"

He frowned. "Elyse got a job as a social worker with Alameda County. Which, if you knew Elyse, doesn't quite fit. I think she got her degree in art history from Sarah Lawrence. After she met Julio, she switched to social work and got a master's degree."

I glanced around Peter's office, mentally comparing it with what Julio might have had in the way of a work environment with an investment banking firm in the city.

"Why did Julio give up finance?"

"He was a true political activist. A child whose eyes had been opened. He wanted to do something more meaningful than making U.S. clients rich on third-world investments. Isabel offered him a partnership, but he'd had enough of banking and securities and wanted to do something for humanity, he said. He enrolled at Hastings, got his degree and came to work for me as soon as he passed the Bar exam."

"How did Elyse feel about the career change?"

He hesitated, made some doodles on the pad. "She made no attempt to hide the fact that Julio's decision to leave investment banking and go to law school was an inconvenience."

"In what way?"

"All the usual female things. She wanted to move out of Berkeley so she could get back to riding, wanted a nicer place to live, a better car, wanted to have a baby. We manage to get enough funding for operating expenses, but our salaries here are modest." He tore off the sheet of doodles, wadded it up, tossed it in the basket behind his desk. "Julio was upset when Elyse got pregnant. But he got over it and was looking forward to being a proud papa." A muscle in his jaw tightened. "Shit! We were *all* looking forward to the two kids growing up together." He pressed his lips together, and turned to stare out the window that overlooked the garden. "I miss him more than I can possibly tell you."

"Would you describe the day of the shooting for me? What time you went out, when you got back. Who knew you were going sailing?"

He turned to face me. The chair creaked as he leaned back and looked thoughtful.

"It was a Friday, the first time last summer when we both had time to sail. Neither of us had any clients scheduled and it was a great day, wind blowing about fifteen knots. The fog burned off early, so we said, what the hell, cleared our desks, and told Rafaela to take off early. We left the marina around eleven, I would say, sailed out the Gate and had a great spinnaker run coming back."

He smiled, paused, seemed lost in memory for several seconds, then shook his head and continued. "We got back to the marina about five, tied her up, pulled out two cans of beer, and then I remember my cell phone rang. I keep it plugged in below to save the batteries. I went below to answer it. There was nobody there. I thought it was the cell phone malfunctioning again. Then I saw Julio fall into the cockpit. I hadn't heard the shots, and I thought he had slipped or something, so I started to come topside. The third bullet ricocheted off the companionway bulkhead, hit me in the shoulder and knocked me down the companionway. Either the guy was a bad shot or he wasn't interested in me."

I thought it very likely the murderer missed on the third shot because Julio was falling, but I didn't interrupt him.

He took a deep breath. "If he'd come onboard, he would have finished me off. And God knows he could have shot Elyse without half trying. They must have passed each other." He was silent for a minute. "The girls weren't even supposed to come back to the marina. We were going to meet up with them at my place for dinner. They were going shopping in the city, but there was some big accident on the bridge, so they came back, went up to the stables, and then came by to surprise us and take us to dinner."

Some surprise.

"Did you telephone for the police?"

He nodded. "It couldn't have been more than two minutes before Elyse came onboard. She started screaming when she saw Julio. I was bleeding pretty bad, but I managed to call 911. There were a few other people on the docks and they came running over when Elyse started screaming. I guess she fell when she got on the boat and hurt herself. The police and paramedics were there in five minutes. You probably know she had a miscarriage later." His voice trailed off. "I was the lucky one," he said hollowly. "I came out with just a stiff shoulder."

"Do you often sail on Fridays?"

"Don't I wish."

"Who, besides Elyse and your wife, knew you were going to be sailing that day?"

He tapped two fingers on the desk, pensive. "It was a spur-of-the-moment thing, so probably only Rafaela. She joked about our interpretation of a casual Friday. I did call her around noon on my cell to check for a call I was expecting. I asked her to give my client the cell number. Maybe Elyse's mother knew. She was going shopping with the girls, I think, then canceled."

I sat in silence for a minute, then asked what cases Julio had handled in his three years with LAUD.

"To start with, a number of small cases. A labor relations dispute down in Hayward, racial discrimination problems in South City, a bunch of immigration files. Prop 2000 was his first big case. Since it had statewide and even national implications, he poured his heart and soul into it. Judith Karamazov worked on the case initially. When we realized the big bucks the plaintiffs were putting behind it, I assigned Julio to help her. They work— they worked well together."

"Judith is one of your attorneys?"

"Yes, Judith Karamazov. She's been with LAUD for five years. Very professional, very competent."

I looked at my notes. "Prop 2000 is the anti-bilingual initiative?"

Aaron nodded. "An extension of the old Prop 227 that turned out to be vague and unenforceable. Specifically, Prop 2000 requires all classes in public schools be taught in English. Julio was multilingual. Fluent in Spanish, French and English. How I envied him. Thanks to a good high school teacher and my mother's cleaning lady, I can defend myself in Spanish, but just barely. The mentality behind an English-only agenda for newly arrived immigrant kids made Julio crazy." He smiled. "Judith kept him on track. And cooled him down. She's had lots of experience with hotheaded men. Her husband is a Basque separatist."

"Is he here? In Berkeley?"

"I'm not sure. I think they're separated. Judith said she had better things to do with her time and education than become a terrorist. Judith is a damned good attorney, but none of us could really speak to the educational issues raised in the aftermath of the election and Prop 2000. That's why we brought in George De Soto."

"Who is De Soto?"

"He's a psychologist, teaches at the university, has done a lot of research in cognitive development."

"Was he working with Julio at the time of the murder?"

"Very closely. They were completing some interrogatories for the next go-around on appeals, which is at the State Supreme Court level."

I looked at my notes and then asked the big question.

"Can you think of anyone who would have wanted Julio dead?"

"I've asked myself that more than once. We tread on lots of toes. After the shooting, we went over Julio's files and looked at the e-mail he'd received. We sometimes get hate mail attacking us for being un-American, for defending immigrants, but nothing so weird that it sounded dangerous. Prop 2000 was Julio's only case that hadn't been settled in the past year. Some were settled with bitterness, but not exactly malice. Many were with big companies. Racial discrimination, sexual harassment. They don't like to pay, but when they do, it's pretty impersonal. Nobody's going to make a vendetta out of settling a discrimination suit."

"What about Julio's computer files? Would it be worth looking at those?"

He frowned. "Julio used a laptop, took it with him everywhere. I haven't seen it since the . . . since the memorial service. I suppose the police have it."

"Would it be possible for me to talk to your other attorneys and the professor, Dr.—?" I consulted my notes. "De Soto?"

He nodded. "Judith Karamazov will be back in the office tomorrow. Felipe De los Santos will be tied up all afternoon preparing for court, but later on in the week might work. I'll speak with them. As for De Soto," he glanced down at his appointment book. "I have a meeting with him this afternoon. I'll set it up. Where can I reach you?"

I gave him my card. "The hotel number is on the back. I'll look forward to your call." I stood, gathered up my belongings. "By the way, Mr. Aaron, would it be possible for me to see the inside of your boat?"

"Camelot?" He shrugged. "Sure. The police literally took her apart. I know the black detective, what's his name, Wineheart, suspected the murder was drug-related." He reached into the left side drawer, pulled out a blue-and-white float with two keys attached. The float was labeled with the slip number. "It's at the Berkeley Marina. The larger key is for the gate on "T" dock. You can drop the key back here or leave it with the Harbor Master."

I put the key in my bag and was about to ask if I could talk to Aaron's wife when the phone on his desk rang. He frowned and pressed the intercom speaker button. "Yes, Rafaela?"

"I'm sorry to interrupt, Mr. Aaron, but it's Judith. I told her you were with the detective, she said it's very important."

Aaron pressed another button, brought the receiver to his ear.

"Judith?"

He listened, his eyes narrowed, and a slight pallor came over his features.

"Good God. Yes, I'll tell her. See you later."

He replaced the receiver slowly and with great care. I noticed his hand was shaking.

"That was Judith Karamazov," he said. "A civil rights attorney was shot in Los Angeles this morning. A man Judith went to school with."

"Anyone arrested?"

He shook his head. "Unidentified gunman."

20

I swiveled in my chair in front of the large window at the hotel's Bay View Lounge and stared out at the whitecaps on the darkening Bay. While I had been at LAUD, the pale November sun had broken through the dramatic gray clouds. Two J-boats were fighting their way back through the wind and chop toward the sailing club next door. At a little after four-thirty, the lounge was sparsely populated. The television monitor over the bar was set to a pre–Monday Night Football commentary, the audio muted. Two men in dark suits conversed at another table in front of the windows. The man in a brown tweed sport coat at the bar had been ogling me since I came in. Ignoring his attempts to make eye contact, I read and reread the news clipping from the afternoon edition of the *Los Angeles Journal* that Judith Karamazov had faxed to Peter Aaron before I left his office.

> An attorney for the Western branch of the Minority Defense Fund (MDF) was shot and killed on the corner of Western and Melrose at 7:30 this morning. Daniel Rivera was Legislative Attorney for the MDF and had recently moved to Los Angeles with his family from Washington, D.C. Witnesses to the shooting say Rivera was approaching the Melrose Building on foot when three shots were fired by a lone gunman in dark glasses, dark hat and tan raincoat, apparently

from somewhere near the revolving door to the building. The gunman then immediately disappeared into the building. Rivera was pronounced dead on arrival at Our Lady of the Angels Medical Center. Rivera's associates could not think of any motive for the attack. Police say they have no suspects.

On the bottom of the sheet there was a scribbled comment:

One of the Hispanic stations received a call this afternoon stating that the Messengers were responsible for the shooting. J.

Another attorney down.

Correction: another Hispanic public-interest attorney down. And who the hell were the Messengers who so unselfishly accepted credit for the hit?

I sipped an icy vermouth with lime and pondered the news clipping. I pulled out my notebook and reviewed the notes from my conversation with Aaron. He'd verified nearly everything Elyse had told me. What she hadn't told me was her dissatisfaction with their limited lifestyle. And what was the source of the ten thousand dollars she'd given me as retainer? I couldn't imagine that her social worker's job had provided much discretionary income. Perhaps Julio had an insurance policy on his life.

Five o'clock. Time to check in with New Millennium before Zelda left for the day. I signed my check, gathered up my coat and bag and ignored the crestfallen face of the man at the bar.

My room was still comfortably warm from the afternoon sun. The drapes were open and blue water and blue sky filled the room. I called Zelda and asked for messages.

"Elyse said she was going to e-mail you. I think she moved or something."

McGillicutty Insurance had reported that the insurance company found no evidence of tampering with the Ghia. Howie of Puget Sound Rentals reported no red paint was found on the bumper of the black Cherokee. Jewel Moon had called once and Petra Von Schnitzenhoff three times.

There were no calls from Nick.

"Guess who filed for divorce today."

I mentally reviewed a list of unstable Friday Harbor couples and gave up.

"Judge Winterbottom," she announced with glee. "Is that justice or what?"

We shared a giggle and I asked about her date with the Seattle yacht broker. The scarf I had loaned her was perfect, she reported, and dinner at the Hunt Room was to die for. But Michael was a total tight-ass who was allergic to dogs, bad-mouthed vegans and ridiculed astrology. She would rather have spent the evening with Dakota. Hans had invited her to come to Berlin. What did I think about enrolling in German class at the community college? I said foreign languages opened new doors. I didn't add that sometimes they were doors that were better left closed.

I dialed my mother's number. Giovanni answered on the second ring. My mother was attending a reading, he said. Without asking, I knew the reading didn't have anything to do with the Mendocino library. He promised to tell her I'd called.

I stared out the window at the white mega-yacht that had just left the Berkeley Marina and remembered I'd forgotten to ask Peter Aaron about talking to his wife, Carmela. I dialed the number for LAUD, got the answering machine and left a message.

I logged on to the laptop to check e-mail. The first message was from Melissa. Did I think it would be all right to invite Gilberto to Mendocino for Thanksgiving, since he couldn't go home to Brazil? She had three papers due this week and didn't have time to see me.

I clicked on Reply and told her I was sure Gilberto

would enjoy learning about American holiday traditions and suggested she check it out with her grandmother. I also said I was impressed with the diligence she was applying to academics. And since she had been majoring in political science, what did she know about a Chiapas uprising?

The second message came from San Juan Percheron Ranch. It was from Elyse.

> *The people who own the Five Fingers house that Campbell was renting are going to sell it. I don't have to move for a month, but it's so remote out here, I can't sleep at night. Rebecca says I can stay here at the ranch until I find something else. What have you found out? Do you think he'll come back?*

Do you think he'll come back? It was the question I'd been avoiding. I couldn't begin to shape an answer because, one, I still had no idea who *he* was, and two, I had no concrete evidence that Campbell's death was anything more than an accident caused by excessive alcohol and excessive speed. I responded with a synopsis of my interviews with Berkeley PD and Peter Aaron and asked her if there had been an insurance policy on Julio.

I logged off and decided to go for a brisk walk around the marina before dark. Clad in warm leggings and my favorite faded blue sweatshirt that said "St. Ann's Inn," I headed out into the early twilight, trying to ignore the fact that I knew even better than Elyse there was no place to hide on San Juan Island. One comforting thought, in a grim sort of way, was that if Elyse's stalker was the one that shot the attorney in L.A. today, he had been too busy to get back to the island.

On the other hand, if he did come back, I knew he would find her.

I had to find him first.

21

On Tuesday the alarm chirped at six-thirty. I turned it off without opening my eyes, and nestled deeper in bed, drifting in that elusive, mysterious state between sleeping and waking that neuropsychologists call theta. Brain activity is slowed, they assure us, and the extraneous intellectual noise that invades our brain during waking hours is filtered out.

For me, it was the most productive period of my day. If I were to leap out of bed at the first sound of the alarm, I'd miss it. So whenever possible, I lingered, floating for a time, following visions behind closed lids, solving problems, planning the day or the rest of my life. More than once, some theta contemplation had solved an irksome case or provided a missing puzzle piece.

The Montenegro case was still very much a puzzle to me, beginning with my client, whose emotions seemed to run the gamut from icy stoicism to tearful hysteria. I wondered what pieces of the puzzle she might be withholding, and I reviewed the list of people I talked to yesterday. Emerson Wineheart and Sandy Silver at BPD. Peter Aaron at LAUD. I hadn't learned anything Detective Wineheart didn't already know. Another attorney had been shot.

The Berkeley PD was not some backwater law enforcement agency. Emerson Wineheart had followed all the right procedures.

The crime-scene unit had been called immediately.

Onlookers were interviewed as potential witnesses.
Divers had retrieved the cartridge casings.
An autopsy had been done even though the cause of death was certainly no mystery.
The crime lab had done its thing.
VICAP had been contacted.

If there was no evidence, there was no evidence, and I was on an investigative wild-goose chase. What had I been thinking of to take the case on?

On that cheery note, I crawled from beneath the bed covers. It was seven o'clock and I had an appointment at nine-thirty with George De Soto, whose message I'd found last night when I returned from my walk and solitary dinner. I turned on the local TV news, peeked through the drapes at the fog-enshrouded Bay, and headed for the shower.

Hot water splashing over my head, I groped for some piece of information I knew was missing, something terribly obvious. Some fact that would either provide more pieces to the puzzle, or better yet, would help me fit together the ones I had. I wasn't ready to believe this was a perfect murder. I turned off the water and reached for the oversize white towel and thought about Julio's laptop computer. I would call Elyse and ask her if she had it.

To get to De Soto's home, I would have to take on the Oakland freeway maze at the end of the morning rush hour. After OJ, coffee, a croissant and *The Chronicle,* I left the hotel at eight-thirty, took University out to Frontage Road, which parallels Highway 80, hoping to advance on the morning commute traffic headed into the city.

Thirty minutes were required to inch my way into the left lanes that exited onto 880 and another fifteen to reach the Walnut Creek exit that was also the exit for the area of Oakland where De Soto lived. I gazed at the cars around me, at the tense faces of the drivers who made this same commute every morning and reversed it every evening. Had they ever questioned the sanity of their lives? And if they had, what would they do? Go raging home and announce they were ripping up roots and moving lock, stock and children to the hinterlands?

I exited onto 51st Street, waited for the traffic signal at Broadway, and nearly missed the left turn onto Moraga. The street curved along the edge of the foot-hills and meandered through tidy neighborhoods of white stucco cottages with red tile roofs that more than hinted at California's Spanish history. I glimpsed hillside areas that had burned out in the terrible fire back in '90, now mostly rebuilt with new houses perched in isolation on the treeless slopes.

I turned left onto Hilltop Drive, right onto Oak Hollow, followed the road for a mile and a quarter and slowed to a stop before number seven.

Leaving the rental car below the entrance to the driveway under one of the trees that gave the street its name, I approached the gate, one side of which was open. Beyond the gate a flagstone walkway, rambling between eucalyptus trees and tall bushes of rhododendrons, led to a tan stuccoed house with a red tile roof. There was a strong smell of earth about the place. At the end of the driveway a two-car garage housed an ancient gray Mercedes roadster and a late-model BMW sedan. As I hesitated, a tall, slender man with salt-and-pepper hair tied back in a long ponytail and a thick mustache emerged from the garage, wiping his hands on a stained towel.

"Good morning," he said, extending his hand. "I'm George De Soto."

I introduced myself, complimented him on the ex-tensive gardens, and followed him up the flagstone path.

The entry hall, tiled with glazed, rust-red Mexican pavers, appeared to run the length of the house. De Soto led me down the hall, past a long, spacious living room decorated with colorful rugs and pillows, lighted with tall windows that overlooked the valley, and into a room that was obviously his study. Like the living room, it also faced the wooded valley. An antique wooden desk and a computer workstation formed an L shape. Piles of papers in neat stacks covered the desktop and a screen saver oscillated on the computer monitor. At the far end of the study, two comfortable-looking upholstered chairs and a low wooden table faced a stone fireplace. A small fire burned in the hearth. De Soto motioned me to one of the chairs and sat opposite me. Muted classical guitar chords drifted from two speakers in the bookcases on either side of the fireplace.

"Peter said you're investigating Julio Montenegro's death."

I reached into my bag for a business card and my notebook. I nodded. "I'm a private investigator. I represent Elyse Montenegro, who believes her husband's killer may be stalking her." He raised his eyebrows and reached for my card. "Apparently the police have exhausted all leads and come to a dead end," I said. "It's possible I'll do the same. However, I've promised my client I'll do my best."

He read the card and frowned. "Friday Harbor, Washington? I thought Julio and Elyse lived in Oakland."

"They did. After her husband's death, Elyse thought she was being followed and came to San Juan Island to stay with a friend. That's where she found me."

"How can I help?"

"Is it all right if I record this?"

He shrugged. "Sure."

"Peter Aaron said you're a psychologist. Do you teach or are you in private practice?"

De Soto leaned back in the chair and steepled his hands. "I've taught at the university the past fifteen years. My specialty is psycholinguistics and psychometrics. I've also taught classes on the psychology of immigration. I'm currently on sabbatical to do a book."

"Could you explain the nature of your relationship

with LAUD? Are you a consultant or advisor or what?"

"I've worked as an occasional consultant for LAUD and other civil rights advocacy groups for a number of years. Sometimes I simply review briefs and pre-trial documents. Sometimes I appear as a witness during court hearings or trials. These are cases involving immigration issues or labor relations disputes or school immigration problems."

"What were you working on with Julio Montenegro?"

He stood up and approached the desk, reached for a stapled document, sat down again and began to leaf through the pages.

"It's a case called *Coalition for English Only versus Gloria Lopez*."

"The result of Prop 2000, the anti-bilingual ed initiative?" I sounded far more knowledgeable than I was.

De Soto nodded. "Prop 2000 holds teachers and administrative personnel personally liable in case of a civil lawsuit by parents or others who might decide the teachers or the school aren't obeying the letter of the law."

"Given all the immigrant students in California schools, how did such an initiative get support?" I asked.

"Basically, the people behind it played on the emotions of the voters who were troubled by immigration and demographic change. By the menace of a brown-skinned takeover. The mainstream journalists were more interested in the polls and who was ahead and who was behind and never bothered to check the statistics they were being fed by the proponents of the initiative. And the people who support bilingual ed—the No on 2000 Campaign—refused to defend it."

Light, firm footsteps came down the hallway and stopped outside the door. There was a knock, and the door opened. A petite woman with almond-shaped eyes and a smooth, unlined face that reflected an exotic Eurasian ancestry stepped inside. Her long, curling dark hair was tied back at the nape of her neck.

She smiled at me. "Sorry to interrupt. I'm Kathryn. You must be the detective Peter told us about. I thought I'd ask if you'd like coffee or something before I leave." She wrinkled her nose at De Soto. "My husband's social graces are somewhat limited."

"I'm Scotia MacKinnon. Thanks, but I had three cups with breakfast." I eyed her leather riding boots and the slightly stained riding breeches. "Looks like you have a date with a horse."

"Actually, with a farrier. See you about four, George?"

He nodded and the door closed. De Soto appeared to be collecting his thoughts.

"So how did LAUD and Julio Montenegro get involved with Prop 2000?" I asked.

"Immediately after the election, LAUD joined a number of school districts and other civil rights action groups in filing a federal lawsuit."

"On what basis?"

"On the basis that the initiative violates the civil rights of 1.4 million California children who don't speak English."

"Why is the state of California responsible for educating kids who don't speak English?"

"It's actually a federal civil rights issue. Let me give you a bit of history." He cleared his throat, glanced at the papers in his lap, and began to speak. I had the feeling he had spoken these words many times before.

"In 1970, a class-action suit was filed in San Francisco. The plaintiffs were a Chinese family named Lau, the defendant was the San Francisco Unified School District. After a number of appeals, the case landed in the Supreme Court of the United States. In 1974 the *Lau v. Nichols* decision was handed down. In a nutshell, the decision required school districts to either teach students in their home language or teach them enough English to be able to participate in classes taught in English."

"I see."

"The implementation of Prop 2000 violates the rights of students protected by the *Lau v. Nichols* decision."

"I'm probably being dense, but isn't it true that the kids would learn English faster if they were, well, immersed in English?"

De Soto narrowed his eyes, stood and moved over to the bookcase next to the fireplace. He picked up one of the small netsuke figurines from the top of the bookcase. "Prop 227, the forerunner of Prop 2000, allowed immigrant students one hundred eighty days of special English-language classes. Prop 2000 mainstreams the students from day one. Regardless of proficiency, they get the same classes as fluent English speakers."

He put the figurine back on the bookcase and turned to me. "I ask you, Ms. MacKinnon, if you were to enter a high school in, shall we say, Moscow, as a monolingual English speaker, do you think you would be ready to compete academically, in, let us say, a physics class, with monolingual Russian speakers?"

"Forgive my ignorance. No, I don't think I'd be able to compete. I wouldn't even be able to survive. And I can't imagine how a teacher could teach such a class." That would teach me to ask stupid questions.

"Precisely." He smoothed the ends of his mustache, picked up the sheaf of papers from the low table, and sat down again. "And neither could the majority of teachers in this state, many of whom are bilingual, experienced, and well trained. In fact, it was one of these teachers that got LAUD involved in the whole mess. Gloria Lopez, her name is. A school principal with twenty years' experience in Los Angeles County schools and president of CELL. California English Language Learners."

He went on to describe how Gloria Lopez had insisted on providing English as a Second Language classes for her students until they tested out as English-proficient. That the CEO watchdogs found out about it and filed a lawsuit against her personally. The school district refused to defend her because she hadn't followed district guidelines and CELL didn't have enough money.

"Gloria Lopez was a single parent with two sons in college and no money to defend herself. And when Julio needed help with the educational policy and language issues, he came to me."

"What's the status of the case? Was it settled?"

De Soto shook his head. "We lost in L.A. County, where we drew a conservative judge. Julio appealed to the district court, where we won, and the plaintiffs then appealed it to the State Supreme Court, where it's awaiting a hearing."

"If you win at the Supreme Court level, would that be a serious setback for the opposition?"

He nodded. "And not only in California. A number of conservatives in other states who've wanted to pass English Only laws have been watching this case like the proverbial hawks."

We sat in silence for several minutes and I had the feeling he was anticipating my next question.

"Do you think this case is nasty enough to have motivated a murder?"

He chewed on the corner of his mouth, started to speak, then stopped. "At one point Julio and Judith Karamazov put together fairly detailed profiles on the money guys behind Prop 2000 and the Coalition for English Only. They half expected to uncover a nest of white supremacists or xenophobes, but all they found was some multimillionaire right-wingers who didn't want their tax dollars used to educate immigrant kids."

"So, in other words, Prop 2000 says 'Immigrants stay away'?"

He nodded. "However, before you jump to conclusions . . ." he began.

"Yes?"

"Prop 2000 was just one of many projects that Julio was involved in. He once showed me a column he was writing for *El Sol Diario*, the newspaper his brother Fernando published in Mexico City. Even to my liberal eyes, it was inflammatory and seditious. With the kinds of stuff Julio wrote, I'm surprised Fernando's not in jail."

"How did that fit with Julio's father as ambassador?"

"He's retired now, but I would imagine it was rather embarrassing." He looked at his watch. "I'm expecting a phone call soon. A contributor to the book I'm doing. Is there anything else I can help you with?"

I stood, put on my coat and picked up my notebook and tape recorder.

"Does your wife know Elyse?"

He nodded. "Kathryn keeps her horse at Tilden Ridge Stables where Elyse was teaching. It's actually on the grounds of the Tilden Ridge School. I believe they rode together a few times."

"Would it be okay if I spoke with her?"

He considered my question, chewed on his lip. "Sure. I'll mention it to Kathryn. Give her a call this evening, if you like."

"I'll do that. Thank you for your time."

He nodded. "My pleasure. Call me if you have any other questions."

He walked me to the front door.

"What's the topic of your book?"

"The politics of education," he said with a wry smile.

22

The fog had burned off and the East Bay was bathed in late-morning sunshine. I drove absently down the hill from De Soto's, turned right on 51st Street, and grabbed the first entrance onto the 880 freeway. I thought about my conversation with De Soto. About the big bucks backing the Coalition for English group. About Julio's vitriolic diatribes against the Mexican government. Criticizing Mexico's ruling political party, from within or outside of Mexico, was not child's play. If the wrong politicians had become the target of Julio's pen—well, assassins on both sides of the border were cheap. It wouldn't be the first time a ruling establishment had protected its own or the long arm of tyranny had extended across international borders.

Emerson Wineheart was right. Julio Montenegro did have his fingers in a lot of pies. Yet it seemed very far-fetched to me that his premature demise could be linked to a school curriculum. This was real life, not the movies.

Traffic was flowing smoothly as the freeway divided. I took the Highway 80 exit that runs along the Bay and headed back to Berkeley. I wanted to do a thorough search of Peter Aaron's boat, but my stomach was making rumbles. I wondered if my favorite Berkeley eatery was still in business, and it was.

Le Cafe Bleu had a large open patio and one could dine al fresco or otherwise. Despite the noonday sun,

I chose otherwise and was ushered into the dim interior of the restaurant by a waitress in white shirt, black tie, black pants and orange hair. The interior designers of Le Cafe Bleu seemed to have chosen Picasso's more depressing masterpieces as their motif. Above my banquette seat, the Old Guitar Player bent over his strings in dreary reflection of his broken heart. On the opposite wall, the Absinthe Drinker contemplated her wastrel life. Lest I get pulled into their morose considerations, I checked my cell phone for messages.

Judith Karamazov had returned to the LAUD office and wanted to meet with me that afternoon at four o'clock at The Rose. The Rose, she explained in precise phrases, was a cafe attached to The French Hotel on Shattuck Avenue near the intersection with Cedar Street. Good. Intuition told me Judith, a woman accustomed to dealing with hotheaded men, might provide some leads.

Probably left from a cell phone, the second message was from Peter Aaron. He said I could talk to his wife at their home in Berkeley on Wednesday morning any time after ten. The address was on Euclid off of Eunice. Would I please not ring the doorbell, because the baby would be sleeping, and would I please be patient with Carmela, her English wasn't very good.

While I'm not what you might call multilingual, after a stint on Narcotics in San Diego and pillow talk with husband number two, who grew up in East Los Angeles, I figured I could probably hold my own with Carmela. Too bad she didn't speak French. Much of my childhood had been spent with children of a French fisherman family on Cape Breton Island.

I listened to the third and fourth messages, which were from Zelda and Melissa, respectively. Zelda was swearing off men. "Can you believe it?" she demanded in an aggrieved voice against something by Bizet. "Hans is only sixteen! What a jerk!" She was leaving on Thursday to drive to Missoula, Montana, to visit her aunt, back by Monday. "Let me know if there's anything you need by Wednesday night. And check your e-mail. Elyse has called three times. She wants to know when you'll be back."

Melissa's message was terse. "Hi, Mom. Check your e-mail for info on Chiapas. Love, M."

The last message was from Nick. He was at the Hotel Careyes Bel Aire, north of Tenacatita. "I had a good meeting with my client, who has as many ideas as he has bucks, which are mucho. Really gorgeous here, Scotty. Tangerine-colored villas on the mountainside, big waves rolling in. An incredible view from the hotel. Oh, yes, and magnificent margaritas. Hope you're making progress with your case. See you soon, love."

Tangerine villas and pounding surf. *Merde!* I ground my teeth in frustration and envy, erased the messages and tried not to snarl at the waitress with the orange hair, who was expounding on the day's lunch specials.

Foregoing the spicy seafood pasta, I ordered the baby lettuce with wild rice, pecans, and snap peas, and a cup of potato leek soup. Chewing on the incomparable San Francisco sourdough, I made a valiant but unsuccessful effort not to imagine my lover lounging on the balcony of the Hotel Careyes, sipping tequila and gazing into the Mexican sunset. Or into the eyes of his client's sexy secretary.

I didn't like the picture and I didn't like the feeling that I had taken on an unsolvable case. I needed some concrete leads, and soon, or I might as well get the hell out of Berkeley. For lack of further inspiration, I decided to check out the interior of the *Camelot*.

The rainbow-colored flags on tall poles that divide University Avenue west of the freeway were whipping in the afternoon breeze off the Bay.

Above "T" dock, the parking lot was mostly deserted and I left the rental car near the bicycle path. The same tattered notices were fluttering on the kiosk. I opened the heavy steel-mesh security gate with Peter Aaron's key. It clanged firmly behind me.

"T" dock was deserted. I stood on Slip 10, gazing at the *Camelot* bobbing in the wind. I climbed aboard and inserted the smaller key into the brass padlock on the companionway. It unlocked easily. I removed the hatch boards and stepped down the companionway into the main salon. Settee cushions of a faded velvety midnight blue surrounded the wooden table with drop leaves. The teak had been freshly oiled. The cabin was private and cozy, and it was hard to imagine a man had lost his life on this boat.

The brass trawler lamp suspended above the table in the main salon swayed as the boat rolled gently in the wind. Behind the galley there was a quarter berth that would sleep one comfortably and two intimately. The large blue sail bag on the quarter berth was marked "Camelot genoa 155." I opened the door at the forward end of the main salon and found the bathroom, nautically known as the head, and a spacious stateroom with a double berth.

I closed the door and moved over to the chart table, where the bulkhead sported the usual navigation toys: Radar, GPS, VHF, radar detector, charting display. On the electrical circuit panel, one small light glowed red. The label opposite the light said "bilge pump." I opened the top of the chart table, glanced idly at the contents. Parallel rules, dividers, a flashlight, a log book, a pair of reading glasses, spare fuses, a Berkeley telephone book. I don't know what I expected to find. Name and address of Julio's killer, perhaps?

I stood in front of the companionway steps and glanced at the louvered cabinet doors above the reefer. An electrical adapter was plugged into the AC outlet immediately to the right of the steps. I picked up the unconnected end. It was an adapter for a cell phone. I remembered then—Peter said his cell phone had rung and he had ducked below just seconds before the first shot was fired. Was the call a coincidence or specifically intended to decoy Peter belowdecks? If the latter, then Julio was the only target. How many people had Peter's cell phone number? Rafaela, the secretary at LAUD, might know.

I replaced the companionway boards, closed and

locked the hatch. I glanced around the cockpit. A square piece of gray duct tape was stuck to the fiberglass bulkhead to the right of the companionway, diagonally across from where the killer would have approached the boat. Idly, I lifted the edge of the tape and discovered it was covering a small hole in the fiberglass. The bullet that had ricocheted before hitting Peter's shoulder? I stared at it and wondered if the same weapon was used in the Denver and L.A. shootings.

Maybe it was time for a drink with Ben Carey.

It was three o'clock when I left the marina. Not enough time to go back to LAUD now. I took a left at the fork on Marina Boulevard. I had just enough time to return to the hotel, check for e-mail from Melissa and get a quick education in Poli Sci 101 before I met Judith Karamazov at The Rose.

23

The Rose was a new addition to the old French Hotel on Shattuck Avenue where many years ago I used to drink café au lait with my friend Raúl, an exceptional poet and perpetual law student whose background resembled Julio's, minus Papa's money. I circled the block three times in search of a parking space, and finally left the rental car in the supermarket lot next door where I could keep an eye on it in the event that the tow-away sign meant what it said.

A few brilliant rays of afternoon sun had managed to escape the clouds, and the vine-covered brick wall of the hotel was a luminescent green. I ordered a tall single mocha from the barrista and scanned the room for the woman with the literary name. In the back of the cafe, a pale man with curly red hair nursed a glass of water and hunched over a crossword puzzle.

At a table near the tall windows overlooking the supermarket parking lot, a thirty-something woman with wild, curly dark hair was watching me. I approached, she stood up and I couldn't avoid the thought that this woman was Elyse Montenegro's physical opposite. Her mop of dark brown hair spilled from under a wine-colored beret onto the shoulders of her black wool cape. She was shorter than I and chunkier. She wore no makeup and her face with high cheekbones looked tired.

"Judith Karamazov?"

She nodded.

"Scotia MacKinnon."

She returned my handshake and sat in the green metal faux wicker chair.

"I really wanted to meet you." She spoke with an intensity that surprised me. "That fucking detective hasn't done a fucking thing to find out who killed Julio."

Ms. Karamazov was angry. I made a noncommittal response, pulled the mini-recorder from my bag, requested and received permission to record our conversation. I pushed the Record button, identified the date, place and interviewee, and suggested she begin by describing her relationship with Julio Montenegro.

Pushing her nearly empty glass around the tabletop, she recounted the work they had done on the *CEO v. Gloria Lopez* case, the details of which pretty much coincided with what George De Soto had told me. Switching to Julio's extracurricular activities, she'd been Julio's campaign manager when he ran for Berkeley City Council. And almost as an afterthought, she said she had gone with him and the FMM to Chiapas.

"FMM?"

"Free Mexico Movement." At my blank face, she added, "A Bay Area group that wanted to help out after the massacres."

I flashed on Melissa's summary of Chiapas: Back in 1994, there had been an attempt at a mini-revolution by a group called the EZLN, based in the southern state of Chiapas. The Zapatista Army for National Liberation. Their goals included better housing, work, food, health and education for all Mexicans. They also wanted a new national constitution. The area became a war zone, a lot of blood was spilled, and eventually a peace treaty, called the San Andreas Accord, was negotiated with the PRI, Mexico's ruling party, in 1996. According to Melissa, allegations of massacres still continued, thousands of indigenous people had been displaced, and the area remained in a state of chaos.

"Julio wanted to meet with the leaders of the uprising. He said he knew Subcomandante Marcos and Comandante Ramona. I don't know from where," she said. "He thought they were going about the revolution in the wrong way. They'd been corresponding by e-mail for a while. So we left the FMM people and finally had a meeting in the middle of the jungle, after the security people nearly killed us." She sighed. "The whole thing was a fiasco. Julio got five minutes with Ramona while I was held under armed guard. Then we were escorted back to the FMM camp. Julio was depressed for weeks."

I decided to get down to brass tacks. "Who hated Julio enough to kill him? Whose toes did he step on too hard?"

She smiled without mirth. "An artichoke grower from the Valley who didn't like Julio messing in farm labor politics? Some dude from SIN? A disgruntled mechanic? Take your pick." She shrugged. "Maybe an assassin from the other side of the border? God knows, he must have offended half the ruling class in Mexico with his column in *El Sol Diario*. He blamed the PRI for virtually every evil in Mexico. Poverty, bank failures, union strikes, infant mortality, you name it. He thought he was safe because he was two thousand miles away."

"What's SIN?" I asked in irritation. Acronyms had become the bane of the English language.

"Stop Immigration Now." She was quiet for a long minute. I glanced out the window. No tow truck was circling the rental car. Two young Asian men came into The Rose, purchased tall glasses of something dark and sat down at the table across the room that the man with red hair had vacated.

"We started getting hate mail on the Internet as soon as we filed an answer to *CEO v. Lopez*," Judith said. "At first it was just ordinary stuff. Lots of people agreeing, lots disagreeing. The ones who agreed with Prop 2000 talked about how the state was going to be overrun by foreigners, about going the way of Canada.

The ones who didn't agree with the initiative blamed everything on neo-Nazis. You get so you can tell the people who just need to get stuff out, and the ones who might be sociopaths. We read all the messages and usually just deleted them. But there were one or two that worried Julio." She paused, took a sip of the dark liquid in her glass and chewed on her full lower lip.

"And they were?"

"One of them called himself the Israel Messenger. He was sending white separatist propaganda, but in a really intelligent way. Julio thought he wanted an intellectual discussion, so he started dialoging with the dude." She paused, shrugged. "We thought it was a man, but who knows. When it got down to discussion of the upcoming white revolution and how the mud people would all be wiped out, Julio decided to cool it and stopped responding."

"What are mud people?"

"Hispanics, Vietnamese, Koreans, Blacks. Anybody who doesn't have white skin. Julio talked to Peter about it, because there was a lot of anti-Semitic stuff." I flashed on the stuff I had been reading in *White Tempest*. Another piece of the puzzle?

"What did Peter say?"

"That there's been anti-Semitism since long before he was born and it will go on long after he's passed on to the hereafter."

"You said there were *two* messages that worried Julio?"

"Yeah, the other one quoted chapter and verse from the Bible about the sinfulness of mixing races, how the country was turning into the Tower of Babel that would be the end of civilization. Julio lost interest real fast." She smiled. "He's not, he wasn't exactly religious."

"Do you have any copies of the messages?"

She shook her head. "I can't even keep up with my own correspondence."

"Do you think Julio kept hard copies of the e-mail?"

She shook her head. "I doubt it." She sighed, emptied her glass. "But they might still be in his Deleted Messages file. I wanted to go back and read them after—" She took a deep breath, and let the tears slide down her face. "After he died, I checked the computer in his office, but I couldn't find his laptop." Without apology or embarrassment, she wiped the tears away.

"Do the police have it?"

She shrugged. "Probably."

I made a mental note to ask Ben about it.

"How well did you know Elyse?" I asked.

She stared at me with hard eyes. "Elyse is a bitch," she said. Her gaze fell to her empty glass. I let the silence grow.

"Would you like another drink?"

"Just a coffee," she said. "Black. I've got about ten more hours of work to do before I sleep tonight."

I processed Judith's sentiments regarding her former colleague's wife and watched the barrista pour the steaming liquid. I returned to the table and put the cup in front of her.

"She's a bitch! She didn't shed one tear at the funeral!"

I flinched at the barrage of angry words.

"He was never good enough for her. All she thought about was horses. She just wanted money, money, money. Fuck." She struck her fist hard on the table, closed her eyes and let the tears flow. Across the room the two Asian men looked at Judith, then looked away. The barrista was watching CNN, or pretending to.

"Were you and Julio lovers?" I asked.

She stared at me without answering.

24

"Were you and Julio lovers," I asked again, gently.

Judith nodded, put her hand over her mouth and began to sob. Her sobs turned to keening. I wondered if I had ever cared for anyone so passionately. The two Asian men stood up and hurried out of the cafe.

After a minute or two, she sat up and I handed her a tissue. She wiped her face, then reached for her drink. "We didn't mean for it to happen. It was when we were in Chiapas. He wanted Elyse to go, but she wouldn't." She paused, her eyes far away. "There's no way to describe what went on there, the brutality, the people without homes, or how incredible Julio was with everyone. And we worked together, days, nights, endlessly. And still there were children without homes, without enough food, without water." She paused. "When we came back from Mexico, all Elyse and Felipe did was bitch at us."

"Felipe De los Santos? The other attorney at LAUD?"

She nodded. "A fucking idiot."

"How so?"

She brushed the tears from beneath her prominent cheekbones and made a futile attempt to tidy the curly locks tumbling out of the beret.

"Felipe complained to Peter that we'd been neglecting our cases, that he'd been doing our work. Peter had to listen to him because he's Carmela's cousin."

So Felipe was Peter's wife's cousin; it was beginning to sound like an international soap opera.

"You don't like Felipe?"

"He's not one of us. Peter hired him to keep Carmela happy."

I waited for more.

"He's an arrogant SOB. Wastes time at our staff meetings complaining about low fees. As if our clients were the Rockefellers. He's never in the office, always off on some 'appointment,' always has stacks of money to spend. And just a little too fond of his cocktails." She chuckled without mirth. "He got a DUI last month. A friend of mine works for the law firm he hired to defend it. It's actually his second one." She played with the handle on her cup and continued without looking up. "Julio didn't trust him. He followed him one night to a warehouse over near the Port of Oakland. There were security guards on duty, so Julio left and went home. The next day he said he was going to send a letter to the police. And he told Peter about it."

"And?"

She shrugged. "Peter said Felipe was a partner in some import-export company."

"Julio didn't buy it?"

She nodded. "Not for a minute. But Julio sometimes saw shadows where there weren't any. A twenty-first-century Don Quixote."

Neither my client nor Detective Wineheart had mentioned a letter from Julio about De los Santos.

"Did Elyse know about you and Julio?"

She shook her head. "God, no. He was going to ask for a divorce, that's why I divorced Izzy. Then she got pregnant and he couldn't." Judith stared into her coffee. "Or wouldn't."

I asked about her husband.

"Izzy? He's back in Spain."

"When did he leave?"

"Last month."

"Did he know about you and Julio?"

She stared at me. "I don't think so."

*   *   *

I left Julio's angry and bereft mistress composing herself over her coffee and retrieved the rental car from the supermarket lot, drove slowly down Shattuck to University and headed West. It was dark and I hadn't returned Peter Aaron's boat keys or made contact with Felipe De los Santos. When I'd called Rafaela on my way to meet Judith at The Rose, she said I could drop the keys through the mail slot and that she expected Felipe back at the office about four o'clock. I'd asked her about any phone calls to Peter on the day of Julio's murder. There were three, she said.

One from Peter at nine-thirty regarding the client he was expecting to hear from.

A second call at eleven-fifteen for Judith from an unidentified woman who didn't speak English.

A third call at twelve forty-eight from a man named Simms who told her Peter was expecting his call and he needed the cell phone number.

Bingo! George Simms a.k.a. Jason Simmons! Elyse's stalker in the black Cherokee. And she had been right on two counts: there *was* a connection between the man who was following her and her husband's murder. And it was more than probable that Simms had mistaken Campbell for Elyse and the accident with the little red Ghia had been no accident. I shivered.

"Do you think I made a mistake in giving Peter's number, Ms. MacKinnon?" Rafaela's voice was anxious. I told her it probably wouldn't have changed anything, reflecting at the same time that her giving out the number might, in fact, have saved Peter from ending up like Julio. Very dead.

Delaware Street was quiet and two of the windows on the LAUD building were lighted. The black Alfa Romeo was parked in the driveway. I stared at the car, thinking about Julio's suspicions, found a miniature flashlight and piece of paper in the bottom of my increasingly cluttered bag, and jotted down the license number.

The outer office was dark. I heard the sounds of a copy machine cranking away from somewhere in the back. I laid Peter Aaron's boat keys on the secretary's desk and moved toward the lighted corridor. "Hello? Anybody here?"

I hesitated, then continued down the corridor to the right, paused outside the office Peter Aaron had pointed out as Felipe De los Santos's. The dark-haired man with the thin mustache looked up from behind his desk, the top of which was covered with files, loose papers, and three black law books. More files were stacked on the floor along with an open black leather attaché case. The tall bookcase to the left of the desk displayed the requisite attorney's reference books, except for the top shelf, which had framed pictures of horses.

"Our offices are closed," the man said. "Perhaps you would like to come back tomorrow." The tone was neutral.

"I'm Scotia MacKinnon." I approached the desk and extended my hand. He stood up, glanced at my hand, then returned the handshake without smiling. "Felipe De los Santos. I'm afraid I'm rather busy."

"I apologize for the interruption," I said. "I represent Elyse Montenegro. Do you have a few minutes?"

"Ah, the lovely Elyse." He murmured rather than spoke her name, and rolled the silver Cross pen between his long, slender fingers. I wondered if his tone was indicative of more than a nodding acquaintance with a colleague's wife. "You are an attorney?" His diction and pronunciation were precise. Only the intonation was Spanish.

I identified my relationship with Elyse, said I had spoken with Peter, and that I wanted to gather as much information as possible about Julio's activities, work-related and otherwise, that might give any hints as to his killer.

De los Santos glanced at his watch. His eyes were brown, fringed with incredibly long, sooty lashes. He ran a hand through the thick dark hair tinged with silver at the temples.

"Well, then, Ms. MacKinnon, you have, how would you say, your work cut out for you. Julio was not careful about people. He spent more time, I think, meddling than working. Mostly meddling in affairs and issues that were not relevant to our work with LAUD."

"Could you be specific?"

He shrugged. "The farm workers of the Salinas Valley. I think he made things worse, not better." He leaned forward. His gaze was earnest. "Let me be frank. Julio was a troublemaker. It didn't matter where he was. And he never stayed at home." His voice was scornful. "All the stupidities about going to Mexico, to Chiapas. As if the government of Mexico couldn't take care of a bunch of ignorant communist peasants."

I tried another tack. "Did you ever work on any cases with Julio?"

He looked down at the yellow lined pad he had been filling with small, precise printing. "We do, we did one case together. A case of discrimination in San Jose." When he looked up, his gaze was angry. "I told Peter I did not want to work with such as Julio. He did not do his homework. He was not a good attorney and he embarrassed me."

"How well did you know Elyse?"

"She is a friend of my cousin Carmela." I saw his gaze go to the shelf of photos in the bookcase. "And she was helpful with my horse when I went to Colombia."

I stood up and studied the photos in the bookcase, in particular the large silver-framed one of Elyse holding the halter of a handsome dark steed. Her hair was longer when the photo was taken, almost waist-length. The wind had tousled its blonde strands and she was laughing at the photographer. I realized I had never heard her laugh or even seen her smile.

"It's a beautiful horse. Thoroughbred?"

He shook his head. "An Arab. A three-year-old.

The finest breeding I could find. Elyse helped in the training. She is excellent with horses."

He stood up and looked at his watch again. "Is there anything else?"

I looked at my notes. "Could you tell me where you were July thirteenth, the afternoon of the murder?"

He stiffened. "I told the police already. I was here in the morning. In the afternoon, I played tennis with my friend Nancy, at her house in Tiburón." His eyes became narrow and challenging.

"I have no reason to doubt your word, Mr. De los Santos. Just one more question. I understand you have other business interests, in addition to your work for LAUD?"

He folded his arms across his chest and his eyes became narrower. "My business is importing. Colombian textiles. It is legitimate. It has nothing to do with LAUD. Or Julio Montenegro. Is there anything else?"

"What is the name of your importing business?"

For a long minute, I was sure he would refuse to answer, then he gave a slight shrug. "It is called Global Imports. And now you will have to excuse me. I have much work to do."

I smiled, closed my notebook, stood up. "That's it. Thank you for your time."

"I will show you out."

I followed him down the lighted corridor. The copy machine was still cranking away. I wondered how many trees were cut each day to support the U.S. legal system. He opened the front door. "Please give my regards to Elyse," he said, turning on an outside light that illuminated the small porch and the sidewalk.

I nodded, thanked him, glanced again at the elegant car in the driveway. The night was cold and thick with fog. I unlocked the rental car, slid inside, quickly locked the door. The light on the porch of the old red house went out. Shivering, I drove slowly down Delaware Street, haunted by the photograph of the laughing, wind-blown face of Elyse Montenegro and the Arabian three-year-old.

25

It was after six when I got back to the Water's Edge.
The parking lot was dark and windy and full of moving shadows, and I ran through the fog and into the
welcoming light of the carpeted corridor. I heard the
phone ringing as I unlocked the door to my room.
Wonder of all wonders, it did *not* stop ringing one
second before I picked it up.

"Scotia MacKinnon."

"Scotia, Ben. How's it going?"

I chuckled, thinking of my recent encounters with
Judith Karamazov and Felipe De los Santos. "Ben,
one could never say my client's husband led a dull
life."

"You have time for a drink?"

"Now?"

"Now."

I mentally reviewed my next tasks.

Call Kathryn De Soto.

Start putting together a dossier on Felipe De los
Santos or have Zelda start one.

Call Elyse's parents.

And find a way to spend some time with my elusive daughter.

I thought about the bullet hole in *Camelot*'s bulkhead and the alleged letter Julio Montenegro sent to
the BPD and the FBI just a week before his death. I
wanted more information about the weapon used at

the L.A. shooting and to find out if the BPD had Julio's laptop.

"Sure. When and where?"

"I'll call you from the bar at your hotel. Half an hour."

I hung up and retrieved my cell phone voice mail. My heart skipped a beat when I heard Nick's voice telling me he was on his way back to Seattle, would try to come up to Friday Harbor this weekend. Could we get together?

I dialed Nick's number at his condo in Seattle and was less than pleased to hear daughter Nicole's chirpy voice on the recording. *Hi, leave a message for Nick or Nicole and we'll call you back.* I did leave a message, with a bit of constraint, saying I'd be back in Friday Harbor on Thursday, please call me. I shrugged off the unpleasant feeling her voice had given me. Had she moved in? Why hadn't Nick mentioned it to me? Why did I have the feeling Nick always managed to surround himself with a barricade of some sort? First the marriage, then the divorce. Then the relocation of his business and the property settlement with his ex. Now it was Nicole's "adjustment." *Merde.* Was there handwriting on the wall I was refusing to read?

There was no message from Melissa and I was tired of pursuing her. It was six-forty. Ben would be arriving in twenty minutes. I searched through my notebook for George De Soto's number. His wife, Kathryn, answered. Her voice was as cordial as she had been in person that morning.

She didn't know Elyse well, she said. She first met her and Julio at a dinner party at the Aarons'. She and Felipe enjoyed chatting with Elyse about horses, found her very knowledgeable. She thought it was a shame Elyse didn't have her own horse. Yes, she, Kathryn had been riding for over fifteen years and kept two horses at Tilden Ridge Stables, and when the stables started interviewing for a part-time instructor, she passed the information on to Elyse. She said Elyse taught a beginning class in English equitation for almost a year, until she discovered she was pregnant. She had also been helping the riding master with a hunter-jumper class.

English equitation, as I recalled, involved the art of riding horses with balance and etiquette, and I imagined a hunter-jumper class was riding over small jumps and fences . . . with the same balance and etiquette. I asked about Elyse's relationship with Felipe De los Santos. She hesitated briefly, then confirmed that my client had exercised Felipe's Arabian when he was traveling, and occasionally provided the same service for several other absent owners. No, she couldn't think of any association between Elyse's work at the stables and Julio's murder. I thanked her and hung up.

The more I learned about Elyse and Julio Montenegro, the more it seemed that their lives had begun a slow, inexorable divergence. Julio had moved away from the world of finance and into the ever-more-convoluted world of political activism and political women. Elyse, through her connections at Tilden Stables, was beginning to edge back into the privileged and expensive milieu of the equine set. When Elyse had declined to accompany Julio to Mexico, he had become involved with Judith Karamazov. And who knew what alliance had blossomed between the laughing, windblown Elyse and the free-spending Felipe De los Santos?

There were several possible ways of getting my hands on some fast info on LAUD's Colombian legislative attorney. I considered and quickly abandoned the idea of trying to go online right then and access the various California state agencies—the corporations records division, the office of the Uniform Commercial Code, the Department of Motor Vehicles—and search for fictitious names, assumed names, federal or state tax liens and driver records. While the information was all public, the catch was that either you had to show up in person or you needed a prepaid account, the cost of which in one case was a hefty $10,000. Besides, that's what I had Zelda for.

It was well after closing time for New Millennium, but she answered on the first ring. She was working late, trying to finish a new promotional brochure for the bank before she took off for Montana.

I passed on what few facts I had discovered on De los Santos, including the tag on the Alfa Romeo and the importing business in Oakland. I asked her to do a quick background check of public records online, and to send me what she could before she left.

"Guess what I got today, boss? A new cell phone. Digital, state of the art, free long distance. Cool, huh?" Zelda's previous cell phone had left a great deal to be desired in dependability. She gave me the cell phone number, I noted it, hung up the phone and sat in the early-evening silence, staring out at my reflection in the glass. My face looked drawn. Suddenly tired in every muscle and feeling very far from anything I could call home, I closed the drapes against the night.

The phone rang. It was Ben, he was in the lobby. I changed into a pair of dark pants and a heavy wine-colored sweater, the brown riding boots that were Melissa's castoffs, did a superficial repair to my face and went to meet my former lover.

26

The years had added a lot of silver to Ben Carey's dark hair, but not a smidgen of flab to his still-trim physique. He stood up and gave me a bear hug. His shoulders were as muscular as I remembered.

"My, my, but you are a sight for sore eyes." He gave me a head-to-toe visual check and I felt myself blushing. I sat down quickly, at a loss for words.

"Is it still the same lucky guy who's making you look so good?" he asked, after the waiter had taken our order. He reached for a handful of salted cashews and watched me.

I told him about Nick, about the on-again, off-again relationship, about Nick's work in Seattle and the house on San Juan Island. The words were pretty, but they sounded hollow to my ears. Ben didn't seem to notice. He was quiet for a minute, then said, "Well, if it couldn't be me, I'm glad you found a good man." He touched my hand lightly, then reached for the foaming mug of beer the waiter put on the table. "I know I wasn't really available to you when we met. And it got worse after that."

"Mary Louise?" I took a swallow of the vermouth, savored its slightly medicinal taste.

"Mary Louise problems and Madame X problems and daughter problems. Karen got pregnant when she was fifteen, fortunately had a miscarriage. And then a year after that, she got into drugs. Madame X, as all good ex-wives do, blamed it all on my lousy parenting skills."

"Ben, I'm so sorry." Any parent of a teenage daughter will tell you that every night they say a prayer of thanks that she's not pregnant, an alcoholic or on drugs. I'd been lucky on all three counts, but I knock on wood just thinking about it.

"I got Karen into rehab, and she's been clean for three years now. Thanks to an engineer friend of mine at Channel 9, she did an internship there as a videocam person, then landed a great job at the Denver PBS affiliate." He took a long swallow of the beer. "After I moved Mary Louise out, I went into therapy myself. That's where I met Sandy. In a therapy group for parents of kids in rehab. A somewhat questionable common interest."

I recalled Sandy's reference to a parenting class.

"She seems like a very nice woman. And probably very fond of you."

He nodded. "That's what worries me." He took a long swallow of beer, emptied the glass and signaled the hovering waiter for another. "Anyhow, moving on to lighter topics, how's your investigation coming? Find anything we didn't?"

I recited a thumbnail summary of my two days of meetings, and mentioned the letter Julio had allegedly sent to the BPD and the FBI regarding what he thought were Felipe De los Santos's shady activities.

Ben nodded. "I vaguely remember a discussion about it after the shooting. I think Wineheart decided to let the FBI check it out." He reached for the small notebook in his shirt pocket. "I'll ask him about it."

"Would you also find out if he checked the files on Julio's laptop computer? Judith Karamazov, one of the other attorneys at LAUD, said they received a lot of hate e-mail."

"Yes, ma'am." He smiled at me. "Any other assignments?"

"What do you know about the L.A. shooting yesterday?"

"You don't miss a beat, do you?"

"I was at LAUD when one of the attorneys found out."

"Similar MO to the Montenegro shooting. Guy appears from nowhere, victim is a Puerto Rican lawyer, he shoots him, disappears. Witnesses gave different descriptions, and you know how reliable those are."

"Same weapons in Denver and L.A.?"

"Different weapons, but all subsonic ammo. In Denver the cartridges were RWS 40-grain hollow point. From the extractor, ejector, and firing-pin marks on the cartridge cases, Wineheart says the weapon was probably a High Standard .22 automatic. They were able to identify the make and caliber, but not the model. LAPD reported a .25 caliber weapon, ammo was Speer 35-grain Gold Dot hollow points. They think it came from a Harrington and Richardson Self-Loading. And a silencer *was* used all three times."

"So it's different perps with different weapons, or . . ." I reached for a handful of cashews and found the dish empty. I made a face.

"Hey, you look hungry. How about some dinner? Force Five has great bouillabaisse."

"Don't distract me. It's either different perps, or one very smart killer who's using a different weapon for each hit."

"Brilliant, my dear, brilliant."

"And all weapons that can be easily acquired on the used gun market."

He picked up the check and peered at it over his reading glasses. I wondered what had happened to his twenty-twenty vision. "And, if the guy is a pro, quickly disposed of after the shooting." He threw down a ten and two ones, pocketed the glasses and stood up. "Let's get out of here."

"Where's Sandy tonight? Maybe she'd like to join us."

"Tired of my company already?" He took my arm in a familiar fashion as we left the lounge. "Okay, okay, get off my case." He grinned. "She should be waiting for us at Force Five just about now. Had to pick up her son at band practice. My car is right outside."

The fog had turned to a drizzle. We drove the half mile or so to the waterfront restaurant in silence. As we crossed the parking lot to the restaurant, the wind off the Bay was in our faces, and I longed for the polar-fleece coat I'd left behind on *'Spray*. Ben reached to open the door of the restaurant and we were pushed back by a boisterous group on their way out. The decibels inside were high. I glanced around; this was the restaurant that the Montenegros and the Aarons never got to that Friday afternoon in July.

Sandy was sitting on a chair in the entryway, frowning slightly until she saw Ben. She stood up and her eyes searched our faces. Ben leaned over and kissed her and the frown lines disappeared. She gave me a bright smile, which I returned. We followed the perky waitress in T-shirt and cargo pants and three-inch platform sandals into the crowded lounge and wedged ourselves around a postage stamp–size table next to the fireplace. The waitress took our drinks order and assured Ben she would come and retrieve us when our table was ready.

Dining with a former lover and his current partner is not one of life's more scintillating experiences. I chatted with Sandy about the rigors of single parenthood, learned she'd grown up on the coast of Maine and, to Ben's surprise (apparently he'd never asked), that she loved to sail. Our conversation on regattas and dinghies and East Coast storms was interrupted by the arrival of our drinks and the announcement that a table was available.

Over Caesar salad and bouillabaisse I steered the conversation back to my case, and asked Ben if the BPD had or was thinking of organizing a special-crimes unit.

"Such as hate crimes?" he said, with his mouth full of sourdough.

I nodded.

"You're thinking that the Montenegro shooting and the other one were racially motivated. That's occurred to us, of course. To answer your question, no, there's no plan for a special-crimes unit. We take each case as it comes and do our best with it."

As the waitress cleared away our plates, Sandy tucked her hand into the crook of Ben's arm, and I suddenly wanted to leave. I realized that in the past Ben and I had spent our time either talking our professions or making love. We'd never had a real friendship. The thought depressed me and the escalating noise was giving me a headache. I declined dessert and couldn't think of a word of light conversation. I was plagued by the thought that the killer was still out there, possibly even on his way back to Friday Harbor to find Elyse, and I was spinning my wheels. I wanted to get back to my room, check on Elyse, find out if Nick had called, maybe call Melissa and collapse.

Ben ordered coffee and chocolate mousse for Sandy, brandy for himself. I looked at my watch, stood up and pulled my jacket over my shoulders, then realized with embarrassment that I didn't have the rental car.

"Ben, I just remembered I need to make some calls before it's too late. Would it be possible for you to run me back to the hotel?"

He looked surprised, but stood up, patted Sandy on the shoulder. "Don't give away my seat, ma'am. Back in ten minutes."

I bade Sandy farewell, we both murmured pleasantries about getting together again. I followed Ben to his car and stood in the drizzle while he unlocked it.

"I hope we weren't boring you."

"Just got overwhelmed all of a sudden with the devastation one dead Mexican attorney left behind. You know how it goes."

"Indeed I do."

Back at the hotel, he walked me to the door, gave me a chaste kiss on the cheek. "Give me a call before you leave, if you have time." He put his hand on my arm. "At the risk of sounding like a broken record, be careful."

I made a face, gave him a hug, and headed for the elevator, anxious to find out if Elyse was still okay, curious to know what Carmela Aaron might add tomorrow morning to the portrait of her cousin, Felipe De los Santos.

27

"Please, come in." Carmela Aaron was significantly younger than her husband. Her tan, unlined face showed dimples when she smiled, which she was doing now. She shifted a dark-haired infant onto her left shoulder and welcomed me with a handshake. Following Peter's instructions, I had knocked softly instead of ringing the doorbell.

She beckoned me into a tiled entryway that opened onto a sunken living room. A fire burned in the fireplace. The Aaron house was a Berkeley cottage design and shone with pride of ownership.

She motioned me to the flowered sofa and stood in the middle of the room, gently rocking the baby.

"I hope I didn't wake him," I said.

She shook her head, looking at the dark downy hair and the tiny face with half-closed eyes. "Emilio not want to sleep yet this morning, but I think now he will," she whispered. "Please excuse me." She disappeared up the stairs off the entrance hall.

I moved away from the fire and glanced across the small dining area to a '50s-style kitchen with a lot of white tile. To the left of the kitchen, French doors opened onto a walled garden. In the dining area, I studied the book titles on the floor-to-ceiling shelves. To the right of the bookcase, a partially opened door revealed a room that appeared to be a study. The drapes were drawn and an art deco lamp on the wooden desk illuminated neat stacks of manila files.

Behind the desk, a glass-fronted wooden cabinet displayed three shelves of handguns and rifles.

Carmela's footsteps came down the stairs.

"That is Peter's office," she said. She opened the door wider, switched on a ceiling light. "This is the last room we have to fix. When we buy the house, it needs a lot of work, but Peter is good with such things." She touched the faded red drapes. "I will make new curtains soon."

I glanced at the gun collection.

"Those belong to Peter's grandfather," she said. "All Browns. I have fear of guns in the house for Emilio, so Peter keep it locked."

I peered at Grandfather Aaron's collection, which included what was commonly called a Colt .45 automatic and a 12-gauge Browning semiautomatic shotgun. The latter was a very popular sporting firearm that dated back to the end of the nineteenth century and was still manufactured in Belgium. In addition to police-academy training, I'd had a crash course in old firearms from the departed Albert, who collected antique handguns along with antique cars.

"My aunt killed with a gun," Carmela said matter-of-factly and led the way back into the living room.

I pondered the syntax of her statement. "Your aunt? She was killed?"

She nodded. "Tío Juan, my uncle, he got very drunk and he shooted her. Because his dinner was cold."

Nothing like a cold dinner to piss a guy off.

Carmela didn't seem to expect a response. She sat on the large hassock in front of the fireplace. "Peter say you want to talk to me about Julio?" She stared down at her clasped hands; pale pink polish covered her delicate, oval fingernails. I reached into my bag and pressed the Record button. Before I could begin the interview, she said, "Peter say Elyse is your, what you say, *cliente*?

I nodded.

"She is okay? She leave without to say good-bye. She never see Emilio."

"Elyse was sad," I said. "And she was afraid."

She blinked quickly against unshed tears and clasped her hands even more tightly. "Perhaps one day we see her again." She opened her mouth to speak, then pressed her lips together, struggling for control.

I opened my notebook. "Carmela, can you tell me about the day Julio was killed?"

She nodded. "Elyse and me, we wanted to go to the city, to buy clothes for the babies. We finded a big accident on the bridge. The traffic was so awful, we go to McDonald's and then we go up to the stables."

"Tilden Ridge Stables?"

Carmela nodded. "At the school. Elyse missed the stables. Since she was *embarasada*, pregnant, her doctor told her not to ride anymore. But the girls want to see her, Kathryn say. The girls in the Stable Club."

"How long were you at the stables?"

"I told the police, we got to the stables about two o'clock, maybe two-thirty. We see the horses, we talk to the girls, then we come back to the marina to surprise Peter and Julio." She took a deep breath, then plunged on fiercely. "It was Julio's fault. I telled Elyse many times, what Julio do was dangerous. I know. The *políticos,* they always win. And if they do not win, they kill you. *Julio estaba loco!* He was even more *loco* than Felipe!"

I wondered what craziness on the part of her cousin she was referring to. Her voice had risen and had a high edge to it.

"Defending *comunistas*, writing terrible things about the Mexico government in *El Diario*, going off to the jungles to find the Zapatistas. *Locura, pura locura!* He wanted Elyse to go to Chiapas with him. I told her not to go. *Julio se enojó conmigo.* Julio, he become very angry with me. Felipe try to talk to Julio and they have, they had a big fight!" She gave a deep sigh. *"Qué horror!"*

I tried to assimilate the information Carmela was

hurling at me, attempting to separate emotion from facts. I decided to start at the beginning.

"Did you meet Elyse and Julio through Peter?"

She shook her head and smiled. "I know Elyse first. She was teaching an English class for foreigners, like me. My English from Colombia is too bad. In class we talk about what sports we like, we discover we both ride horses. Elyse introduce me to Kathryn and to Julio and then to Peter. Peter and me, we get married and have Emilio."

It was far more happily ever after than Elyse's tale.

I asked when she had immigrated to the U.S. and learned of the long wait for visas for herself and her cousin, Felipe De los Santos; that Felipe had been raised by Carmela's parents on their ranch near Medellín after Felipe's mother, Carmela's Tía Marta, was shot. The emigration from Colombia was instigated by Carmela's father, she said, who foresaw increasing political unrest in their region between the police and the guerillas and the drug dealers. Carmela also hinted that Felipe's acquaintances in Colombia were less than desirable. "His girlfriend, she was very rich. She used drugs and she drived my mother crazy. She wanted to get married with Felipe." She sighed deeply. "Felipe is my cousin. I love him, but he drinks very much, like my uncle. I also think he use *las drogas*." She pleated her blue cotton skirt and continued her tale.

"My father, he selled horses for our tickets. We arrive here to live with my mother's cousin in San Francisco. In Colombia I was a teacher, so in San Francisco I go to work for the school district. Not to teach, because I not able to go back to university, but like *una examinadora*." She paused, at a loss for words, and tried to explain. "You know, when new students come to school in San Francisco, they get tested. I do that. I tested in Spanish."

"Tell me what happened when you and Elyse came to the marina on the afternoon Julio was shot."

She took a deep breath. "We come in Elyse's little red car, and we both have much trouble to get down from the car." She smiled a sad smile. "Because our bellies, they are getting big. We are laughing so hard, and then I have to go to the *baño*, to the rest room. Elyse went down to the boat. When I come back, I hear screaming and some people are running to the gate."

"Did you see anyone come out of the gate?"

She shrugged. "Three or four people run out of the gate, because they are afraid. People are running all around. I think the *asesino* runned away, *se escapó*." She twisted her hands again. "I try and try to get in to the gate, then the police come, and I scream so much they let me in. Elyse was on the boat, but she have much pain. Julio, he is on the floor in the boat, and Peter is with him and blood is coming out of his shoulder. Then the ambulance come and take her and Julio and Peter away. It was so awful. *Una pesadilla*." She shivered.

She was right. It was a nightmare.

"The police take me to the hospital." She blinked and the inevitable tears came down. "I tell her, I tell her, just like in my country."

She swallowed, wiped her eyes with her skirt.

"Did Felipe De los Santos come to the marina that afternoon?"

She looked surprised at my question, then shook her head. "No, I called him at his office when I am at the hospital, there is no one there. But he say he was with his girlfriend." She made a face. "Nancy. Just like his girlfriend in Colombia. She live in a big house in Tiburón, and she drive a big car, but she is *basura*! Garbage."

She probably meant "trash," but I didn't correct her.

"What happened after you got to the hospital?"

She stared into the fire, remembering. "Julio is died when we get to the hospital and Elyse finded out she have a, how do you say, *un malparto*?"

"A miscarriage."

She nodded. "She called her mother and father.

They come to the hospital and her father wanted Elyse to go to their house, but she say no, and her mother cried a lot."

"Do you know why Elyse didn't want to go and stay with her parents?"

"She say it was like to be a traitor to Julio."

"A traitor in what way?"

"Elyse's father was not happy that Julio not take good care of her. When Julio go to Mexico without her, she is sad. Her father told her to divorce from Julio." She paused. "But I say that is wrong. Divorce is a problem, not a solution," she said firmly.

Amen.

There was one more avenue I wanted to explore, and I knew I had to tread lightly.

"Carmela, did Felipe and Julio work well together?"

"No!" She shook her head. "Felipe did not like to work with Julio. He told Peter that Julio was not doing a good job, that he should work and not to go around like a *gitano*, a gypsy. Felipe felt sorry for Elyse, so he paid her to take care of his horse when he go to Colombia."

"Did Felipe go to Colombia often?"

She considered the question, drew somewhat into herself, and clasped her hands tightly.

"He go to Colombia to take care of family business."

I wondered what family business was left. Felipe's mother had been killed and I would imagine his father had received some sort of jail term.

"What do you know about Felipe's importing business?"

"Importing business?" Her dark eyes stared at me without blinking. "I know nothing of this importing."

Before I could pursue what I had learned while talking with Judith Karamazov, and as if on cue, we heard the cry of infant Emilio. Carmela leaped to her feet and looked toward the stairs. "I have to go to Emilio."

I looked at her and gathered up my belongings.

"Thank you for your help, Carmela. If you think of anything else, please call me." I handed her my card.

She took the card without looking at it, glanced anxiously again toward the stairs, then smiled and shook my hand.

"Please give Elyse for me an *abrazo. Es mi buena amiga.*"

I walked to the car, thinking that by the time this nightmare was over, Elyse was going to need a *buena amiga.*

I started the car and sat there while it idled, contemplating my next move. There were no messages on the cell phone, nothing from Zelda on De los Santos.

I pawed through to the bottom of my canvas carryall, retrieved the East Bay map I'd had the forethought to buy this morning. I spread it out on the steering wheel, found where 40th Street in Oakland intersects with Adeline, and headed down Eunice Street in the late-morning mist.

Next stop: the residence of Elyse and Julio Montenegro.

28

The Oakland address Elyse had given me was on 60th Street in a culturally and racially diverse neighborhood of small single-family dwellings whose inhabitants either had modest incomes or wanted to make a social statement. I guessed both might have been motivations for the Montenegros.

The small plots of land surrounding the houses were, for the most part, neat and well kept, but apparently, like their counterparts in far more affluent areas, left something to be desired in safety. Wrought-iron bars, some decorative, some plainly institutional in nature, covered the windows on most of the houses where a sign or decal announced that the property was protected by one or another security system.

I coasted to a stop before a small yellow frame residence with white trim on the windows, locked the doors of the rental car, and approached the house. Beside the door, four red geraniums were gallantly blooming in dry soil in a cracked terra cotta pot. I keyed in the combination for the alarm Elyse had given me, unlocked the deadbolt and stepped inside. The house smelled as if my client had forgotten to take out the garbage before she left.

A minuscule entrance hall with a bare, dark wood floor opened into the small living room. Two tall big-leaf ficus plants, now dead, stood near the windows, their leaves cracked and dusty. Beyond the living room, I glimpsed a kitchen with orange Formica countertops and heard a refrigerator that sounded as if it was not long for this world. The place reminded me of my own starving-student lodgings from long ago, after husband number one had departed for the Seychelles.

Despite the bright yellow-and-orange sofa cushions, and the almost new beige velour sofa that filled most of the small room, I couldn't visualize Elyse sitting in the Naugahyde recliner or preparing a meal on the orange Formica countertops. A green light on the front of a television set blinked untiringly. Six or eight CDs in their plastic cases lay on the floor in front of a set of shelving from where they had apparently toppled. The eclectic sampling included UB40, Luther Vandross, Tupac Shakur, Carman MacRae, cafe singer Andrea Marcovicci, and the jazz singer Jane Monheit.

In the bookcase behind the sofa, the titles ran the gamut of Julio's activities: two thick volumes on contract law; *Litigation in the California Courts*; Chomsky's *Manufacturing Consent* and *Secrets, Lies and Democracy*; *El Laberinto la Soledad*; *L'etranger*; *Hate Crimes in America*; several novels by Dostoevsky and Sartre; a leather-bound volume of the complete works of Federico García Lorca.

I looked through the stacks of old Spanish-language newspapers and magazines, some dating back several years. *Tiempo*, *La Jornada*, *El Financiero*, *El Sol Diario*. And taking up the entire bottom shelf, stacks of *Covert Action Quarterly*, all arranged in chronological order.

Where, I wondered, in this accumulation of law and literature and politics, was there anything of Elyse? Where were the books of Renaissance and modern art? The tomes on social services? The treatises on English equitation? Had she already removed them? Or had she been so overshadowed by the relentless political activism of her husband that the woman Elyse had ceased to exist?

In the kitchen, the refrigerator was still churning away. I hit it hard with my hand and was rewarded with silence. Inside I found a glass carafe half filled with moldy orange juice, three unopened cartons of nonfat key lime yogurt. The freezer contained frozen vegetables and microwave meals. Tracking the smell of something rotten, I opened the white painted cupboard door below the sink and stepped back in self-defense. Slightly brown pieces of plastic wrap that had once covered something from the sea lay crumpled on the bottom of the plastic wastebasket. I considered removing it, but couldn't think of what to do with it, so I closed the door and continued my reconnoiter, trying not to breathe deeply.

A thin layer of dust covered the maple bedroom furniture. The blue sheets on the unmade king-sized bed were rumpled; the bed filled most of the room. A woman's white cardigan sweater and a long black skirt had been flung on the bed, along with pale pink cotton bikini underwear and several black leather belts. A closet ran along one entire end of the small room. I peered past the open closet door. Elyse had probably left behind more than she had taken, and apparently was unable to deal with the disposal of Julio's clothing. Men's coats and jackets, trousers and dress shirts still in plastic sacks from the laundry, hung beside long dresses and skirts. Men's and women's shoes lay intermingled on the floor of the closet. I closed the door to the bedroom and opened the door to the immediate right, unprepared for its contents.

Late-morning sun radiated through the white gossamer curtains. A blue-and-pink bassinet sat in front of the white-curtained window and a changing table stood along one wall. From the ceiling over the bassinet hung a plastic mobile, its pink-and-blue miniature teddy bears moving ever so gently in some small zephyr of air, illuminated in the rays of yellow sunshine. A pale blue braided rug provided a soft oval in front of the white louvered doors of the closet, which I did not open. Rather, I returned to the hallway and closed the door of the tiny nursery behind me and stood for a moment, reflecting that I would have done exactly what Elyse did. Flee to friends from a safer time.

"Ma'am?"

I whirled around. A man of some seventy years in a dirty Mexican guayabera, faded blue jeans and purple running shoes stood in the living room. His long gray-white hair was neatly combed and hung down his back. My eyes flicked to the open entry door behind him. Living on a remote island had made me careless.

"Yes? Can I help you?" I moved away from the nursery and into the living room.

"I just wondered, ma'am, are you the family?" Faded blue eyes peered at me over wire-rimmed glasses.

"I'm Scotia MacKinnon."

"Well, ma'am, I'm White Knight. I live next door." He motioned back toward the entrance and to his left. "Sure was an awful thing, the killing. Did the police ever find out who done it?"

"Did you know the Montenegros, Mr. . . . . Knight?"

He shrugged, and stared at the piece of paper in his hand. "He wasn't never here, not much. Always coming and going with his briefcase and black valise. And when he was home, there was always that noise till all hours of the night."

"Noise?"

"You know, that Meskin music. Salsa, I think they call it. And sometimes he played the guitar till two or three o'clock in the morning."

"That must have been difficult for you."

He nodded. "I tried to be friends with the missus after. Invited her over for coffee one day, but she turned me down cold." His deeply wrinkled face expressed his disappointment, then he shrugged. "Haven't seen her for quite a bit. This is kind of a dangerous neighborhood to just leave a house empty. Them kids down the block'll carry away anything that's not chained down. And I ain't gonna try to stop them. They's got guns, you know." He sniffed and looked at the paper again.

"Have you seen anyone trying to break in?"

He shook his head. "Not exactly. But I sure was suspicious when the burglar alarm dude came by."

"Burglar alarm dude?"

He nodded. "Right after Miz Montenegro left. I remember it, because I was sitting in my window writing the letter. To the city council, you know, about our little park down the street they're going to sell to a big supermarket chain. I don't want them to do it. I take Imogene over there every day. Imogene's my dog. They's plenty of places they could put a supermarket. Don't have to be right in the middle of our park."

I could feel a draft from the front door. "While you were sitting there writing your letter, Mr. Knight, what did you see?" I asked, refraining from discussing another Berkeley park that nearly caused a revolution.

"I saw this dude in a brown uniform with a van. Gray, I think it was. Couldn't tell what he looked like, 'cause he had on dark shades. No reason for shades on a foggy day, but those druggies, they always wear shades." He twisted his mouth. "Had a sign on it, the van." He held the paper away from his eyes and peered at it. "The sign said, 'Bay Area Locksmiths.' Even had this telephone number on the sign. I suspicioned right away he wasn't no locksmith, so I called it, and there's no such number. He went right up to the door with his tool kit."

"Did the man open the door?"

"Not while I was looking, he didn't. I watched him for a while and in a couple of minutes he got back in the van and drove off. Never saw him again." He shrugged. "Course, he could of come back at night."

"Did you report your suspicions to the police?"

"Nope." He shook his head. "I don't mess with the police."

"I see."

He put the scrap of paper in his jeans pocket and shuffled to the door. "Gotta go and walk Imogene before the park goes away." He paused in the open door. "Tell Miz Montenegro I'm real sorry about her husband. Nobody should have that happen, even if they are hoity-toity."

"Thank you, Mr. Knight."

"My pleasure, ma'am."

The door closed behind him.

I gathered up my bag from the sofa and followed him out, reset the alarm and headed for the rental car. Inside the car, I locked the doors and started the motor. There was a tapping on my window and I turned to see White Knight standing beside the car. I rolled down the window an inch.

"Ma'am, I didn't call the police, but I did write down the license number. Maybe it'll help you find the killer. Mr. Montenegro helped me get Imogene back after they took her away to the animal shelter when I had my triple bypass and I'd like to help if I could." He passed the wrinkled scrap of paper through the window. I looked at the seven-figure alphanumeric printed in small block letters.

I thanked White Knight, wished him luck with the park, and watched him shuffle away down the sidewalk with the small spaniel whose steps matched its owner's.

29

The noontime traffic gridlock on Ashby Avenue between Telegraph and San Pablo Avenues provided me
half an hour of snaillike travel time to collect my
thoughts on the morning's interviews. If I had learned
nothing else from Carmela Aaron, it was that increased familiarity with Felipe De los Santos was unlikely to inspire increased admiration. If one could
believe Carmela and her mother, Felipe's choice of
female companions, both in Colombia and in California, left much to be desired. It would appear that Felipe, like his father before him, had an alcohol
problem. I wondered if the genetic legacy extended
to violence.

Below San Pablo Avenue, I jumped the light,
slipped into a right lane in front of a delivery truck
from Home Depot and headed for the entrance to
Highway 80. At the convenience store, I collected a
meatball sandwich and a Pepsi, then headed for the
hotel, eager to know what Zelda had uncovered on
LAUD's legislative Don Juan. I was equally eager to
pass on the scrap of paper White Knight had given
me, for whatever it might be worth.

The message light on my room phone was blinking.
The first message was from Melissa: Gilberto had a
meeting of the Brazilian Club tonight and she was
bringing her car into Berkeley to get the oil changed.
Did I want to have dinner? She'd call about five.

The second message was from Zelda. She'd done a

preliminary on De los Santos that she'd sent by e-mail and she was running out of time. Should she turn the request over to DataTech? She was leaving on the red-eye tomorrow.

I downloaded the file on De los Santos.

Preliminary report on Felipe De los Santos

Born: *September 13, 1962, Bogota, Colombia*
Citizenship: *Colombia*
Education: *Ll. B., Hastings School of Law, San Francisco, CA 1997*
Career: *Clerk, De Angelo & Gomez, San Francisco, 1995–97*
Legislative Staff Attorney, Latin American Union for Defense, Berkeley, CA, 1997–present
Other business affiliations: *Partner, Global Imports, Inc., Oakland, CA; partner, California Van Lines, Oakland, CA*
Police record: *San Rafael, CA. DUI, December 19, 1998; acquitted.*
Tiburón, CA. Arrested for assault, April 2000. No charges filed.

I dialed New Millennium.

"Yes?" Zelda's voice was sharp and frantic.

"Thanks for the report. I'll review it and decide if we need any more from DataTech. Before you leave, can you check a tag for me? Shouldn't be too hard." I read her the tag number White Knight had provided.

"I'll get on it right away. Anything else?"

"Any word from Elyse?"

"Nada."

I reread the report on Felipe. Carmela's cousin seemed to be expanding his business ventures, and I was willing to bet that both my client and Carmela knew more about Felipe's import-export activities than either admitted. Since it was apparent from my conversations with both Judith and Carmela that there had been no love lost between Julio Montenegro and

Felipe De los Santos, and if Global Imports was a cover, and if De los Santos thought Julio had uncovered it, to what lengths would he go to protect himself?

I stared at the report and decided to forward it to Sergeant Wineheart at the Berkeley PD, along with a note asking if he had sent Julio's exposé of De los Santos's activities to the FBI.

It was nearly two o'clock. I chewed my cold meatball sandwich, spilled two globs of tomato sauce on my white shirt, balled up the stack of stained paper napkins and deposited them in the wastebasket beside the desk. I sipped on the Pepsi and stared out the window. Except for my appointment with Elyse's parents on Thursday morning, I had run out of avenues to explore.

The earlier sunny sky had gone partly overcast and dark clouds were gathering out beyond the Golden Gate. The room felt hot and stuffy. Feeling slightly claustrophobic, I threw on my jacket and headed out, trudging north beyond the hotel until the two-lane road dead-ended at the waterside park on San Francisco Bay. Here, on warmer afternoons, colorful kites would have been flying from the green hillsides. There were no kite flyers today. I stood on the windy hillside, hands in my pockets, and watched the whitecaps accumulating on the blue-gray waters of the Bay. A few dauntless sailors tacked along, sharply heeled, to the north of the municipal pier. For once, I had no desire to join them in the biting wind. I felt antsy and cold and apprehensive, and I wanted to go home.

Melissa didn't call, but rather appeared at my door at five-thirty. When I'd last seen her over Labor Day weekend, her honey-blonde hair had been straight and shoulder length; now it was no more than two inches long anywhere on her head and appeared to have undergone an extensive treatment of styling mousse. I gave her a hug and uttered silent thanks that there were no visible body piercings, no nose or tongue rings or worse. She wriggled out of black high-top shoes with thick lug soles and tossed her dark-blue parka on the bed nearest the TV.

"You're so not going to like this, Mom, but I'll show you anyway."

She pulled down the top of the white sock on her right foot and displayed a slender ankle. "Pretty cool, huh? Just like the ones you used to read to me when I was little."

I stared at the multicolored iridescent fire-breathing dragon tattoo that coiled sinuously between her ankle bone and Achilles tendon. We had been "dialoging" for years over the subject of tattoos. "Cool," I agreed with a smile. "I particularly like the flame." It might have been worse. It might have been a boy's name, or a cult icon. "You hungry?" I asked, knowing the answer.

She reached for the TV remote on the bedside table. "Starving. Can we order up room service?"

"Sure." I handed her the menu. With Melissa, it had always been important to attend to first things first.

I watched her sitting cross-legged in her oversize denim overalls and white T-shirt, simultaneously surfing the cable channels and flipping through the extensive room-service menu. Melissa was tall and willowy like my mother and looked like she worked out every day; in fact, she was a couch potato whenever possible and lived on junk food. A perfect exemplar of Generation X, female gender.

"Can we get a pepperoni pizza and some Cokes delivered?"

I detested pepperoni so she compromised on a large size half-and-half pepperoni and tomato/mushroom and called the local pizza franchise, which promised to deliver within forty minutes or our order would be free.

"So, tell me about Gilberto." I settled into the chair by the window.

She tried to hide a grin, continued her channel surfing, stopped at Nick at Nite, whose current offer-

ing was an ebullient black-and-white version of Lucy
Arnez trading '50s-style insults with her best friend,
Ethel.

"He's the best," Melissa said. "Want to see a picture?" She reached for the parka and pulled a photo
out of the side pocket.

I stared at the full-length shot of Melissa and a smiling slender young man with dark curly hair. Gilberto
had one arm flung over her shoulder; both were wearing blue jeans and parkas. He was about her height,
which, at five feet eight inches, is three inches taller
than I am.

"And where's he from in Brazil?"

"Brasilia. His father's an industrialist. You know."

I smiled, interpreting the "you know" as meaning
she was clueless as to what an industrialist was.

"His sister Zidia's really nice. We've been doing
e-mail. She's exactly my age."

"What's Gilberto studying?"

"Business. He ended up at St. Mary's because his
mother went there. She's American. He's a year behind me and he wants to transfer to Stanford next
year. And get an MBA." She tore her attention away
from Lucy and Ethel, who were exiting stage left arm
in arm. "Could we afford Stanford? I mean, if I'm still
with Gilberto and I transferred there?"

We might be able to; the proceeds from the sale of
the house in St. Francis Wood had been substantial
and were well invested, but I wasn't about to encourage college transfers based on short-term infatuations.
For better or worse, my career in law enforcement
had begun the day I spied Melissa's father standing in
the registration line for criminal psychology at San
Francisco State when I was a freshman. Although it
had no connection whatsoever to my declared major
in library science, I had manipulated my way into the
class with him, six months later we were married, and
four years later I was a divorced single mother of a
three-year-old.

"That might depend on your grades," I hedged, noting that Lucy and Ethel had been replaced by the Brady Bunch. "They haven't exactly been in the top ten percent, have they?"

"Mother!" She frowned and glared at me from the golden brown eyes she inherited from her father. "Do you *always* have to talk about my *grades*?! Besides, they're okay this semester except for economics and that's because the instructor is an idiot. He's way too monotone and goes off on these weird tangents. He won't even hold study sessions before exams. Can you *believe* it? I was telling Grandma about it and she said she knew someone who could probably get me a dance scholarship." Her gaze was riveted on the TV screen, where the Brady Bunch was breakfasting. It had always astonished me that she preferred the '50s sitcoms to the shoot-'em-up violence, sex and drugs entertainment most of her contemporaries thrived on. "And I don't understand why you flipped when I suggested it." She turned to face me. "Sometimes you sound like you don't even *like* Grandma. What's *with* you two?"

What was with me and Jewel Moon?

I stared at Melissa and wondered how much I could or should tell her and where to start. Should I begin with Jewel Moon running away from our home in St. Ann's Bay when I was five? The infrequent postcards from Boston, then Denver and finally San Francisco, and the slow realization that she would never return? Or the long days of my childhood curled in my grandmother MacKinnon's padded window seat overlooking the ocean while I waited for my father to return from a fishing trip? Melissa already knew of the frigid winter storm in the North Atlantic that had claimed his and my grandfather's life, but I had never talked about the painful transition from the rocky green mountains of Cape Breton Island to urban communal living with Jewel Moon and her lover Giovanni in San Francisco's Haight-Ashbury district—the infamous playground of the '60s Flower Children—after my grandmother died. I had always doled out information on my pre-Melissa existence on a need-to-know basis. At this moment, her need to know was postponed by a knock on the door and the arrival of our gigantic pizza.

I joined her on the bed and we devoured the hot, cheesy concoction and washed it down with sips of icy Classic Coke.

"Mom, do we still have family on Cape Breton Island?"

I nodded. "Cousin Anne, your grandpa's brother's daughter. Sometimes I get a Christmas card from her. She lives in Halifax. She's got a son about your age."

"I think it would be cool to visit her sometime." The Brady Bunch had retired for the night and I returned to the subject of her political science studies while she found a channel broadcasting a fifteen-day Double-Oh-Seven marathon.

"You said you had a paper due this week. How's that going?"

She stared at the two dark-haired females fighting to the death to determine which would be worthy of the gypsy chief's son in *From Russia with Love*. "It's for a class called History of Terrorism. We read the *Unabomber Manifesto* and we have to write an analysis of it."

"Did it make any sense?"

She turned slowly toward me, frowning. "I know you're going to think I'm pretty weird, but there's a whole lot of stuff I agree with."

"For example?" I closed the drapes and returned to stretch out on my bed, pillows behind my shoulders.

"I think the main message was that we think we have freedom, but as society becomes more and more technologically based, we have less and less power over our lives." Double-Oh-Seven and the gypsy tribe forgotten, she rested her elbow on one knee and leaned her chin on her hand. "Like technology seems to make our lives easier, but the stable social framework we used to have, and the family ties and small communities we used to have, no longer exist. And nobody really has any power, because all the big decisions are made by politicians and big corporations. And they always lie anyway, it sucks. Like maybe only five hundred or a thousand people in the whole world make all the decisions."

It was the longest intellectual discourse I had ever heard from the lips of my daughter. "Sounds like you've given this a lot of thought."

She stared vacantly at the TV screen and continued, "What I could most understand was what he said about there not being any security in our lives."

"You mean because of crime?"

She shook her head. "No. It's things like how do you know that the maintenance men at a nuclear power plant are doing what they should so there's not going to be a meltdown? Or do you know if the stuff you buy at the supermarket's been genetically altered. Like that food that got recalled because it was made with genetically altered corn that wasn't approved for human consumption." She paused, intent on Sean Connery embracing his leading lady. "A long time ago," she continued, "when people lived in caves, they worried about *physical* security and getting enough to eat, but they could fight in self-defense and go out and kill a mastodon or whatever they ate in those days. One of the big points of the *Manifesto* is that now, in a technological society, we're threatened by things like environmental pollution and invasion of privacy and constant government regulation. Psychological threats that we're powerless to do anything about."

I flashed on my conversation with Jared a week ago and his comments about the rising mutiny against federal regulations. "Does the *Manifesto* see any hope for modern society?"

She shook her head. "He says that the advanced industrial technological society *has* to regulate people completely in order to function, and that as it grows, our freedom and power will keep on shrinking. He says there's no way to reform the system. Only a revolution can change it and that's why he started building bombs. To get people's attention before it's too late."

"And so the ends justify the means?"

"That's what I've still got to discuss in the paper. And I have to compare and contrast it with two other examples of domestic terrorism. I was supposed to finish it tonight, but I wanted to see you. What are you doing down here, anyway?" She stood up, slithered out of her overalls, and climbed under the bed covers.

I gave her a synopsis of the Montenegro case so far.

"The guy who got murdered sounds like one of the leftists the *Manifesto* talks about," she said. "You know, those people who get involved in causes and look like they're really compassionate, but they're just doing it for power or so they have something to do. And if our society didn't have any social problems, they'd invent some so they'd have an excuse to protest something." She yawned, hit the Off button on the remote. " 'Night, Mom. I'm too tired to drive back. Would you please wake me at six? I've got an eight o'clock tomorrow."

" 'Night, Melissa. Dream of angels." I stared down pridefully at the boyish blonde head on the pillow, touched her smooth cheek. I set the alarm on the clock radio, undressed and crawled into my own bed, pondering Melissa's description of Julio as a leftist in search of a cause. As I drifted off, I wondered if his murder and the attacks on the two other attorneys were part of some far larger, darker piece of domestic terrorism than I had previously imagined.

30

Fog and drizzle covered the East Bay on Thursday morning. I stared at the gridlock traffic at the Bay Bridge Toll Plaza, knew I'd be late for my nine-thirty appointment with Elyse's parents, and wondered if a face-to-face meeting was necessary or if I could have done an interview by phone. Given what I'd heard from Judith Karamazov and Carmela Aaron, I expected little more than tears from *mater*, and some version of "I told her so" from *pater*. The Muehlers lived in Sea Cliff, which is way to hell and gone on the other side of the city, and I had a one-thirty flight out of San Francisco back to Seattle.

I had awakened Melissa at six. In a sleepy voice she'd agreed not to change her major before the end of the term, and I'd approved the new dress for the homecoming dance. I was back in bed as the door closed behind her and slept until seven-thirty, after which I'd showered and packed, grabbed a juice and coffee, and headed out to play in city-bound morning traffic.

The Bank of America clock tower showed nine-fifteen as I came off the bridge. I checked my mental map of the city, darted across three lanes of traffic and exited on Laguna-Fell, which took me through the Haight-Ashbury and out to 19th Avenue.

Two blocks beyond California Street I turned left onto Lake Street. The light drizzle had become rain,

and at 37th Avenue, I turned in through the gates that
separate the highly affluent from ordinary mortals.

Sea Cliff is a manicured community that lies along
the oceanfront between the Presidio and Land's End.
The architecture of Sea Cliff houses is eclectic, and
the Muehler's imposing, many-gabled, three-story
brick-and-timber French Normandy residence at number Sixteen Paseo del Mar added to the diversity.

I stepped under the portico and lifted the heavy
brass knocker on the wooden door. From within re-
sounded a two-toned chime. A few seconds passed,
then the door opened.

Alice Muehler's eyes were the same aquamarine as
Elyse's, but there the resemblance ended. Her hair
was carefully colored an artificial blonde and styled in
a smooth pageboy. Her makeup was perfect and mask-
like over what had once probably been fine skin. Her
ivory lounging pajamas were silky and luxurious. She
had a green ceramic cup and saucer in her hand.

"Mrs. Muehler?"

She frowned, nodding. "I'm sorry, whatever you're
selling, my husband doesn't—"

"Mrs. Muehler, I'm Scotia MacKinnon. I'm sorry
I'm late."

She looked at me in bewilderment, still frowning.

"I called yesterday," I said. "Your husband said I
could talk with the two of you about Julio Montenegro's death." I handed her my business card.

"Oh." She held the card away from her and
squinted at it. "Friday Harbor. That's where Elyse is.
Is Elyse all right?" There was anxiety in her voice.

"Your daughter is safe, Mrs. Muehler," I said, praying I was telling the truth. "Is your husband at home?"

"No, he's not. And Will didn't tell me about the
appointment." She hesitated, glancing down at her attire, her eyes darting from side to side. She gave a
half smile and shrugged. "I'm so sorry. It's not the
first thing he forgot to tell me. Please come in."

From the spacious tiled hallway, an open curving
stairway led to an upper level. She ushered me into

an immaculate, exquisitely furnished room. A pair of tortoiseshell reading glasses lay on an opened newspaper that was spread on the marble-topped coffee table. She collected the newspaper and glasses, motioned me to the moss-green velvet sofa, and offered a welcome cup of coffee. As she headed back toward the hall, her heel caught on the silk oriental rug. She steadied herself against the doorway and disappeared. I picked up Mrs. Muehler's coffee cup, sniffed the liquid, and understood why she had tripped.

I inspected the room, dazzled by its opulence. An enormous stone fireplace filled one end of the room. Gold silk drapes hung on either side of long windows that overlooked the ocean and the Golden Gate Bridge. The rounded hills of Marin County were barely visible through the rain. A collection of porcelain figures, all cats, gamboled on the table behind me.

Alice Muehler returned with a green cup and saucer that matched her own. I watched her approach the sofa unsteadily. She rearranged the needlepoint pillows between us and apologized for her husband's absence. He left for a meeting with a client before she got up, she said.

I complimented her on the house and pulled out my pen and notebook.

"Thank you." She gazed around the room. "It's not really my taste. I would have preferred something more modern, more California, but Will prefers this style." She shrugged. "I was studying design when I met Will. When he proposed, I dropped out of school and we moved to New York. Will never wanted me to work." She stared into her cup. "So I redecorate instead." She flashed an artificial smile.

I asked if I might tape-record our conversation. She nodded and asked, "Have the police found new evidence?"

I shook my head, plunged in and told her about Elyse's suspicion that she was being followed and Campbell's fatal accident with the Ghia. I also related Elyse's suspicion that she had been the target.

Her face paled. She looked down in consternation as the cup rattled against the saucer and gave a sharp cry. She set the cup and saucer on the coffee table with a small crash. Black liquid splashed onto the marble top.

"Oh, poor Campbell. That poor, poor child." She pulled a linen handkerchief from the pocket of her pajamas and wiped her eyes.

"I knew he'd try to find Elyse," she said. "Will said he wouldn't, that he only wanted Julio. But I knew it. That monster. As if it wasn't enough that she lost the baby, my grandchild."

I asked where she and her husband had been on the afternoon of Julio's murder and Elyse's miscarriage.

"I was here all day," she said. "Elyse asked me to go shopping with her and her little friend from Colombia, but the Garden Society had a walking tour in Sea Cliff and I had to be here. I made some orange madeleines for the group." She smiled. "It was so lovely. I used my grandmother's silver service, and I was starting to clear away when the hospital called." She inhaled deeply, as if in need of oxygen, and blinked rapidly. "We didn't know Julio was—had been—killed until we got there." She closed her eyes, and her body swayed slightly. "Julio was a good boy. But he associated with such . . . such unsuitable people."

"And your husband? Was he at home the day of the murder?"

"He played golf in the morning. He always plays golf on Fridays. He came in, I think it was about one or two o'clock. Will was upset with all the people in the house." She was silent, remembering. "So he went into his study. He played with, he took down the— I think he took down the collection."

"What collection is that?"

"Will has a fine collection of toy soldiers. Hessian soldiers. One of the finest in the world. He started collecting them when he was a boy. He was an only child, you know. The soldiers are a great comfort to

him. Elyse used to give him one every Christmas.
That's what he was doing when the hospital called and
we heard about the miscarriage. And I guess he was
so upset, he pushed them all on the floor. At least,
that's where I found them the next morning."

She looked at me with imploring eyes. "Will had
such fine plans for Elyse. She was like . . . like, I guess
you could say, a trophy. He always wanted the very
best for her. She had ballet lessons and piano lessons
and art lessons. He never got over that she wanted to
be a social worker. He couldn't imagine why anybody
would want to work with those . . . those people."
She took a long swallow from the cup. "He planned
for her to marry the son of one of his partners, you
know. At the investment firm he worked at in New
York. He told her he would take her mare if
she married Julio. Gypsy's Legend. She won so many
trophies with her." She stared into the cup, as if it
were reflecting old memories or misplaced dreams.
"And when they eloped, Will went to the stables and
loaded up the horse and took it to an auction. He
didn't want to, but Will always keeps his word."

I thought about the dangers of parental threats and
remembered the day eleven-year-old Melissa packed
her rucksack and said she never wanted to live with
me again. I threatened to get rid of her silk mice if
she left. Fortunately, I did not have to make good on
the threat and she never knew I loved the tiny rodents
as much as she did.

"Julio told her he would buy the horse back, but
he never did." Her voice was forlorn. "It broke her
heart." She lapsed into silence and sipped her coffee.

"How would you describe the relationship between
your husband and your son-in-law, Mrs. Muehler?"

She looked at me and her eyes widened. "Oh," she
said in confusion. "Well, you know, they never could
agree on—on politics. I always told Will he shouldn't
bait Julio like that. Will is very conservative. He always—"

The phone shrilled. "Oh, that's probably Will now. Please excuse me."

She took a gulp from her cup, stood, steadied herself and scurried into the hall. I heard the murmur of her voice, a silence, a short response, and she returned to the doorway of the living room.

"That was Will. He apologizes for not being here. The Lincoln Town Car is on the fritz, and he wants me to go and pick him up. He's over on California Street. It's not far. Will you excuse me, please?" I checked my watch. Ten-fifteen. I wondered if I would make my plane.

"Certainly."

"Just make yourself at home," she said, moving toward the entrance hall. She reached into a closet and pulled out a long camel-hair coat. "If you want more coffee, ask Rosa, she's in the kitchen." She gave me a quick smile, and disappeared. A door opened and closed and I heard the sound of the garage door lifting. I walked to the window in the hall, saw a polished silver Mercedes sedan back out of the garage and drive away. The garage door closed. I hoped the Mercedes would make it back in one piece.

31

Make yourself at home. Dangerous words to utter to a private investigator. I stood, stretched, and walked into the Muehler's elegant hallway, intrigued by the massive double doors opposite the living room. From behind another door I heard dishes rattling.

Make yourself at home. I repeated the words to myself, walked softly to the tall double doors, opened one, and peered in. I felt like Alice in Wonderland. Or that I had just stepped through the back of the wardrobe. Floor-to-ceiling bookshelves of a rich, dark reddish wood covered the walls of the library. Sable velvet dressed the windows, and dominating the center of the room, hundreds of toy soldiers waited at attention or engaged in maneuvers on a massive wooden table that could have come straight out of *Passage to India.* Two armchairs, upholstered in a claret-colored tapestry, were arranged on either side of the table.

There was a computer and printer, on a carved wooden desk at the end of the room opposite the windows. The left-hand drawer of the desk was open a few inches. I glanced at it, then looked back over my shoulder through the open library doors. The kitchen door was still closed.

Wilhelm Muehler was no more a suspect than any of the other individuals I'd talked to in the past four days, but opportunity seldom knocks twice. I pulled the drawer farther open, leafed through the files, stopped at one labeled "Current Year Taxes." I had no interest in Herr Muehler's income; I was interested in his social-security number, that magical nine-digit identification with which all secrets may be accessed.

I copied the SSN onto a scrap of paper, slid the paper into the jacket of my blazer and replaced the file folder in the drawer.

An abstract geometric screen saver was undulating on the monitor. I touched the keyboard. The Eudora mail window, identical to mine, appeared. The Inbox window was open; the status line at the bottom of the screen said "No new messages." Idly, I scrolled down to Sent Mail. Again, all was blank. Either Wilhelm didn't receive much mail or he was more efficient than I in managing it.

I clicked on Deleted messages and was rewarded.

I scrolled through the twenty-three deleted messages and was about to return to the first screen when one name caught my attention. I remembered something Judith Karamazov had said. I double-clicked on the name and read the one-word message. I stared at the screen, noticed the open box of new floppy disks beside the computer, and glanced at my watch. Ten forty-five. I clicked back to the Desktop, found the Recycle Bin, and uploaded. The garage door was opening. I inserted one of the floppies into the disc drive, clicked on Copy, waited for the green light to go out, went back to the Deleted messages, and hit Copy again.

A car door slammed, then another. The green light was still on, and my mouth was dry. The garage door was closing. Finally, the green light disappeared. I hit the Eject button on the drive and slid the floppy into my pocket. I glanced down at the desk one last time and spied another floppy disk. The label said "Quicken 2000 backup." Without considering what Muehler might do when he discovered it missing, I grabbed it and walked rapidly to the open door of the library.

Footsteps approached the hall doorway from the garage. I raced through the hall and pushed open the swinging door into the kitchen. A small Hispanic woman in a black dress turned away from the stainless-steel sink.

"Yes, *señora*?"

"Hi, Rosa. Mrs. Muehler said there might be more coffee." I was breathless and I muttered a silent prayer that I hadn't left my first cup in the library.

"I fix." Rosa wiped her hands on her white apron. I heard the hall door open and concentrated on the steaming black liquid the maid was pouring into a clean cup.

"You want it like the *señora*?"

"Excuse me?

"The *señora* take the coffee with the *licor*." She opened a cupboard and took out a bottle of Remy Martin.

I shook my head, took the cup, thanked her, and moved back through the swinging door.

Alice Muehler was hanging her husband's charcoal wool topcoat in the hall closet. A tall, distinguished man with a decisive face and iron-gray hair looked sharply at me, smiled, and extended his hand.

"Sorry to have been delayed, Ms. MacKinnon. Please come into the library."

He glanced back at his wife. "Perhaps you could get dressed now, Alice."

Without answering him or looking at me, Elyse's mother began to climb the curving stairs. She moved upward slowly, carrying her green cup and saucer.

I retrieved my bag from the living room and followed Elyse's father back into the dramatic, book-lined room, feeling like the proverbial feline with yellow chin feathers. I glanced at the computer and breathed an inaudible sigh of relief. The screen saver had returned to its geometric undulations.

Muehler indicated one of the tapestried chairs and we faced each other across the table. His eyes were a clear, pale blue, and despite his receding hairline, he was supremely handsome. His demeanor was that of a powerful, successful alpha male who had nothing to

prove. His world was everything Julio Montenegro's
was not.

Controlled, white, rich.

"You mentioned on the phone that my daughter
hired you to find Julio's murderer. How can I help?"

I reached into my bag for my notebook and tape
recorder. "I'm trying to collect as much information
as I can to put together a complete picture. May I
record our conversation?"

Muehler glanced at the recorder and opened both
palms.

"Certainly. I have nothing to hide. I would do anything to help Elyse."

"Just for the record, would you tell me how you
spent the day of Julio's death?"

"That was a terrible day." He sighed and leaned
back in the chair. "In the morning, I had a golf date
with a client over in Marin. We played at the Meadow
Club, had lunch, and I arrived back here, oh, around
two o'clock. My wife had some people over. Some
sort of community thing. I was reviewing a client's
portfolio when the hospital called. We went right over
to Berkeley. We learned about the miscarriage and
tried to persuade Elyse to move back home as soon
as the hospital released her."

"And did she?"

He frowned. "If you have children, Ms. MacKinnon,
you know they don't always act wisely. Unfortunately,
Elyse had some sort of illusion that I didn't like Julio,
that she would be betraying his memory to come and
stay with us." He shook his head. "I had nothing
against Julio personally. My own parents were immigrants. I only wanted the best for my little girl and he
wasn't exactly providing it. And I wish she had talked
to me before she ran off to that island to live with
Campbell."

"Your wife told you about Campbell's accident?"

He nodded. "Very sad. We've known Campbell
since she and Elyse were children. They were also
roommates at Sarah Lawrence. I'll call Mrs. Sawyer

today." He clasped his hands together on the table and frowned. "I hesitate to mention it, but you should know that Campbell had a history of instability."

"In what way?"

"She's had treatment for various sorts of substance abuse. Alcohol, even cocaine."

"Elyse believes that Campbell's accident was caused by Julio's killer."

He sighed deeply. "My poor Elyse. That is patently ridiculous. Elyse saw nothing, she identified no one. Both she and her mother have become quite paranoid. If I could get Elyse to come home, I know I could help her."

"Who do you think killed your son-in-law?"

Muehler gave a mirthless laugh. "Any one of a dozen people on either side of the border."

"For example?"

"When you called, you said you had talked to Peter Aaron and his wife, and to that Russian attorney Julio was working with. I'm sure they must have mentioned all the inappropriate involvements he had." He shrugged. "That principal he defended in Los Angeles against the Coalition for English Only, the Salinas labor problems. I believe he was writing a highly inflammatory column for his brother's newspaper in Mexico City. As you and I both know, Ms. MacKinnon, what goes around comes around. I only regret that my little girl has suffered so much."

For whatever reason, I was not going to get anything helpful from this man and I didn't want to miss my flight back to Seattle for nothing. I glanced at my watch and pulled a business card from my bag, placed it on the table and stood up. "I have to leave to catch an airplane, Mr. Muehler. I appreciate your speaking with me. Please let me know if you think of anything that might help with the investigation."

Muehler stood and extended his hand. "I will do that." The phone on his desk rang. He answered it, then covered the mouthpiece and turned to me.

"I'll see myself out," I said.

He nodded and returned to the phone call.

Alice Muehler was standing beside the front door, dressed in a gray wool pant suit. She opened the door for me. I clasped her outstretched hand, and on a whim, gave her a hug. Her body was thin and fragile, and she was fragrant with brandy.

"Please, ask Elyse to call me." Her voice was a whisper, her face looked pinched.

"I will. And you call me if you think of anything that might help."

I gave her a card and hurried to the car. She was still standing in the doorway as I drove away.

Traffic was thick on 19th Avenue, but the rain was diminishing. Alice Muehler's anguished face continued to trouble me as I manipulated the rental car into a left-hand lane on Highway 280. I scrolled through the list of people I had talked to in the last four days and reviewed what I had learned from each. I pondered the antagonism between my client's husband and his associate, De los Santos, and speculated on the love triangle between Julio and Judith Karamazov and my client. Did Elyse know about Julio's philandering? Did Judith's terrorist husband ever suspect his wife was unfaithful?

At the check-in counter, I learned my Alaska Airlines flight would be delayed. Boarding pass in hand, I made my way to the Business Center, logged on to the Internet, found a message from Zelda.

California tags on the van from Berkeley are expired but I finagled a VIN #. It was registered in Idaho last year. J. J. Sykes, 9653 Shadow Mountain Road, Coeur d'Alene. I'll check it out when I go through there this afternoon.

A name and an address! Thank God for White Knight! I took a deep breath and called Zelda. I didn't know yet what the connection was between J. J. Sykes and Julio Montenegro and Felipe De los Santos, but I knew for damn sure I didn't want my outrageous red-haired assistant pursuing a serial murderer through the mountains of Idaho. The phone rang and rang again and on the third ring was picked up.

"This cellular customer has traveled outside the reception area. Please try your call again later."

Merde! If Zelda could get a state-of-the-art cell phone, why the hell couldn't she have gotten voice mail. It was twelve-fifteen. If she had left Friday Harbor on the red-eye that morning, she should be somewhere east of Seattle by now, probably on the other side of the Snoqualmie Pass, which wasn't renowned for its great cell phone reception. Until she decided to call me, I had no way of reaching her.

PART III

Violence does, in truth, recoil upon the violent and the schemer falls into the pit which he digs for another.

—Sir Arthur Conan Doyle

32

The blond, clean-shaven man paced in front of his computer workstation. The headache was bad again. It had been almost blinding during the last part of the drive from Spokane when the snow started. It was good to be home again, but he hadn't seen Snowy since he'd been back. He missed her. He just wanted to settle in for a while, maybe do some trapping or varmint hunting. But he had to go back to the island and finish the job. No way around it. Damn.

He thought about how it had all begun at the Rendezvous, way back after the Ruby Ridge shooting. The Rendezvous was by invitation only, and he had been there only because of his receiving the Sharpshooter Award at the training camp. Funny how the littlest things can change your life. This guy had asked for his e-mail address, but he hadn't really thought any more about it. Then one day there was a message, asking if they could talk. And they had, and the job seemed heaven-made.

Track down and exterminate one of the mongrels.
Work alone. Leave no evidence. Leave no witnesses.
Report when you're done.

It had been so easy to drive to California and find the big-mouth mongrel lawyer. An assignment from God. No doubt about it. The only problem with Berkeley was when the wife showed up. She wasn't supposed to be there. But that was a glitch and he'd just have to take care of it as soon as the snow melted. And then *he could move on. The MO worked in Denver and Los Angeles. It would work again. He snickered and thought about how he'd just kept extending the assignment.*

Shoulders hunched, he stood up, stretched, and tried to get rid of the stiffness from the long drive. Across the room he pressed his thumb on the small rectangular box above the doorknob, listened for the distinctive click of the lock, and jerked open the heavy metal door that separated his living quarters from the body shop. He flicked on the overhead light, stared at the van, resplendent in its new coat of dark-red body paint. He'd been very careful to repaint the van and get new plates each time. He frowned, walked around the vehicle. This job had been done too fast and he was afraid it would start to peel. And he couldn't take the time to redo the interior paint.

After yesterday's snowstorm, all those service calls had come in and it had seemed best to respond to them, make sure he was doing his job as always. The dependable mountain mechanic.

Yesterday morning he'd gone out to the Weber place to fix the alternator on the Ford pickup. Around one o'clock a whiney woman on the other side of the lake needed a battery charge. Just when he'd been about to leave for Wallace, Georgina's dad called with an electrical problem that had taken two hours to fix.

When he'd gotten to Wallace, Corrine was busy, and he'd drunk too many beers while he waited for her. Then he didn't remember much until he woke up in the van in his yard this morning. He smiled ruefully. Really stupid to pay for something you couldn't remember enjoying. He looked at his watch. If he got all the messes cleaned up, there was time to head back to Wallace tomorrow night. This time he'd find Corrine first, drink beer afterwards. The paint should be dry by Sunday, snow should be melted. He'd pack up the stuff, head out early, drive straight through. Be back by Wednesday or Thursday, all the loose ends taken care of.

He looked around for Snowy one more time, then closed the door to the shop and spread a map out on his desk. It was a straight shot through on Interstate 90 to Seattle. He could leave the van at the airport and pick up a rental car, like last time. Or just drive the van to Anacortes. He didn't like it, hated breaking his own rules, but nobody on the island had seen it. He wanted to be back by Thanksgiving. His mother always made pumpkin pie with whipped cream and he'd promised he'd have dinner with her. Then he'd lay low 'til after the holidays and take a nice drive south. Southeast Florida might be a great place to kill two birds with one stone.

He smiled, replaced the map in the drawer and noticed the credit-card slip. Rocky Mountain Rentals in Denver. Shit! He thought he'd destroyed all that paper. He tore the yellow slip into small pieces, dropped them into an ashtray on the desk and set fire to it. The scraps of paper burned into small black crisps. The headache was getting worse. What else had he forgotten? Where was Snowy?

33

This file is password protected.

I read the message again. It was the same for all the files I had copied from Wilhelm Muehler's hard drive to the floppy disk. Sent messages, Deleted messages, and Muehler's entire set of files in the Recycle Bin.

Friday was not beginning well. I'd flown in on Harbor Airlines last flight the night before, had gotten back to *'Spray* about eight, and had fallen into a restless sleep. Around one a.m., the mainsail halyard had started slapping against the mast, and I'd be damned if I was going to go up on deck in the wind and rain to move it. While I watched the digital display on the clock radio go all the way from one-thirty to fourten, I contemplated Julio Montenegro's multinational misadventures, tried to read *White Tempest*, and wondered when I'd hear from Zelda. I finally dozed off and awoke at seven when Calico squeezed through the partially open porthole in the small aft cabin and leaped onto my pillow with her wet feet. After that, I gave up, tried unsuccessfully to call Zelda again, took my shower and headed for the office, wondering if Elyse had responded to Zelda's request for Julio's laptop computer. Or if Zelda had remembered to call her.

Now my computer was refusing to open Muehler's files. If Zelda were here, it would be a *fait accompli*. But she wasn't and I still hadn't heard from her. There were a number of other competent computer techies in Friday Harbor, and I was clueless as to what the files I'd copied might contain, but they were not for public distribution. Not yet.

There *was* one person whose discretion was probably beyond reproach and he was pretty good with computers. I flipped through the Rolodex and stared at Jared Saperstein's card. For reasons I couldn't define, I decided not to call. Feeling like the proverbial fish out of water, trying not to fret about Zelda or Nick, I went downstairs and got a cup of Soraya's weak coffee. Back upstairs I checked my e-mail again. Three new messages. None was from Zelda.

Feeling guilty for having neglected my other cases, I read Brian MacGregor's message first.

> *Ocean Dancer has departed New Zealand.*
> *Bartender at the Royal Flush reports that*
> *Petrovsky and crew are en route to Sydney.*
> *Await your instructions.*

I fired back instructions to grab Harrison in Sydney, wishing I'd retained the bartender at the Royal Flush. The next message was from my darling daughter and I wished I hadn't opened it.

> *Mummy, Gilberto invited me to go to Brazil*
> *with him over Christmas break. He says*
> *he'll pay for my ticket. Can I go? Love,*
> *Melissa.*

Whenever Melissa calls me *Mummy* there's trouble brewing. I decided to let that one sit for a while. Maybe Gilberto would withdraw the invitation after three days over Thanksgiving with Jewel Moon.

The last message was from Angela. Matthew was in a snit again, had gone off on a fishing trip with his friend Herman without so much as a by-your-leave. Providing my Hungarian hunk hadn't made me a better offer, would I like to meet her and Allison Fisher

for an early supper, say five o'clock at Roche Harbor
on Sunday? Since the whereabouts of my Hungarian
hunk were still unknown, I typed back that I'd be
happy to join her and Allison, and was about to log
off when a new message popped up.

This one was from Zelda!

> *I hate this @#$%* cell phone. I checked the*
> *Shadow Mountain address in Coeur*
> *d'Alene. No such place. I have another idea on*
> *how to find him. I'll call you later. Z.*

I stared at the message and typed a reply.

> *Stay away from this Sykes, wherever he is!*
> *Call me ASAP so we can make a plan.*

Hopefully she was on her way to Missoula and I
could stop feeling guilty for not having gone to
Idaho myself.

Downstairs the stack of mail slid through the slot
and hit the floor. Lured by the possibility of a check
from Property Casualty, I was about to go and retrieve
it when the phone rang. Zelda, a fervent believer in
telepathy, would not have been surprised to hear the
voice on the other end of the line, but I was.

I glanced down at the Rolodex that was still open
to Jared Saperstein's card. Coincidences are not telepathy, I assured myself. Jared had some information he
thought might be useful in the Montenegro matter, he
said. He was cooking Thai chicken soup. Would I like
to have dinner with him tonight?

"I'd be delighted, Jared. What time?"

"Seven o'clock, 895 Georgia Street, Number 4."

*Some information that might be useful in the Monte-
negro matter.* Whatever Jared had found out, it would
be useful. Unless he was about to pass on more gems
from Holmes and Watson.

I put together an interim report on my Berkeley activities for Elyse, along with a list of expenses incurred

to date, requested that she contact me regarding Julio's laptop computer, and e-mailed the message off.

It was noon. I needed a walk, I had promised Nick I'd check on his yellow cat while he was away, and I should give *DragonSpray* some TLC before I went to Jared's. I tidied up the office and was about to give myself the rest of Friday off when the phone rang.

It was my passive-aggressive client.

"I just got your message." Elyse's voice was even smaller than the last time we talked. I wondered if she would become mute before we found her husband's murderer.

"Do you have the laptop?"

"I've been storing it."

"At the Five Fingers House?"

"No, at Island Storage on Cattle Point Road."

"How can I get it?"

"It's in unit 17. The combination is 4444. Just . . . just go ahead and look at it. It doesn't matter anymore."

I wondered what didn't matter anymore and remembered another of my questions she hadn't answered.

"Did Julio have life insurance, Elyse?"

"Yes."

"Who was the beneficiary?"

"I was."

"What was the amount of the policy?"

There was silence for a minute. "Five hundred thousand dollars."

No wonder she hadn't blinked at my fee. "Did Julio take out the policy?"

"No. I mean, he couldn't afford anything like that."

"Who did?"

Another long pause. "I don't know."

An insurance policy for half a million dollars with my client as the beneficiary. Was she lying about not knowing who bought it? "What do you mean, you don't know?"

There was another long silence. "I really don't know. About a month after Julio—" I heard an intake of breath and she continued, "I got a phone call from an insurance agent. He said he needed a copy of the death certificate and then he would send me a check."

"Did you receive the check?"

"Yes."

"What did you do with it?"

"I deposited it in my account."

"What company was the insurance agent with?"

"Lloyd's of London."

"Could LAUD have taken out the policy?"

"I asked Peter and he said no."

At Island Storage, the tumblers on the brass padlock for unit 17 fell into place in a horizontal line and the hasp separated from the lock. The tall, cambered metal door rolled upward and I spied a black zippered computer case, the only item in the small unit that wasn't boxed. I stared at the case, shrugged and opened the zipper. If there was nothing left on it, or nothing of importance on it, I'd just leave it there. Surprised that it powered up on the battery alone, and waiting for Windows to load, I contemplated my client's credibility. Obviously, Elyse had had the laptop in her possession since before she hired me. Why hadn't she mentioned it? Who was she protecting?

There was no disk in the floppy drive. I checked the contents of the hard drive, found seven document files. Skipping files whose names included "2000," which I figured would be Julio's LAUD files on Prop 2000, I opened the one called *"fdls.doc."* It was a ten-page dossier on Felipe De los Santos who, according to the concluding statements in the document, was using Global Imports, Inc., as a cover to launder revenues Julio suspected came from the Berkeley end of a pipeline of cocaine that began in Colombia, traversed the west coast of Mexico, and surfaced somewhere in Alameda County. Julio had cited dates and places and his case was pretty convincing. I stared at the screen and thought about Elyse exercising Felipe's Arabian mare during his "family business" trips to Colombia and Carmela's wide-eyed, "I know nothing of this importing" protestation. I speculated on the anonymous insurance policy and remembered that Felipe was fond of wealthy women. What could be better than a wealthy widow? Especially one who liked horses and was as pretty as Elyse.

I closed the file and clicked on *fdlsbpd.doc.* On July 6, seven days before his death, Julio wrote letters to the Berkeley PD, to the IRS and to the FBI, attaching the dossier on Felipe.

Exactly as Judith Karamazov had described.

Felipe supposedly was with his girlfriend the afternoon Julio was shot. Did Sergeant Wineheart ever verify his alibi? I pulled the cell phone from my jacket pocket and dialed what I remembered as the number for the Berkeley PD. Instead, I got the hotline for the Berkeley Psychics, who offered to answer three life questions for free. Some of my life questions are probably better left unanswered, so I declined the offer. I wanted to get back to the office and check the laptop for deleted files. I could call Wineheart from there. I dialed Zelda's cell phone number.

"This customer has traveled outside the cellular area. Please try your call again later."

Back at the office, the red light on the answering machine was blinking. The message was from Jewel Moon. "Giovanni canceled his trip to Phoenix. Please let me know *right away* if you're coming down for Thanksgiving. It's only six days away, and I need to know how many spinach quiches to make." I called her, explained that I wouldn't be going to Mendocino because I was in the midst of a demanding investigation, and wished her well with the quiches.

Familial niceties concluded, I booted up Julio's laptop, found the Recycle Bin icon on the desktop, and scrolled through the fifteen file names. For each file name, I clicked on the Properties button, which gave me the creation and deletion dates of the file.

Twenty-three e-mail messages had been deleted last night; my client had been busy.

I checked the deleted messages. Nothing regarding Felipe De los Santos, but as I scrolled down and opened and read the deletions one by one, I understood what didn't matter to Elyse anymore.

Sometimes in Spanish, sometimes in English, occasionally in French, Julio had left behind a trail of billets doux to and from Judith Karamazov, spanning January to May of this year. What had happened in May? When did Elyse discover her husband's indiscretions? Were there other floppy disks she hadn't turned over? What other files were missing?

I stared at the Montenegro file, which was nearly an inch thick, locked up my office and went downstairs. New Millennium was silent. I gave the office a cursory once-over and was about to lock up when the front door opened. It was Sheldon Wainwright, Port Angeles ship's pilot and Zelda's ardent admirer. His tall bearded frame was wrapped in a black-and-red checked woodsman's jacket and a black watch cap covered most of his curly dark hair. He looked big and burly and rough, but I knew he was a sheep in wolf's clothing.

"Hi, Scotia. Zelda around?"

"Gone to visit her aunt in Montana. Back next week."

He frowned and chewed on one side of his face.

"Do you know if she's got any plans for Thanksgiving?"

"Haven't a clue, Shel. Why don't you check back on Monday or Tuesday?" If she wasn't already promised to Michael or Hans or some new cyberspace suitor, he might have a chance. And maybe by then the Idaho puzzle would be solved, and the office would be resounding once again with operatic arias and aromatic with popcorn.

Little did I know.

34

It was four-thirty when I got back to *DragonSpray*, and I finished hosing down the decks about five-thirty. Scrubbing seagull excrement off the decks in fifteen knots of wind is not my favorite pastime, and the exercise had given me ample time to wonder why I didn't sell *'Spray* and move into a cozy condo above the harbor like a normal woman. Or find a man that wasn't out slaying litigious dragons or consoling a neurotic, overindulged daughter.

I put my boots below to dry out, peeled off my damp wool socks, and checked the message light on the answering machine for the tenth time in two hours. Damn! Where was Zelda? Why hadn't Nick checked in? The last message I'd received from him was on Wednesday while I was still in Berkeley. He said he'd be back this weekend and planned to come over to the island. At his nomadic worst, this wasn't like him. Now I was beginning to *worry*.

How had he traveled from Costa Careyes to Mexico City?

What airline did he take from Mexico City to Seattle? Did the mechanics that checked the plane in Mexico know what they were doing?

Or did one of them drink too much tequila the night before or have an altercation with his mistress?

I dialed Nick's office number and got the answering machine. A call to his condo got me daughter Nicole's sugary outgoing message. Maybe I'd have better luck with Elyse. I didn't.

Rebecca answered the phone at the ranch. She felt shitty, thought she was getting the flu, Elyse had left several hours ago to go out to the Five Fingers house and pack up the rest of her stuff. Rebecca's son, Gregg, had gone with her.

"Is Gregg up here for good?" I asked.

She sneezed twice before answering. "He handed in his resignation at Microsoft. He's promised to stay here and take care of the ranch so I can go to New Zealand with Lars."

She promised to have Elyse call me when she returned.

Not in a mood to trek up to the showers at the Port, I turned up the heat, stripped down and bathed myself in *'Spray*'s miniature shower stall, dried off, and anointed my body in pink Country Apple body lotion. I'm not the Shalimar type and the wholesome fragrance lifted my spirits. I could hear rain on the deck and I chose a thick black turtleneck sweater, a clean pair of blue jeans and a pair of well-worn, soft-soled boots, my customary winter attire.

On the way up the hill to Jared's, I stopped at the corner grocery for the requisite bottle of wine, an Australian Chardonnay, and produced a cheery smile for my host, who opened the door in a well-used white chef's apron, whisked away my fleece coat and ushered me into his warm and cluttered kitchen. Jared's yellow Lab approached to sniff my pant legs, then returned to sprawl on the tattered braided rug beside the old gas range. From the living room came the scent of wood smoke and the sound of violins. Beethoven, I thought.

"Let's save the good wine for later," Jared said. "I'm working on a bottle of Barefoot Chard. Would you like your usual?" He held up a bottle of Martini and Rossi dry vermouth.

"How nice of you to remember."

He smiled, poured the pale liquid over ice, added a

twist of lime, and handed me the glass with a flourish. "In case you hadn't noticed, lady, I'm more than just a pretty face. Now, grab a stool and keep me company while I get the rice started."

I climbed up on the wooden bar stool and watched my portly, balding friend measure the water and rice and add coconut milk to the soup, thankful that I knew so many men who liked to cook.

"Tell me what you discovered down on the Barbary Coast. Did you solve the case and bring the elusive murderer to justice? Or is your mettle still being tested?"

"No to the first, and yes to the second. What's that you're adding to the soup?"

"Lemon grass."

"How did you learn Thai cooking?"

He answered without looking up. "I spent four years in Bangkok. For two of those, I had the good fortune to enjoy the company of a lovely Thai lady who taught me many things, one of which was her native cuisine."

Thai women are legendary for their beauty. I wondered what had happened to her. Jared offered no further information and I sipped my drink in silence, wondering when I would receive the background reports from DataTech on Muehler and De los Santos. I also wished the license-plate number on the van from Oakland hadn't turned out to be a dud.

"To get back to your question," I said, "the most significant link to the Montenegro murder seems to be the Denver and L.A. shootings."

"Remember Holmes's theory of progressive homicide?" he said. "That subsequent murders will occur in order to cover up evidence or to silence witnesses to the original murder?"

"I remember. And you were right." I sipped the vermouth and watched Jared's hands as he sliced cucumbers. Strong, capable, blunt-fingered hands. "The Berkeley PD detective is working with the FBI, I *think*. And I did manage to get my sticky fingers on one or two bits of information that *may* lead to others. But it's all pretty murky."

Jared put the salads aside, threw the cucumber peelings in the sack under the sink, and smiled mischievously. "And so now you'd like to know, 'Does this old lecher really have any useful information for me, or was he just trying to lure me into his den of iniquity for dishonorable reasons?' "

"Well?"

"The answer is yes and yes."

He glanced at my glass, and put the lid on the soup pot. "When I wrote the article for the *Gazette* after Campbell's accident, I was never able to verify who had called for the EMS unit. Your buddy Angela took last week off and the substitute dispatcher at the sheriff's office was having a hard time deciphering her records, and then said she couldn't release the information without Nigel's permission." He poured a few drops of white wine vinegar, sprinkled sesame seeds over the cucumbers and continued without looking up. "The sheriff didn't return my call, so I didn't get the information until Angela got back to the office." He lifted plates and rice bowls from the cupboard, counted out two sets of utensils from the drawer, and disappeared in the direction of the living room.

I drained my glass and swirled the ice in the bottom. I wondered about Angela's sudden absence from the office. Maybe the red nightie hadn't done the trick. Maybe the philosophical differences couldn't be sugarcoated anymore.

"The accident was called into the sheriff on a cell phone with a Seattle number," he went on. "More vermouth?"

I shook my head. He carried the salad bowls to the round wooden table in front of the fireplace and returned to the kitchen, turned the flame under the rice to low. "I called the number, got a voice message. A man's voice. I left a message to call me, which he did yesterday morning while I was out." He reached into his left shirt pocket, pulled out a slip of white paper, glanced at it and handed it to me.

I squinted at the scribbles. "Arthur Smith, 1200 Center Road, Tukwila, WA." The phone number was a 206 area code.

"I called him back," Jared continued. "He said he and a lady friend were coming down from Mt. Dallas the afternoon of Campbell Sawyer's accident. They saw a black Jeep Cherokee way ahead of them, saw the Cherokee ram the red Ghia twice, saw the Ghia go off the road and the Cherokee disappear down the hill. Apparently concluding this was a San Juan Island brand of road rage, Smith and his companion called the accident in from their cell phone, turned around and hightailed it to the other side of the mountain and left on the next ferry for Anacortes. Or so he says."

If Arthur Smith had been telling the truth, then Elyse had been right. It wasn't an accident and the perp would be back.

"I asked why they didn't make a report in person," Jared said. "I got a lot of vague answers about how his friend had to get back home early, and they didn't want to miss the ferry. But my sixth sense, which is pretty good, tells me the lady friend might be married or didn't want to be identified for some reason. He didn't exactly refuse to give me her name, but neither did I get it. And I checked the reverse street directory. His address is a mail drop."

Jared removed his apron, refilled his glass. "Anyway, you have the phone number if you want to follow up."

And next time Elyse wouldn't be so lucky.

"Now, Ms. Private Investigator, if you'll be so kind as to put the spring rolls and rice on the table, I'll open the wine and you can enlighten me about the cast of characters you unearthed in Berkeley."

I took the plate of fresh spring rolls and the bowl of rice. "Off the record?"

"Off the record until you tell me otherwise." He moved over to the CD player next to the fireplace, replaced the magazine of CDs and sat down. The opening movement of Prokofiev's *Three Oranges* filled the cozy room.

The soup was savory with ginger and coconut. Between mouthfuls I summarized my meetings with the Berkeley PD and the Aarons and George De Soto and Judith Karamazov. I described the pink-and-blue nursery frozen in time at the Montenegro residence. I related my encounter with White Knight and Imogene; described Felipe De los Santos and his importing endeavors; Julio Montenegro's dossier on his Colombian associate; and the background info Zelda had unearthed on De los Santos. I also told him about the tag on the gray van that pointed to a mountain lane in Idaho.

Prokofiev segued into Tchaikovsky. Jared listened to my narration, emptied his bowl, and watched me as I elaborated on my meeting at Sea Cliff with Elyse's parents.

"Wilhelm Muehler. Sounds like good Teutonic stock." He ladled more soup into his bowl and added a dollop of rice. I mentioned the tiny Hessian soldiers and the horse that had been summarily sold when Elyse had disobeyed the paternal dictum and married Julio.

Jared smiled and took a sip of wine. "When my daughter Janet married her first husband, a no-good, beer-drinking unemployed lout, I lost my temper and yelled a lot. I don't remember selling any of her possessions."

He speared two slices of cucumber with his fork, chewed thoughtfully and swallowed.

"So. Let's see if I have this right. You have a grieving young widow from a good family. A deceased civil rights attorney who was delving into politics on both sides of the border. A passionate and sorrowful mistress separated or divorced from a Basque terrorist, whereabouts unknown. A sad colleague who is soldiering on. A possibly shady colleague from Colombia whose nefarious activities were being investigated by the deceased. A consulting professor who suspects sinister assassins from south of the border. And to round out the cast, there's the alcoholic mother of the grieving widow and the distinguished, graying patriarch who can't do enough for—what did you call her? The trophy daughter?" He smiled and raised his dark bushy eyebrows. "Not too bad, my dear, not too bad."

"Thank you, Dr. Watson."

"So, who do you think done it?"

"If I had to make a guess right now, my number-one suspect would be De los Santos. But quite frankly, lots of people could have wanted Julio out of the way."

"True, but who wanted him out of the way enough to murder him?"

I shook my head and finally voiced the vague, formless suspicions that had been lingering in the back of my mind. "Jared, I've been reading your journalist friend's book, *White Tempest*. It was written ten years ago. Is that stuff still going on?"

Jared looked at me sharply. "Why do you ask?"

I related what Judith had said about the hate mail she and Julio received after they took up Gloria Lopez's defense against the Coalition for English Only.

"I wouldn't worry about the e-mail." He shrugged. "You should've seen the stuff I got when I was with the *L.A. Times*. It goes with the territory. Doesn't sound like there were any death threats." He frowned. "However, that van in Berkeley you traced to Idaho? That could be another can of worms entirely." He stood up. "Coffee?" I nodded and helped clear the table.

We settled in with our coffee. Jared pulled a pipe from his sweater pocket, filled and lit it. I sipped my Kenyan Roast and watched the curly dark hairs on the back of his hands.

He regarded me with narrowed eyes through a haze of blue smoke. "Something is brewing out there. It's hard to put your finger on exactly what it is or what it means to people like you and me. But in the hinterlands there's a great wave of immense dissatisfaction with the federal government. I'm not just talking about the known political or religious groups like the Klan and Aryan Nation or Christian Identity. I'm talking about ordinary white, middle-class Anglo-Saxon citizens whose son or daughter thinks they lost a college slot to a student who isn't white. Or a million owners of small farms who've lost their family heritage either because of foreclosures, or subsidies that dried up, or unpaid taxes."

He paused and I continued the litany. "Or Oregon loggers who can't log the forests anymore because of the spotted owl? And Puget Sound fishermen who can't fish because the salmon is on the endangered species list?"

"Exactly. You're a quick study. And none of these people are neo-Nazis, none are long-hairs, and most don't use drugs."

He went into the kitchen and returned to refill our coffee cups. "Pernod? I forgot to ask."

"Please." A burst of rain pelleted the windows. He returned to the table with two cordial glasses and a decanter of the milky chartreuse liquid with such an infamous history.

"A lot of folks think the dissidents are just a bunch of old farts who don't want to keep up with the times. Let me assure you, dear lady, there are many twenty- and thirty- and forty-year-olds that want their sons to bear arms as soon as they can walk and want their kids to recite the Lord's Prayer and the Pledge of Allegiance in an English-only, all-white school.

I listened and felt the hairs rise on my forearms. It was all coming together. "And to this," I said slowly, "you add the insanities of Waco and Ruby Ridge and assault weapons available at your neighborhood gun shop or even online. Do I have the picture right?"

He nodded. "Except for one important element: the Internet. It's given verbal power—some would say verbal napalm—to every dissident in the country with access to a PC. And now we have a bubbling cauldron of incipient domestic terrorism."

He drew a deep breath. "Sorry, I got a bit carried away. And off the subject. I know you asked the question in the context of your case. Well, bilingual education is a big, big threat to a lot of people. And it's a cultural and political threat, not an educational threat. Which I'm sure you've already figured out."

I nodded, thinking that the projects Julio Montenegro had been involved in would have set off alarms in half the population of the U.S.

We sat in silence and listened to the wind and rain. Jared's pipe went out and he relit it.

"I think it was George Bernard Shaw who said or wrote that murder is an extreme form of censorship," he said.

Someone had wanted to censor Julio, and wanted it badly enough to commit murder.

The wind blew more rain against the windows. The fire crackled. We listened to Schubert and finished our pernod and traded updates on our respective daughters, agreed that parenting didn't end at the age of majority. Jared wished me luck with Melissa's Brazilian beau, refused my offer of help with dishes; I declined his offer of a ride back to the Port. He held my coat for me and I put my hands in the pockets and found the floppy disk.

"Jared, this might or might not contain important information. I borrowed it, shall we say, from Wilhelm Muehler. Would you see if you could open the files?"

"A purloined disk? Why does it sound so much more mundane than a letter?" He took the disk and gave me a long hug. "I'll be happy to, beautiful lady, first thing in the morning."

I hugged him back, and went outside into the cold rain. As I was about to step off the deck, he called after me. "Don't forget, Scotia, I am not Prince Hamlet."

No! Am not Prince Hamlet nor was meant to be.

Am an attendant lord, one that will do, to swell a progress, start a scene or two.

"The Love Song of J. Alfred Prufrock." I'd had to memorize it for a high school poetry contest, under the eagle eye of Grandmother Jessica, who was an Eliot devotee.

I waved and headed off to the Port in the rain, smiling at Jared's courageous self-knowledge, wondering if I belonged in a book called *Women Who Always Choose the Wrong Men.*

35

Murder is an extreme form of censorship.

It was my first coherent thought on Saturday morning as I awakened to Calico's soft purring beside my pillow. When I'd returned last night, Henry's *Pumpkin Seed* had been dark and Calico was huddled in *DragonSpray*'s cockpit, drenched and miserable. I had scooped her up and taken her below, and now we both shared silent thanks that last night's gale had blown away to wherever November storms in Puget Sound blow away to.

It was eight-thirty. I snuggled deeper under the fluffy white comforter, still half asleep, and pondered Jared's quotation. Someone had wanted to censor Julio and was willing to commit murder to accomplish it. I was mentally scrolling through my list of suspects when the phone rang.

I reached for the portable receiver I'd left on the ledge above my berth, managed to drop it on the cabin floor, and retrieved it just as the answering machine was clicking on.

It was Nick and he was back in Seattle.

He wanted to get together but needed a few days to catch up on loose ends and move Nicole into her own digs. He'd tell me all about it.

"Scotty, I've had enough Mexican sun for a while. I can't wait to get back to the island. How about I come up on Wednesday and we take '*Spray* to Victoria? I know Thursday's not Thanksgiving in Canada, but I'll treat you to a five-course dinner at the Empress Hotel anyway. What do you say?" Before I could respond, my call-waiting tone sounded, I asked Nick to hold and pressed the Flash button.

It was Jared. "Have you heard from Zelda?"

"No. Were you able to open any of the files?"

"Just three of them," he said. "And there's not much there of interest. The rest all require a password and they're beyond my expertise. I'm on my way down to the *Gazette* to work on next week's editorial. Shall I drop the disk off at the boat?"

I knew Jared had more on his mind than the purloined disk. And not only did I still have Nick on hold, I'm not one of those fortunate females who arise from sleep with sparkling eyes and dewy skin. I suggested he drop the disk through the mail slot at the Olde Gazette Building. He agreed in a disappointed voice and hung up.

I returned to Nick and we arranged a rendezvous at his house on the island on Wednesday night. "I've got a lot to tell you," he said. "And I'd like to spend some quiet time." I couldn't have agreed more. I carefully placed the phone back on the ledge with a ridiculous smirk on my face.

The smirk was swiftly erased by the next phone call. It was Zelda.

"Hi, boss, hope I'm not interrupting any romantic sleep-in."

"In my dreams. Where are you?"

"Missoula, where else?"

Where else, indeed.

"That address on the vehicle you asked me to trace? The one I got from the DMV in Boise? It was fictitious. No such place as Shadow Mountain Road. So I came on to Missoula."

"Why didn't you call?"

"Cell phone wouldn't work. No reception out there in the mountains. Then when I got to my aunt's, she'd invited the whole family over for dinner. Cousins I hadn't seen for years. I forgot. Sorry." I heard the crackling of paper, then she continued between bites of something crunchy. "I fretted about the address all day yesterday, and last night about midnight I went over to my cousin's and borrowed his computer and started surfing the Net. I figured if the guy who had the van in Berkeley was the same one who gave the phony address to the DMV, he might be using it for e-mail as well and I could find his log-in name."

"Did you?"

"Sure enough, about two a.m. this morning. J. J. Sykes has at least four log-in names, which are—" She paused and there was more rustling of papers. "Here they are:. *jjs0001@mountain.net, Imessenger@mountain.net, simms@pclake.com,* and—"

She paused for effect, and I felt shivers up and down my arms. Simms again! The name he had used in Friday Harbor *and* in Berkeley the day Julio was killed! And I-Messenger was the name in one of the e-mail messages Judith Karamazov had mentioned. We were making progress!

"—ta-da!" she crowed. *"Mechanic@mountain.net."*

"What's the ta-da for?"

"Oh, come on, boss, don't tell me you're not a Bronson fan?"

I frowned, searching for the connection.

"Bronson, as in *The Mechanic*? Mechanic, as in hit man?"

Hit man.

I stared at the phone and remembered my conversation with Judith. The hate mail after the Prop 2000 suit was filed. *A mechanic in the mountains. Mechanic @mountain.net.* A hit man.

Whose hit man?!

"This morning," she continued, "Aunt Janette left on a gambling junket to Reno with six lady friends. Says she forgot to tell me about it. Anyway, I've had enough of Missoula, so I'm heading back. But I'm thinking about making a short detour through Wallace."

"Wallace, Idaho? That funky old silver-mining

town?" I vaguely recalled a pit stop when Albert and I and Melissa drove to Yellowstone a number of years ago, a trip memorable for the frequent stops to replenish the motor oil in the antique Cadillac and Melissa's hourly bouts of motion sickness.

"One and the same. I spent my sixteenth summer in Missoula, and Cousin Kenneth, who was several years my senior, spent many a summer evening tipping a few with the boys at the Silver Ass Saloon in Wallace. And"—she paused dramatically—"if Auntie's worst fears were true, carousing with the FFB ladies. Anyway, since I'm going right by there on my way back, how about I stop in for a beer and see what I can find out about J. J. Sykes? If he lives anywhere within fifty miles of Wallace, somebody at the Silver Ass will know him. It's just like Friday Harbor."

I could think of many differences between Wallace, Idaho, and Friday Harbor, Washington, and a little voice nudged me to tell her to forget Wallace and J. J. Sykes and to head straight back for the island. A second voice whispered that if a few more pieces of the puzzle could be uncovered, a serial murderer might be apprehended. The second voice won.

"One beer and you're out of there," I said in a stern voice. I reminded her of the political climate in northern Idaho.

"Not to worry. There are a lot more skiers and snow boarders here than political dissidents. Besides, they'll love me in my black leather miniskirt."

I sighed. "Call me when you get to Wallace."

"Will do. Over and out."

I hung up the phone, pictured Zelda in thigh-high black leather perched on a bar stool at the Silver Ass, and shrugged. What could go wrong in broad daylight in a small town like Wallace? And what the hell were FFB ladies?

36

Since Jared had had no success in opening Muehler's locked files, I couldn't think of any reason to rush off to the office on a Saturday morning. Zelda was safe for the time being; Elyse was back to ignoring my calls; and neither Ben Carey nor Sergeant Wineheart had responded to anything I'd sent them. And Nick, thank God for small favors, was moving Nicole into her own apartment. Except for any information Zelda might eke out in the hills of Idaho, the two other loose ends were the reports on Wilhelm Muehler and Felipe De los Santos that I'd requested from DataTech before I left San Francisco. I wondered if, by chance, they were sitting in my e-mail Inbox.

'Spray had rocked on her lines most of the night, but the wind was calm now, and rays of November sun were invading the forward porthole. Calico sat expectantly in the galley, making breakfast noises. I reached one hand from beneath the comforter and turned on the weather radio. It had been almost a month since I'd had 'Spray away from the dock, and a brisk sail might do wonders for my fragmented state of mind. Sailing in the San Juans had its pluses and minuses, with many days of calm winds. The secret, I'd found, was to go out on the edge of a storm, either as it approached or after it departed. And if I could believe the Weather Center of Environment Canada, the monster storm promised yesterday had been downgraded and this would be a perfect day for a sail.

*. . . for today, Saturday, November 17, early-
morning showers, then partial clearing with afternoon sun breaks. Chance of precipitation forty
percent today, sixty percent tonight, eighty percent
Sunday. . . . Juan de Fuca Strait small-craft advi-
sory in effect. Winds southwest ten to fifteen
knots, rising to fifteen to twenty knots this evening. Rain developing near midnight.*

I listened to the remainder of the forecast. Apparently, the front that had been headed down from the
Queen Charlottes had stalled over Vancouver Island,
but would move across Vancouver Island tomorrow
and head for the British Columbia mainland. I
checked the tide tables: maximum flood at 1318, slack
water at 1501, maximum ebb at 1811. Perfect! I could
sail up San Juan Channel to Wasp Passage with the
incoming tide, turn around about three o'clock, and
sail back to Friday Harbor with the ebb.

I stared at the phone and wondered if I could talk
Angela into an afternoon on the water.

A telephone call revealed that she was deeply depressed over Matt's behavior, and she, like Rebecca,
thought she was getting the flu. And, she added with
an apology, Allison had a hot new prospect for the
Brown Island listing she hadn't been able to sell for
six months, so dinner at Roche Harbor tonight, which
I had forgotten about anyway, was also off.

A single-handed sail it would be.

After a shampoo and shower and the depressing
realization that my body was beginning to put on its
predictable layer of winter fat, I left Calico sitting in
the cockpit daintily cleaning Captain's Stew from her
whiskers and headed uphill for a fresh cinnamon roll,
coffee, and the *Seattle Times*. Coming out of the bakery, I ran into Jared. Allison Fisher, Angela's bridge
partner, looking suntanned and sexy as hell in a black
wool blazer, scarlet silk shirt and black miniskirt, was
with him. Her blonde hair was curly and her lipstick

perfect. She checked out my naked face, shapeless sweatshirt and worn boat shoes, gave me a big smile and an exuberant greeting. I wondered why she wasn't out peddling real estate.

"Hi, lady." Jared tapped my *Times*. "Looks like you've got a perfect Saturday planned. I left the disk at your office. Sorry about not being able to open the files."

"Not a problem," I said, wondering what the two of them were doing together.

Jared patted my arm and followed Allison inside. I stared after them for a minute, then headed down the hill. It didn't require very much gray matter to determine that Allison's hot new prospect had nothing to do with real estate.

Back on *'Spray* I devoured the cinnamon roll, stowed everything moveable, donned my life vest-in Coast Guard jargon, a personal flotation device, or PFD—started up the engine, and accepted Henry's offer to cast me off. His redheaded girlfriend was back. She watched Henry untie *DragonSpray*'s dock lines and guide the boat out into the fairway.

Outside the breakwater I hoisted the mainsail, unfurled the headsail and cut the diesel engine. Patches of blue sky were widening and the wind was a pleasant eight knots or so. Past the university labs on the north edge of the harbor, I fell off to a comfortable beam reach.

Ordinarily, sailing alone erased the problems of the world from my mind. I would do what needed to be done and concentrate on the wind and weather and trim of the sails. I would forget about Nick or Melissa or Jewel Moon. Or uncommunicative clients and their unsolvable problems.

But today it was not to be. I couldn't shake off a sense of anxiety, of helplessness, of the nagging feeling that some malign energy had been set in motion and I was powerless to halt it.

A movement of white caught my eye: the Washington State Ferry was coming out of Wasp Passage. I steered toward Shaw Island, tightened the sheets, and

the boat heeled sharply. Surprised, I checked the anemometer, that convenient little meter that told me the
velocity of the wind at the top of the mast. The digital
readout said thirteen knots.

The ferry passed and the more intrepid passengers
on the windy upper deck waved. I returned their
greetings and decided to sail around Jones Island
counterclockwise. Hopefully the wind would hold on
the north side, which would put me back in San Juan
Channel about two-thirty or three o'clock at slack
water, that very short interval of time between the
ebb and the flood tides.

Sailing downwind, I let my mind pick over the mul-
titude of loose ends in the Montenegro case. *Merde!*
I had forgotten to check for the DataTech reports on
Muehler and De los Santos before I left. And for sure,
something about De los Santos didn't ring true. Or
was it something about Elyse Montenegro and De los
Santos? And what about the anonymous half-million-
dollar insurance policy on the deceased? How could a
person be insured for that amount without a stringent
physical exam? Or could such an exam be purchased
for the right price?

I adjusted the sheet on the mainsail and contemplated the probability that Elyse's stalker, the unidentified driver of the black Cherokee that Jared's source
had described, would return to the island to finish his
task. If the stalker had committed the other two murders in Denver and Los Angeles, then we had a serial
killer. And right now Zelda was somewhere in Idaho
attempting to gather evidence that would tie the three
killings to a mountain mechanic.

I knew from my training in law enforcement that
serial killers were often very angry. With each killing,
they lost a little more of their conscience. Whether
from genetic predisposition or as the result of being
raised in an environment of abuse, such killers lacked
feelings of remorse or guilt. With each attack, they
became more daring and felt more powerful. But that
still didn't explain what was motivating Julio's mur-

derer. Did we have a Dahmer or a Kaczynski? Was this guy Sykes or Simms a renegade sociopath or a political extremist looking for a twenty-first-century version of Hitler's "final solution"? Was he working alone or representing a group? I couldn't quite put the motivation together.

Philosophical questions aside, the fact remained that if the killer's target had been Elyse Montenegro instead of Campbell Sawyer, he must be aware of his mistake by now, and it was just a matter of time before he returned to hunt down my client. He could well be on his way at this very minute. I wondered why I'd had no response whatsoever from Ben Carey or Sergeant Wineheart.

The wind held all the way to the entrance to Wasp Passage and I gybed up Spring Passage between Jones and Orcas Islands without resorting to the engine, totally unprepared for the unforgiving blast of wind that hit me as I rounded Jones to come back down San Juan Channel. I looked at the rails in the water with chagrin. Knowing I'd never make it all the way back to Friday Harbor with so much sail up, I ducked back behind Jones, fastened on my safety harness, and reduced the mainsail. So much for believing the meteorologists!

Half an hour later, with two reefs in the mainsail and the headsail partially furled, 'Spray was headed down San Juan Channel. The sun had disappeared, the water was gray-green and covered in whitecaps. The wind was gusting at twenty-three knots, and the combination of ebbing tide against a rising wind was sure to make for a choppy sea and a nasty trip back to Friday Harbor.

I have great respect for the ocean, and sometimes fear it as well, and I will never forget the devastating winter storm in the North Atlantic that claimed the lives of my father and grandfather when I was twelve. For some reason, I remember my grandfather most clearly. A tall burly man with dark hair, green eyes, and a big voice, who decided that Sarah Josephine was far too much of a name "for such a wee lassie," and Scotia it was thereafter.

A large wave crashed over *DragonSpray*'s bow. Point Caution was abeam and the anemometer was reporting thirty-two knots. I made the executive decision to put on the engine and drop the sails, terribly grateful I'd had the sense to add lazy-jacks a year ago. I steered up into the wind, furled the headsail and released the main halyard, the line that holds the mainsail up. The big white sail slid down the track in the mast and folded itself obediently into the embracing lines of the lazy-jacks, and I was on my way home.

The harbor was covered in whitecaps. I attached the fenders and envisioned a messy single-handed docking. A cell phone call roused my lascivious dock mate and Henry was dutifully standing on G-73 ready to receive the lines as I approached the dock.

I tossed him the bow line, put the engine in neutral, and clambered onto the dock with the stern line. "Thanks, Henry."

"Looks a little breezy out there," he said, cleating off the line.

"A bit more than predicted."

"Blowing forty knots over at Rosario. Ferry from Anacortes has been canceled. Another big storm headed down from Alaska tomorrow. By the way, Scotia, there was a woman here looking for you. A tall blonde. Didn't want to tell me what she wanted. Looked kind of worried."

A tall blonde. Elyse. She ought to be worried. I wondered what it would take to get her to stay out of sight.

I waved Henry back to his Saturday afternoon recreation, put two spring lines on *'Spray* and went below. The cabin was cold. I turned on the heat, called the ranch and left a message for Elyse. The red button on the answering machine was flashing. The message was from my itinerant assistant and had come in five minutes ago. I called her back.

37

"Where are you?" Recently all my phone conversations with Zelda seemed to begin with this question.

"In Wallace, where else?"

"It's almost six o'clock. Did you and Dakota check out the Silver Ass Saloon?"

"Yeah, we got here about three. The Silver Ass welcomes bikers, pikers, and ladies of the night, but it does not allow canine companions. So I had to leave Dakota in the Morris and I've been bonding with Malcolm."

"Who's Malcolm?" I asked in annoyance.

"He's the bartender and it turns out he's practically my cousin. He grew up in Missoula and his older brother married my aunt's cousin." She paused. "Or maybe it was his father. Anyway, he's lived around here a long time and I can tell you that not a lot happens in Wallace that Malcolm doesn't know about." She paused and I heard her chewing on something. Couldn't I ever have a conversation with this woman when she wasn't eating?

"I can also tell you that secrets are as rare in Wallace as they are in the fair village of Friday Harbor."

Which is extremely rare.

Zelda's MO at the Silver Ass, she reported, had been to order a beer and inquire as to the availability of a mechanic who could fix her fictitious overheating engine. She'd been whiling away the time over several mugs of the local draft brew while Almost-Cousin

Malcolm supplied the names of three local mechanics, two of whom turned out to be closed on Saturday afternoon. There was, however, a mobile mechanic who might be able to help her. Jamie Sykes, the mountain mechanic.

"How about that!" she said.

Sykes again. The owner of the van from Berkeley, a.k.a. George Simms.

"I call this guy a couple of times," she continued. "No answer. Pretty soon it's five o'clock and I order another beer and Yvonne—that's the waitress— Yvonne has a beer and she tells me how her fiancé just packed up and left her after five years and went off with the high school principal's wife. Then I start whining about the car and how I don't have much money and how am I going to get back to Seattle and my job on Monday. So Yvonne says, not to worry, if I don't get the car fixed, I can bunk in with her, but she's pretty sure Jamie will come in. She says he's a real hunk, and he's got a sweetie in Wallace, name of Corrine, FFB. Then these two bikers came in and—"

"Stop. What the hell is FFB?"

"Fucks for bucks. Gee, boss." She chortled and made a sound of amazement at my naiveté, then continued. "Anyway, as I was saying, these two bikers wanted a game of billiards, but since I promised to call you, and this stupid cell phone wouldn't work in the bar, I said I had to go and walk my dog and I came out and called you."

Which was all well and good, so far. What was *not* well and good was that Zelda was now about to return to the bar for a game of billiards and to await the arrival of the mountain mechanic.

"Forget it, Zelda. Get your tush out of there! This is a job for the FBI!"

"Hold on, boss, I have to go back and pay my bill. Besides, I promised Yvonne I'd tell her how to find the online singles network. She says there's nobody worth giving the time of day to in Wallace."

"Pay your bill and don't make any waves. And under no circumstances are you to approach Sykes or try any surveillance. I'm not licensed in the state of Idaho. If you get in trouble, nobody's going to bail you out."

"Okay, okay!"

Before I could caution her about the storm forecast for Sunday, the connection went dead. I stared at the phone, wishing not for the first time that when Zelda got her allotment of super brains, she'd also received a commensurate portion of common sense.

I poured three fingers of dry vermouth over ice, filled it to the top with club soda, checked e-mail, and began to read the two reports from DataTech.

DataTech Confidential report #1101874: Wilhelm Freidrich Muehler

Born*: November 13, 1944 to Hans and Freida Muehler, naturalized U.S. citizens who emigrated from Germany in 1938, in New York City*

Education: *Brandywine Military Academy; graduated magna cum laude from Princeton University with B.A. in Economics in 1966; White House Intern Summer 1967; MBA in Economics from Princeton University, 1968*

Marital status: *Married to Alice Wharton for 34 years. One child, Elyse Christine, age 31*

Religion*: Member, United Episcopalian Church*

Career: *1968–1972 Commodities trader, Empire Investments, NYC; 1972–1981 Registered Financial Advisor, Straus & Schultz overseas Commodities, NYC; 1982–1995 Partner, Straus & Muehler Financial, NYC; 1996 Opened private consulting office in San Francisco, Muehler Financial, Inc.*

Politics: *Republican. Supporter of the World*

> *Heritage Foundation; Plato Institute; Center for International Studies; National Taxpayer Foundation*
> **Club Memberships:** *San Francisco Country Club; World Collector's Club*
> **Professional Associations:** *International Society of Investment Consultants; Goethe Association*
> **Police Record:** *None*
> **F.B.I. Record:** *None*
> **F.I.T. Taxes due:** *None*
> **Childhood hobby:** *Collected miniature antique soldiers; currently owns world's largest collection of Colonial India and Wehrmacht miniatures*
> **Childhood pet:** *German shepherd named Adolf*
> **Credit rating:** *Top 1%*

There were no surprises in the report, nothing to indicate that Wilhelm's relationship with the deceased was anything other than what he had described. I thought it exemplary that the son of an immigrant ended up at Princeton. Overall, the report described a well-educated, law-abiding East Coast financier of conservative political leanings with a stable marriage.

No sinister associations, no police record, no criminal connections.

I added more soda and ice to my glass and read the second report. It duplicated Zelda's report and went on from there to reflect a *persona* that was less than lily-white.

Confidential Report 1101875: Felipe Rodriguez De los Santos

Born: *September 13, 1962, Bogota, Colombia*
Citizenship: *Colombia*

Education: *Ll. B., Hastings School of Law, San Francisco, CA 1997*
Marriages: *None on record*
Career: *Clerk, De Angelo & Gomez, San Francisco, 1995–97; Legislative Staff Attorney, Latin American Union for Defense, 1997–present*
Other business affiliations: *Partner, Global Imports, Inc., Oakland, CA; Partner, California Van Lines, Oakland, CA*
Police record: *San Rafael, CA: DUI, December 19, 1998. Acquitted. Tiburon, CA: Reported for domestic violence, April 1999, no charges filed; Berkeley, CA: Arrested for carrying a concealed weapon without a permit, June 1999, Case under investigation; Oakland, CA: DUI, August 2000, case pending*
F.I.T. Taxes due: *Subject has never filed a U.S. tax return; currently under investigation.*
California Franchise Tax Board: *Subject has never filed a California tax return; currently under investigation*

Assault, two DUIs, carrying a concealed weapon without a permit. The last offense at least should get him disbarred in the state of California. I dutifully forwarded the report to Sergeant Wineheart, although I suspected that he already knew a lot more about De los Santos than he would ever share with me.

The cabin was getting warmer and I peeled off my sailing jacket, polar-fleece pants and boots and donned the faded flannel Mickey Mouse nightshirt Melissa had insisted I buy at Disneyland ten years ago. I hadn't had anything to eat since the cinnamon roll this morning. The cupboard above the reefer yielded up a cardboard box of instant tomato soup. I opened it, added water, and put it on to heat. I stared at the blank TV monitor without enthusiasm, searched for the remote control and clicked my way through the program menu until I found an old rerun of *Law and Order* that I watched over spoonfuls of hot soup and stale soda crackers. I followed that with a National Geo special on "Savage Mountains" that contained dazzling four-color footage of landslides and mudslides and avalanches. It would be an excellent promotional piece for life on the prairies.

At ten o'clock, I'd had enough. The wind seemed to have dropped completely, but the calm felt menacing. I hoped Zelda had had enough sense to stop over in Spokane and not get caught in a storm in the mountain passes.

I glanced around the cabin. I should have been sleepy after the afternoon spent fighting wind and waves, but I wasn't. I heated a cup of milk, added Ovaltine, wrapped myself in the chenille robe and climbed up to the deck. The moon was nearly obscured by high, fast-moving clouds. I stood there for a long time in the cold night air, clasping the warm cup, sipping the malty liquid, absorbing the utter loneliness of the night. Henry's boat was dark once again. The docks were deserted and the bell on Reid Rock clanged a dire warning of unseen rocks and reefs and punctuated the admonition with green and white flashes of light.

The cold air overcame me. Shivering, I descended into the cabin warmth and dialed Zelda's cell phone number, wishing I'd asked her to call me when she left Wallace.

"This customer has traveled outside the cellular area. Please try your call again."

I washed my face, crawled under the white comforter and fell asleep with a deep sense of apprehension that wove itself into restless dreams of raging winds and crashing waves.

38

Sunday was not a day I would voluntarily have chosen for travel in a small plane over open water and mountain ranges. The premonition of impending disaster that had accompanied my restless sleep and storm-drenched dreams on Saturday night had not dissipated as I awoke to rain on the cabin roof. Instead, the sense of dread had progressed to fingernail-chewing helplessness, which was validated by reality when the phone rang at seven-thirty a.m.

"It's me, Zelda." Her words were slow and slurred.

"Where are you? Did you make it across the mountains?"

There was a pause, more fuzzy words. "I got myself in a lil' bit of trouble."

"Such as?"

"I can't walk and I can't drive. I can't fly back because of Dakota. Can you come and get me?"

Merde! I took a deep breath. "Were you in an accident?"

"Sort of. I got shot at and I've got a broken leg. I'm in the hospital and I think he got away."

"Dakota?!"

"No, Sykes."

"I told you to stay the hell away from him!" *Merde encore!* "Wherever you are, stay there! Don't move a finger. Don't go *anywhere*."

"Not likely," she said. "Cousin Malco'm won't let me."

Thank God for Cousin Malcolm.

I wanted to know who had shot at her and why. But knowing Zelda, I also knew that a request for details would be counterproductive at this moment. I scribbled down the address and phone number of the Panhandle Medical Facility in Coeur d'Alene, Idaho, wished I had a friend among law enforcement in Idaho, which I hadn't, and asked Zelda if she or Malcolm had any idea where the closest airport was. Malcolm said I could fly into Spokane, about forty-five minutes away, and United and Southwest flew there from Seattle. I would have to rent a car in Spokane. Or maybe I could get a charter flight into Coeur d' Alene with Big Mountain Charters. Malcolm's daughter was a pilot with Big Mountain.

If I had needed to fly out of Friday Harbor during the summer on an hour's notice, I wouldn't have had a prayer. But on that blowy, wet morning in late November, I was the only passenger on the Harbor Airlines eleven-thirty flight to Seattle. It wasn't the worst winter flight I've ever had over Juan de Fuca and Puget Sound, but I spent the last gut-wrenching fifteen minutes with my eyes closed, seriously contemplating replacing Zelda Jones, either with someone who would stay put at the Olde Gazette Building and do background investigations, or with an honest-to-goodness experienced operative who would follow orders.

I connected with a Southwest flight in Seattle at one-thirty. After another white-knuckled, hour-long flight over the Cascades, I landed in crisp sunshine in Spokane, picked up a rental car and followed the freeway east into Idaho. The roadsides were bordered with soft, fresh snow. It had been more than ten years since my last trip through the Sawtooth Mountains, and while nothing in the west was very wild anymore, there had been no diminishment in the awesome, towering snow-covered mountain peaks or the lush pine and cedar forests. As I drove toward Coeur d'Alene, I tried unsuccessfully to reconcile the wholesome outdoor atmosphere of hikers and canoers and skiers with what I knew about militia compounds and ethnic cleansing American-style.

"I'm sorry," Zelda said. "I know it was stupid, but I thought I could help." She was pale, her face devoid of makeup. A small rectangular patch of tape and gauze covered a portion of her brow and forehead. The hennaed hair was uncombed and her right leg was encased in a white plaster cast from the knee down. The Panhandle Medical Center's standard-issue gown was not *haute* anything, and I couldn't repress the thought that her ethnic dressing had suffered a blow, at least temporarily.

"This is Cousin Malcolm. Malcolm, this is Scotia. He's the bartender at the Silver Ass. He saved my life."

She gestured toward her companion, a thin, bearded, white-haired man who had stood up as I entered the room.

I extended my hand and felt it embraced by a warm sinewy palm. "A pleasure, Malcolm." The man smiled and offered me his chair, then pulled another one close to the bed and sat.

"I didn't exactly save her life. But it sure did help that Doris and me were related. 'Course, if this one would have followed my advice, and stayed out of Doris's back pasture, she wouldn't of gotten in trouble."

So there was a back pasture somewhere. I slid out of my jacket and sat next to the bed, figuring it would be a waste of breath to mention that Zelda never followed anyone's advice, and wondering if I should just plunge *in media res* and ask what Zelda was doing in Doris's back pasture, why Doris wanted to shoot Zelda, and who in the hell was Doris anyway. Or should I go back and start at the beginning, wherever that might be?

"I really tried to call you back last night," Zelda said, "but the cell phone wouldn't work from the bar,

and after Jamie came in, I figured it was too dangerous. And then things got complicated." She patted the
plaster cast. "This really looks worse than it is. I can
go home as soon as the doctor comes by."

Home being five hundred-plus miles away and her
leg in a cast, it was clear what my function was to be.

"We talked yesterday about six o'clock, Zelda," I
said in a neutral voice. "You were going to go back
to the Silver Ass Saloon, pay your bill and leave.
What happened?"

Before she could reply, Malcolm stood up. "I guess
you two ladies need to talk in private." He offered to
go down to the hospital's cafe and bring back coffee.
I said a silent prayer of thanks for modern hospitals
with amenities and accepted with alacrity. Zelda
wanted tomato juice.

"You've been doing some illegal sleuthing," I
prompted her when Malcolm left. "Want to tell me
about it?"

"Are you mad at me?"

"Actually, I am. But I was also worried about you.
So you found him?"

She nodded. "His name is Jamie Sykes, like I told
you. He's a gorgeous hunk with a mind like a steel
trap. He lives somewhere down near the south end of
the lake and I'm honestly not sure I could find my
way back there again if my life depended on it." She
shuddered. "Which it probably does! Or somebody's
does." She reached for the glass of water on the bedside table. I noticed her hands were shaking. I wondered if it was fear or a hangover.

"I thought we had a conversation several months
ago about private investigation without a license."

She gave me a hangdog look and said that she'd
returned to the Silver Ass after she talked to me, ordered up the Saturday night special of BBQ ribs and
baked beans and another mug of local draft, and accepted the two bikers' challenge to a game of billiards.

"I beat the bikers, hands down. They sulked a bit,
refused a second game and went and picked up a cou-

ple of hussies at the bar. So I went back to chitchatting with Malcolm, who thinks I should move back to Montana.''

Hooray for Malcolm.

"Around eight o'clock, when I'm about to explode from all the beer and lies I've told, Yvonne gives me a nod and I see this delectable hunk take a seat at the bar. Tight blue jeans, incredible shoulders, tall, lean and gorgeous." She shuddered. "Gorgeous."

"And at this point no little bells went off?" I asked. "No little voice said, 'Zelda, this man could be a murderer, get your ass out of here'?"

She ignored my sarcasm. "Yvonne introduces us and after checking out my boobs and legs, which I must admit were the best in the bar, he offers to buy me a drink. Which I accepted. I couldn't drink any more beer, so I started drinking rum and cokes. And then I tell him my mechanical problems. To which he politely tells me he'd love to help, but he has plans for the evening and is leaving town early Sunday morning and won't be back until Thanksgiving. I tell him no problem, and we have another drink.''

By nine o'clock, she reported, the delectable hunk was lending one ear to her creative life history and keeping one eye on the door.

"I can see him getting mad that his sweetie hasn't showed," she continued, "so I try to keep his mind on lighter topics. He tells me about his high school drama club, and all the plays he was in, and how he wanted to be an actor."

She paused and looked as if she were in pain. "I have a terrible hangover." She sighed and continued with her story. "This part is really kind of sad. Apparently, he could have had a college scholarship to study theater, but his old man refused to fill out the financial application and made him turn it down. After that, it was football. He was the star end until his career was ruined by some low-life mongrel wetback that intentionally kicked him in the kneecap. That kneecap kept him out of Vietnam and ruined his life."

She frowned. "You ever hear the term 'mongrel'?"

I nodded, thinking of my conversation with Judith. Mongrel and mud people: white-supremacist terms for nonwhite and mixed races.

"When he started talking about the knee, his eyes were getting narrower and narrower," she went on, "so I decided to change the subject and we talked about movies, and it turned out we have a lot in common." She raised her hands above her head, interlaced her fingers, stretched, and resumed her narration.

"Such as?"

"All the Exterminator films and Bruce Lee stuff and Bronson, of all things. About eleven o'clock, I'm tired and drunk and worried about Dakota being in the car so long without being able to pee. I'm trying to figure out how to extricate myself and find a place to lay my head for the night when out of the blue, he asks if I'd like to come back to his place for a nightcap. It's only about twenty minutes away, and we could watch a Bronson video and then tomorrow morning before he leaves, he can look at the Morris."

"You didn't!?"

She shook her head. "Even *I'm* not that dumb. But it gave me an idea. If he only lived twenty minutes away, I could follow him, stay out of sight, and find out where he lived. Then when he left on his trip, I could, like, maybe check out his house."

I shook my head in disbelief.

"So I told him I'd had too much to drink, which wasn't a lie, and that I had already paid for a motel room in Wallace, and if I didn't get the car fixed, I'd give him a call."

"And he left?"

"Yeah, but here the plot thickened a little. Just as Sykes was walking out, this blonde tart in a skirt a lot shorter than mine came charging in the door and he grabbed her arm and they left together. I dashed over to pay my bill, but Malcolm didn't buy my lie about a motel, probably because I didn't know the name of any motels, and it had started snowing. And then I guess I got tired of lying and I told him I had to find out where Sykes lived."

"Did you tell him why?"

"I said he might be stalking a nice woman I know."

"What did Malcolm say?"

"Said it wouldn't surprise him. After he dropped out of high school, Jamie started getting into fights. I got the idea he did time."

"And I told her," interjected Malcolm, "there was no way I was letting her go skulking around them back roads by herself in a snowstorm. Particularly in that ridiculous little car!" Malcolm had returned, hands full of foam cups and a brown paper bag. He had brought not only steaming coffee for me and tomato juice and crackers for Zelda, but also a dozen chocolate chip walnut cookies, three or four of which I figured would deceive my stomach into thinking it had been given lunch.

"Ladies, I'm gonna have to push on," he said, taking a cookie from the bag. "Have to pick up my grandson and then be to work at five." He looked at Zelda fondly and shook her hand with quaint formality.

"If you two gals need a place to lay your heads tonight, you let me know. Or just come by for a drink. And let me know when you want to pick up Dakota. I'll keep him with me."

Zelda blew her savior a kiss. "Thanks, Malcolm. I owe you." He gave me a salute, gathered up his green plaid logger's jacket and was gone. Zelda rubbed her head above the bandage, took a bite of cracker, and sighed.

"To make a long story short, when we came out of the bar, Sykes was gone, but Malcolm knew where he lived. We took Malcolm's truck and finally got to a place way out in the boonies that Malcolm said was right next to his cousin Doris's place, so I convinced him we should sneak in from the back, since we didn't know if Sykes was home or not."

Amateur sleuthing at its finest.

"Which is where Doris comes in?"

"Ye—eah. Like I said, she's Sykes's neighbor. About ninety-five years old. When we went through her field to come up behind Sykes's cabin, this big, bright light comes on and then there's bullets flying over our heads. I think she only stopped shooting when Malcolm yelled at her. She's his mother's cousin twice removed, or something."

"Did she hit your leg?"

Zelda bit her lip. "No. But when she started shooting, I dropped my flashlight and tripped over some stones that were all covered with snow, and I fell in an old feeding trough. Doris came running out with her shotgun and this big can of bear spray, but then she felt terrible when she saw I couldn't get up. They put me in a wheelbarrow and I had to ride in the bed of the truck all the way back to town. In the snowstorm!"

"Where was Sykes while all this shooting was going on?"

"Not at home, obviously." She shrugged. "And after all that, I haven't a clue as to whether Sykes is even the guy you want or not. Not one of my better evenings." She peered at me from under her long lashes. I burst out laughing and she joined in.

"Welcome to Surveillance 101, my dear."

"Nice to have some levity on the ward, ladies."

It was Zelda's doctor, a Pierce Brosnan look-alike in regulation white smock and stethoscope, who, after perusing Zelda's chart, pronounced her well enough to leave, as long as she kept the cast dry and checked in with her regular doctor when she got home.

Tagging along as Zelda was wheeled down the corridor to the elevator and officially discharged on the first floor, I concluded it was possible Zelda had gleaned more information than she realized. Sykes's grudge against a "mongrel wetback" would be consistent for someone who had shot three Hispanic attorneys; and as for the "trip" Sykes had planned, either he was going to make another hit or, in a worst-case scenario, he would return to the island to get rid of the woman he perceived to be a witness to the first killing, my client. And he expected to be back home by Thanksgiving, which was only four days away.

While Zelda was signing forms and accepting small plastic ampules of antibiotics, I called the Berkeley PD, actually talked to Wineheart, and gave him an update on what we had discovered on Sykes. He thanked me in a noncommittal voice and disconnected.

39

It was well past dark and the moon had not yet risen when I pulled out of the parking lot of the small, rustic Kootenai Lodge in Coeur d'Alene and followed the signs to Highway 97 south. After checking Zelda out of the medical center around five, we had driven east to the historical silver-mining town of Wallace, reconnected with Malcolm at the Silver Ass, and retrieved Dakota and his BBQ rib bone from behind the bar.

For an outrageous fee, the rental-car company in Spokane agreed to pick up the rental car from the Silver Ass. With Zelda and her cast and crutches wedged into the backseat of the Morris Minor, and Dakota folded into the passenger seat beside me, I made a fast stop at the Chinese buffet and then transported both cripple and canine to the Lodge. After extracting her solemn oath to keep the door locked and not leave the motel for any reason whatsoever, I headed into the hills.

Before leaving the motel, I had studied the scribbled map Zelda had drawn on the back of an old brown paper sack as she and Malcolm had pursued their quarry over the back mountain roads late last night. With Malcolm's help, we had attempted to label the roads, but somewhere near Stone Creek Road and Sherman Ranch Road, Malcolm had started shaking his head and couldn't remember road names, and I'd known it was going to get dicey.

By my best calculations, Sykes's cabin was located
on or near the southeastern tip of Lake Coeur d'
Alene. Now, sitting in the Morris in pitch blackness
at a fork in the road, I felt a cold trickle of doubt
teasing the back of my neck. I was lost and I had two
choices: I could take the left fork and continue ahead
on Sherman Ranch Road, or take the right one onto
an unmarked, unpaved dirt road that was little more
than two tracks through the snow. Both directions
were heavily wooded. I studied Zelda's cartography
under the beam of my flashlight, decided that the
squiggle in the fold of the paper indicated a turn to
the right.

There were no lights in any direction, and Malcolm
had assured me that Doris had Quilting Club on Sunday night at her niece's place and would probably get
dropped back off at her place by ten. He suggested I
be long gone by then. I got the distinct impression
from Malcolm's tone that only Zelda's fracture had
saved her from a nocturnal sojourn in the county jail.
It was seven-fifty and I wasn't going to press my luck.
I shifted the Morris into low gear, turned the steering
wheel to the right, and hoped the road wasn't a
dead end.

A mile beyond the fork, the dirt road began climbing, wound around several blind curves, and descended through a thick stand of cedar trees, beyond
which I glimpsed moonlight on water and a cluster of
dark farm buildings silhouetted against the bright
light.

Doris had left her yard light on.

I continued slowly along the road until I saw a mailbox beside a grassy drive on the right-hand side. I
stopped beside the mailbox and focused the beam of
the flashlight on the rectangular black letters. *W. and
D. Dodge.* I wondered how long it had been since W.
Dodge had received mail there. Sykes's cabin supposedly lay a quarter of a mile beyond the Dodge place
and backed up to a river or a lake, Malcolm wasn't
sure which. He just remembered attending a big family

reunion there when he was a kid, and picking a fight with his cousin and ending up with a black eye.

I rolled down my window and crept along the road. A hundred yards or so beyond the Dodge mailbox, spying what looked like a lane intersecting the road on the left-hand side, I pulled into the lane. The wheels of the little car started to spin, then dug into the snow and frozen ground, and I came to a standstill inside a field. I cut the headlights and stepped out. The night was silent and crisply cold and a crescent of moon was rising over the trees. No shadows moved. I reached into the Morris for my heavy jacket and buttoned it on over my sweater and blue jeans, wishing I'd had the foresight to pack my long johns.

From the glove compartment I retrieved the Smith and Wesson .38 revolver Malcolm had brought out from behind the bar and insisted I carry. Along with my old Nikon, I pocketed my lock picks and the flashlight, locked the Morris and moved along the side of the road toward Sykes's place. I trod carefully, grateful for my thick boots, avoiding frozen patches of snow or rough dirt, reminding myself that I was in enemy territory.

The second mailbox on the right was new and gleamed in the moonlight beside a stand of cedar trees. No letters identified the owner. And unlike Doris's place, no trees sheltered Sykes's cabin. It sat in a clearing, a long shedlike affair with a larger, squarish addition at the back. I stood near the mailbox, in the shadow of the trees. Nothing moved. The silence and remoteness were pervasive and within the stillness I could hear the occasional faint sounds of nocturnal critters. All that was lacking was the howl of a timber wolf.

The house was dark, but I fully suspected that Sykes, like his neighbor, would have a yard light equipped with a motion detector. As soon as I moved toward the house, I'd be lit up like a suspect in a police lineup. I'd bet that as a good survivalist, he'd own an arsenal that included a rifle with a scope.

There were no vehicles in the driveway. Either Sykes was gone or the now-infamous van was stowed away for the night. I picked up a stone from near my foot, circled around the perimeter of the moonlit clearing until I could see an entry door, and tossed the stone onto the porch of the cabin. The stone bounced, rolled, and came to rest near the door. I waited.

No light came on, no dog barked, no shotgun spoke.

I tossed another stone. The silence continued. The moon moved slowly higher, illuminating the driveway. I stared at it, seeing only one set of tracks through last night's snow. Were they coming in or going out? I couldn't be positive and I didn't want to walk over to inspect the tracks in the moonlight.

Moving along the shadows toward the cabin, one step at a time, I reached into my jacket pocket and felt the lock picks that my detective second husband had taught me to use a long time ago. Under his tutelage, I had developed a real talent for breaking and entering. I'd brought gloves, but they were thin leather and already my fingers were icy.

Somewhere under the porch, a small animal scurried. I continued walking across the frozen yard, keeping to the side that was in moon shadow, and stepped tentatively onto the porch. There was no snow there and no boards creaked and nothing moved. No curtains shifted behind the casement windows. I tried the door handle, found it locked, shone the flashlight beam on it, and exercised the talent I had discovered for breaking and entering, praying that I wouldn't break off a pick inside the lock. If I did, I was screwed, and the last thing I wanted to do was leave anything behind. Despite that my fingers were shaking from cold and fear, the lock turned, I pulled the .38 from my pocket, and was inside the cabin.

40

I stood motionless just inside the open door for what seemed like forever, scanning the room, ready to bolt. I saw no telltale red light of a P.I.R., the passive infrared beam that, when broken, would trigger a shrieking alarm here and notify a remote police dispatcher of a prowler on the premises.

The cabin smelled of wood smoke, but the temperature was no more than fifty degrees. Rays of moonlight began to stream through a window, illuminating the one-room cabin with a cold white light. The room appeared to be empty.

To my left I made out a small kitchen with a table and two chairs. At the opposite end of the room stood a studio couch and a bureau. A computer workstation on a long wooden table occupied one wall. I clicked on the flashlight, scanned all corners of the room, approached the one open door, beyond which I spied a lavatory and toilet. The room was lit by the glow of a small night-light. The glass door on the small shower stall stood open; a damp towel lay crumpled in front of it. The bathroom smelled of a pungent musky aftershave.

I glanced through the front windows onto the moonlit yard. The luminous dial on my watch said nine-fifteen. I shone the flashlight around the perimeter walls, observed a large door at the end of the cabin opposite the kitchen. The door was metal and smooth and cold to my touch, and I couldn't find a lock in it.

I finally realized that the door must be secured with some sort of high-tech device, probably requiring a fingerprint or other digital evidence of identity. Since I'd left San Francisco, I hadn't kept up on state-of-the-art security devices; however, a recent issue of *P.I. Magazine* had described fingerprint and palm-print readers and eye scans. It was all a growing science called biometrics that used to be confined to spy movies. Someday soon, old lock picks would end up in antique stores or museums.

I put my nose near the door casing and sniffed. Gasoline, I thought, or maybe diesel. I wondered what Sykes kept behind the door that required security that couldn't be breeched by an imposter, or an intruder such as myself.

There was a thump on the front porch and I whirled around, flattened myself against the wall, the .38 ready. I inhaled slowly, trying to slow the thudding of my heart. I swallowed, listening to the silence, then something white drifted through the door and padded across the kitchen floor into a streak of moonlight. A large white cat. I smiled and moved out into the room, and the cat bolted back onto the porch, where it sat on the top step and stared into the house.

No shadows moved. On the long table all the computer components were neatly shrouded in plastic covers: the CPU, the printer, the scanner, even the keyboard. I focused the beam of the flashlight on the row of books above the table: *The Road Back*, *Unfriendly Persuasion*, *Mountain Survival*, *The Turner Diaries*; a volume titled *Big Sister is Watching You*; two loose-leaf binders marked *New Report* and *Taking Aim*; a mail-order catalog from the Militia of Montana.

There was a door beside the wood stove. It had a normal deadbolt lock, and here the lock picks worked their magic. I focused the flashlight inside and it was there I hit pay dirt. As I stared at the contents, I wondered if things would have turned out differently if Sykes's daddy had let him become an actor.

The closet was filled with props.

Four pairs of dark glasses, three windbreakers, a yellow foul-weather jacket, a tan raincoat, a pair of boat shoes, a pair of moccasins, a pair of wingtips. Several tubes of theatrical makeup. Four packages of men's hair dye. Mustaches in assorted colors to match the four wigs in assorted colors and lengths. Six pairs of men's leather gloves. An old hatbox of sports caps embroidered with the names of various clubs and teams. *East Bay Sailing Club*, *Denver Mountaineers*, *Los Angeles Earthquakes*, *Miami Gators*. A serial killer's map of geographical millinery. When did he plan the Miami hit? Before or after Thanksgiving? Before or after he hunted down my client?

Not to my surprise, the closet also housed an impressive handgun collection, including a Beretta Model 70, a High Standard Dura-Matic and a Harrington and Richardson Self-Loader that I would have given long odds ballistics could match. He had been smart enough to use different weapons for each hit, but hadn't been able to part from the toys.

There were also two combat knives, an AR-15 semi-automatic rifle and hundreds of rounds of .223 ammunition.

A warehouse for assassins.

I glanced over my shoulder at the quiet room, where the temperature was dropping, and pulled the Nikon from my pocket.

I photographed it all: the hats, the guns, the ammo; the disguises, the hair dye; the large self-adhesive decals advertising "Bay Area Locksmiths" and "Denver Plumbing Supplies"; the scrapbook of newspaper clippings headlining the three murders; a photo album documenting the education of a militiaman.

I closed and locked the closet. It was nine forty-five. I glanced through the front window again. The tops of the trees along the road were illuminated; a car was coming up the hill above the Dodge place. Either Doris was returning early from the Quilting Society or the owner whose cabin I was searching and

on whose property I was trespassing was returning
from an evening with one of his FFB ladies. Either
way, it was time to take a hike.

I moved swiftly to the door, closed it and heard the
lock spring shut behind me. The white cat was perched
on the porch railing. It watched me, a motionless marble statue in the moonlight. I stared back for a second,
then melted into the dark shadows behind the cabin
and began making my way to the road. The car lights
crested the hill, approached what would have been the
driveway at the Dodge place, and turned in. I exhaled
a long sigh of pure relief.

I was convinced that Sykes had left this morning
and was by this time many miles to the west. Now my
greatest fear was that he would get to Elyse before I
could get back to Friday Harbor.

41

"Friday Harbor! This ferry is now arriving Friday Harbor. Please return to your vehicles. All walk-on passengers will disembark from the car deck. Friday Harbor!"

I unfolded myself from the long bench seat in the booth on the passenger lounge and prepared to return to the Morris on the lower car deck of the Washington State Ferry. The last forty-five minutes on the *Kaleetan*, after it left Orcas Island and before we docked in Friday Harbor, had seemed more like ten hours. It was, in fact, exactly twenty-four hours since I'd completed my search of Sykes's cabin and returned to the motel in Coeur d'Alene. After a call to my client at the Percheron Ranch—warning her of Sykes's probable return to the island—and a call to Ben Carey requesting that he alert the San Juan County Sheriff's Department, I had followed the snoozing Zelda and Dakota to dreamland.

We'd bailed out of Idaho as early as I could get my eyes open the next morning, and the entire five hundred twenty-five-mile journey—past Spokane and the rolling hills of the Palouse wheat country, across the Columbia River and over the snowy Cascade range, down into Seattle, Highway 90 all the way—was a blur.

Tucked into the little Morris with Dakota and my physically incapacitated assistant and her accoutrements, I had suffered Zelda's incessant chatter all the way across the state of Washington, mostly about how she had screwed everything up, and now Sykes was ahead of us, and it was all her fault, and had I heard from Elyse? I hadn't. The fact that my cell phone's batteries had died and I'd forgotten to bring the recharging adapter for the cigarette lighter did nothing to improve my mood. I told her about the expanded report on Felipe De los Santos and the Muehler files that neither I nor Jared had been able to open. We agreed that it was possible De los Santos fit into the murder somehow— possibly he had hired Sykes—but anything on Muehler at this point was probably superfluous.

Our only stops had been for fast food and brief walkabouts for Dakota. We'd arrived at the ferry terminal in Anacortes with just enough time to make the evening milk run that stops at Lopez, Shaw, and Orcas Islands before arriving in Friday Harbor.

Now that we were back on the island, Zelda was quiet most of the way out to Davison Head. I helped her into the house, told her to lock all the doors, and headed back to town. I hadn't seen any other cars after we left town, nor did I meet any on my return trip. Back at the parking lot above the Port, I sat in the Morris for several minutes. It was twelve-fifteen. Nothing had followed me and nothing moved. It wasn't legal to leave the car there without a permit, but I would deal with it on Tuesday. I felt as if I had been away for weeks. I extricated my aching body from the car, grabbed my bag and headed for *Dragonspray,* on orange alert all the way.

When I left *DragonSpray* on Tuesday morning, Henry, attired in a white shirt, red tie and dark sports coat, was checking the dock lines on *Pumpkin Seed.* The morning was gray, chill and overcast. The wind seemed to be coming out of the north. I commented on his businesslike appearance.

"Got an escrow closing in Mt. Vernon this morning. Hope the ferries are still running when I get done. According to Canadian Weather, the front's stalled over Vancouver Island. Don't like the feel of it. Could be a big old nor'easter headed our way. Good thing you got back when you did."

I had also listened to the weather forecast, as I do every morning. There was a .968 millibar low a hundred miles south of Tofino on the west coast of Vancouver Island. High winds and colder temperatures were predicted. I agreed the sky looked ominous, reminded him about replacing the frayed power cord while he was in Anacortes, and headed up the hill for my coffee and a maple bar.

I'd found the red light blinking rapidly on the answering machine when I'd returned to the boat last night, a signal that there'd been a power outage after I'd left on Sunday. I wondered what messages I'd missed. My cell phone had recharged overnight and showed two missed messages. Both were hang-ups and the call log showed the Percheron Ranch number for one and what I thought was Jared Saperstein's number for the other. Rebecca Underwood answered my early-morning call to the ranch, reported that Elyse was out feeding the yearlings, and promised to ask her to call me.

Still on orange alert, the Beretta resting snugly in its shoulder holster under my polar-fleece vest and parka, I scanned the streets for an unfamiliar van of whatever color. I stopped by Radio Shack and left the Idaho roll of film for developing. They promised a set of jumbo prints within an hour.

I had told Zelda to stay at home, and now New Millennium was cold and dark. A brown manila envelope with my name on it was propped against the pencil holder on Zelda's desk. The disk that Jared had dropped off on Saturday. After the report I'd received from DataTech on Wilhelm Muehler, I doubted the locked files would yield anything substantial. I picked up Saturday's and Monday's mail from below the mail slot, gave it a cursory look-through, and stacked it on Zelda's desk.

Upstairs, I turned on the wall heater, emptied the brown envelope, and read Jared's handwritten note.

*Thanks for sharing the soup last night. I
printed out what files I could open. The rest
require a password. Sorry. J.*

I leafed through the pages he'd printed out: two
memos from Muehler to several people regarding pur-
chase of an overseas mutual fund, and a letter to
someone named Larry inquiring about his health.

And that was it.

The remainder of the messages in the Recycle Bin
would require a password. I stared at the little 3½"
plastic disk holder, then reached into my bag and
pulled out the two reports I'd received from DataTech
on Saturday. I separated the one on Elyse's father,
clipped it to the floppy disk and left both in the
brown envelope.

There was a new e-mail message from Ben Carey:
He had spoken with Sheriff Bishop, who said he'd be
on the alert for Sykes, and Felipe De los Santos had
disappeared. Why was I not surprised?

I was about to call Elyse at San Juan Percherons
one more time when I heard the sound of canine toe-
nails on the plank floor downstairs.

"We're here!"

I went to the door and looked down the stairway.
It was Zelda, on crutches, grinning, accompanied by
a tail-wagging Dakota. She was wearing the widest
bell-bottom pants I had ever seen, both legs of which
were slit up to the thigh. I was impressed with her
ability to create an instant fashion statement.

"I couldn't stay home, knowing that SOB is wandering around somewhere. I had to do something. Sheldon brought us to town, and he'll pick us up in an
hour." She hobbled over to her desk chair and sat
down heavily. Her crutches fell to the floor. I started
to tell her there wasn't really anything she needed to
do—that she would be safer and more comfortable at
home, then I shrugged.

Zelda had no concept of orange alert.

*   *   *

I stared out the window at the brown leaves whipping along the street in the wind, and called a widowed friend of mine who owns a small B & B on the west side of the island up above the state park. I told her I was sending her a special guest and she promised to prepare a second-floor room. Cora Mae is a sweet innocent, and I did not upset her by telling her why Elyse needed the room, an omission I was to regret bitterly. I then called my client one more time. Gregg answered the phone and went in search of Elyse. She answered immediately.

"Scotia, he's back! What shall I do?" Her little-girl voice had an edge of hysteria.

I felt my throat tighten. *He must have been just ahead of us all the way from Coeur d'Alene.*

"A dark-red van followed Gregg and me when we went to Roche Harbor last night. This morning I saw it drive past the corral when I was working with the two-year-olds."

"I want you to leave the ranch immediately," I said. "Have someone drive you out to the Golden Poppy B & B. It's on West Side Road, above the state park. Cora Mae, the innkeeper, is a friend of mine. She's expecting you. Go to your room and stay out of sight until you hear from me. Do you understand?"

There was a silence, then she agreed. "Gregg will drive me. He has to go to Anacortes. We're out of feed."

"One more thing, Elyse. Do you have any more of Julio's files, perhaps on floppy disks?"

She did, and she would have Gregg drop them at my office when he came to town.

I called the sheriff's office. Sheriff Bishop was working on a case over on Waldron Island, expected back at four o'clock, the office administrator said. The deputy was at the high school conducting a DARE session on self-esteem. I asked for Angela. She said the sheriff had heard from Ben Carey and had discussed Sykes at that morning's briefing session. Nobody had reported anything suspicious. "He's back," I said. "Elyse and

Gregg have seen him twice." She promised to get hold of a deputy and have him call me.

I glanced at my watch, anxious to get my hands on the photos I'd taken at Sykes's cabin. They should be done by now.

After discouraging the Radio Shack sales clerk who wanted to sell me a new digital camera, I tore open the envelope and stood at the store counter staring at the results of my photographic handiwork. The shots of the disguises and the rest of the contents of the mountain mechanic's closet had turned out well, and the headlines I'd photographed in the scrapbook fairly leaped off the paper.

East Bay attorney shot at municipal marina.
Denver lawyer ambushed at courthouse.
Civil rights attorney attacked in Los Angeles.

I stared at the photo of a page of snapshots of a tall, fit man in camouflage clothing, holding an assault rifle. Had someone hired this man to kill Julio Montenegro and the other two attorneys or was he acting on his own?

My cell phone rang.

"Hi, it's Zelda. A handsome man was just here asking for you."

"Nick!?" What was he doing on the island? He wasn't supposed to come up until Wednesday. And me tracking down a killer and looking like a zombie after a fifteen-hour trip across the state of Washington and five hours sleep.

"Not *that* handsome. Older. He'll be back in half an hour or so. Must be from out of town. He was headed for the Topsail Inn."

The visitor had declined to give his name, said it was important that he see me as soon as possible. "And one more thing," she said.

"Yes?"

"Sheldon just got here. He saw a red Dodge van

parked in front of the Topsail this morning. Washington plates, some guy with long hair got in and drove up Spring Street. Just thought I'd mention it."

The same van Elyse had seen. Sykes didn't seem to care who saw him. Not a good sign.

An opera I'd never heard before greeted me at New Millennium, but Zelda's chair was empty. There were two envelopes in my mail cubby. I read the note on the top one. "*Gregg Underwood left this for you. I'm going home. Let me know if I can help. Zelda.*"

Julio Montenegro's missing files.

I raced upstairs, inserted the floppy disk Gregg had left into my computer and began to open the files, one by one. "wtm1.doc" was a dossier on Elyse's father not unlike the one I had received from DataTech. The second file, however, "wtm2.doc," began where the first left off. I read it with increasing astonishment and disbelief, and was about to reread it when a tall figure appeared in the doorway.

"Good afternoon, Ms. MacKinnon. I hope I'm not intruding. Your charming redheaded receptionist seems to have disappeared, so I took the liberty of coming up."

Startled, I whirled around from the monitor screen and stared into the handsome face of the man whose dossier I was just reading. A dossier delineating Wilhelm Muehler's association with no less than four anti–federal government, white-supremacist and gun-owners groups, and a group called OWN, or One White America. OWN was the group that had put up big bucks, along with the Coalition for English Only, to support the prosecution of Gloria Lopez, Julio's client.

No wonder they hadn't agreed on politics!

I took a deep breath, glanced at the monitor, noted that my nautical screen saver was displaying colorful sailboats under spinnaker, and decided two could play the same game.

I smiled cordially. "Not at all, Mr. Muehler. Have a seat."

He folded his tall frame into the same wicker chair his daughter had first sat in only two weeks ago and unbuttoned his gray wool topcoat.

"I know you must be surprised to see me, but after you left on Thursday, my wife and I talked it over and decided all this has gone far enough. I spoke with Elyse Saturday and told her I was coming up to get her." I wondered if Herr Muehler knew that women in the U.S. were emancipated a number of decades ago.

"I see." I folded my hands together on the desk blotter to keep them from shaking.

Muehler frowned and tapped one perfectly manicured index finger on my desk. "I'm sure you must agree with the police at this point, there really are no suspects. Sad, but sometimes it's that way." He slid his right hand into the inside breast pocket of his jacket. Reflexes still good, I reached quickly under my vest, then I saw him remove a black checkbook identical to the one Elyse had, and a silver Waterman pen.

"I'd be more than happy to reimburse you for your time and expenses and add a bonus." He looked at me, silver pen in the air.

I swallowed with difficulty. My money karma was definitely improving.

"Mr. Muehler, Elyse has already given me a retainer, and whether she decides to stay on the island or return to San Francisco is entirely between the two of you. But your son-in-law's killer is still at large. Your daughter feels that she's in danger and I agree with her. I've already notified the sheriff."

"Elyse in danger! That's impossible!" He stood up and the wicker chair fell over behind him.

"Why impossible?" I asked.

He pressed his lips together. Two deep vertical lines appeared between his eyebrows. He reached for the overturned chair and set it upright with a harsh sound. "My daughter is suffering from a broken heart and her agitation is quite understandable. I've had enough of this circus. I'm going to the ranch and get her. Good day to you!"

I stared at the empty space left by the retreating figure, glanced down at my desktop and noticed for the first time the second envelope I'd grabbed from the mail cubby along with Julio's files. There was another note in Zelda's handwriting. *"Success! This should add a whole new dimension. Call in the troops! Zelda. P. S. The password was Adolf."*

I emptied the envelope. The floppy disk that contained Muehler's locked files fell out, along with a stack of printed pages. I leafed through the sheets of fine print. The same files Jared had printed. *Merde.* Then I found the last three pages: three one-line messages addressed to *whiteonwhite@bay.com.*

I read them and read them again.

Latin American Union for Defense. Done
Rocky Mountain Center for Legal Defense. Done
Western Center for Minority Defense. Done

Finally, it all made sense. I understood who the mountain mechanic was working for. Zelda was right; it was time for reinforcements.

After getting Ben Carey's answering machine and ditto for Sergeant Wineheart, I e-mailed and faxed the three messages from the locked files to both of them.

Then I dialed Angela. She'd reached the sheriff over on Waldron, who'd failed to exhibit any particular concern for "Miz. Fletcher's latest paranoia." "He said when he sees something suspicious, he'll look into it," Angela reported. "Until something happens, there's nothing he can do." She muttered several expletives. "But I'm expecting the deputy back any minute. I'll have him call you."

I called the ranch to confirm that Elyse had gotten away safely. Rebecca answered. She'd just gotten back from the doctor. "What's going on, Scotia?" she asked in a hoarse voice. "There's a note from Gregg saying he's taking Elyse out to the Golden Poppy. And Big Boy is missing."

I gave her a synopsis of the last few days' events and wondered what it meant that her dog was gone.

"I wonder why Elyse didn't mention it," she said with a cough.

"Her father is also looking for her. When he gets to the ranch, you don't know where she is. Do you understand?"

There was a moment of silence. It is very hard to get honest people to lie, even under circumstances such as this. "Okay, Scotia. Her father did call her on Saturday and she got very upset. I'll tell him I don't know where she is. Good luck." Then I called the Golden Poppy.

"Cora Mae, is Elyse there?"

"Oh, Scotia, yes, that nice young man brought her and the big dog out about an hour ago. I gave her the pretty yellow room upstairs with a private bath. We don't usually allow animals, but it's off season, so I made an exception. Do you want to speak to her?"

I did, and she left the phone and returned a minute later.

"Scotia, I just remembered. She went out a few minutes ago."

"Went out!" I screamed. "Where the bloody hell did she go? I told her to stay in her room."

"She said something about losing a bracelet down at the state park. She said she had to go look for it. I was on the phone, so I didn't hear exactly what she said. What's wrong, Scotia?"

I took a deep breath. "I'm sorry, Cora Mae, but what's *wrong* is that her husband's murderer is on the island! Looking for *her*! That's the reason I sent her over to stay with you!"

"Oh, my, I had no idea. Why didn't you tell me? She took the dog with her. Do you want me to go and look for her?"

Merde! Merde encore! Big Boy would be zero protection against an armed killer like Sykes. I told Cora Mae I'd look for Elyse myself, gave her my cell number, and she promised to call if she heard anything.

42

I tore down the stairs and out of the office. There was no sign of Muehler and no sign of a red van. I raced across the theater parking lot, took the steps two at a time behind the courthouse and ran across First Street. The steps on the stairway behind the Legion Post were slick from all the recent rain. Only the sturdy handrail saved me from a nasty tumble. A cold wind was gusting up from the harbor. I noted with chagrin that Zelda's Morris had a citation on it, and headed for the Volvo.

I sped up Spring Street, turned right on Second, ignored the stop sign on Blair, and barreled out of town.

It was raining, a hard cold rain. It looked like Henry was right about the nor'easter. And Nick due to fly up to the island with his partner tomorrow in that little Arrow! The cell phone rang. It was Jared.

"Scotia, I just talked to Angela. Are you okay?"

"I'm on my way out to the state park to find my bimbo client. Where are you?"

"Trying to get back from Lopez in a private boat. It's really nasty out here. What can I do to help?"

I thought for a minute, trying to formulate a plan.

"I'm going to try to pick up Elyse. Unless I can get hold of a deputy or the sheriff, I think we'll make a run for *DragonSpray*. Meet us there!"

I turned onto Mitchell Bay Road, furious at Elyse's lack of common sense. She'd put her life in danger to

recover a charm bracelet. What a total airhead! She
exhibited a mental age of six and needed a full-time
keeper.

It was three forty-five when I got to the park; the
sign outside said that it closed at dusk. I left the Volvo
parked along the stone wall outside the park facing
out, took the Beretta from my holster, made sure
there was a round in the chamber, checked the safety.
I locked the car and pulled on my knit hat. The wind
slammed me as I sprinted into the park. One vehicle
was parked under the trees: a dark-red Dodge van
with Washington plates.

Sykes's van! I was too late!

The wind was gusting off the water and I raced past
the comfort stations, down the trail that leads to the
whale watch site. The sky was darkening. A large red
container ship was wallowing its way through the gray-
green, whitecapped waters of the Strait, rolling in the
swells. I scanned the rocky trail that wound down to
the lighthouse. There was no sign of Elyse. She could
be anywhere. My eyes scanned to the left, along the
narrow trail where it dipped and meandered above
Dead Man's Bay.

Then I saw him: a tall hiker with dark hair and a
mustache. He was wearing a dark-blue hooded parka
and blue jeans. Despite the hirsute appearance, I had
no doubt whatsoever that the hiker was Zelda's handsome score from the Silver Ass Saloon. Julio's murderer and Elyse's stalker. Jamie Sykes, the mountain
mechanic.

He was approximately a quarter of a mile away and
must have circled around to the trail that comes up
from the other end of the park. Frantic, I scanned the
hillside and finally spotted Elyse, head down, walking
away from me, climbing steadily downhill on the most
precipitous part of the trail, where one misstep virtually guaranteed a fall of several hundred feet to the
sharp black rocks and frothing waters below. The big
multicolored dog was trotting happily ahead of her.

Both of them heading directly into the arms of Jamie Sykes.

As I pounded along the narrow path, she came up on a rise and stooped down and then I could see neither her nor Big Boy. I screamed. The wind must have carried my voice. She stood up, turned, and waved. The wind blew her long hair across her face. I pointed beyond her. She looked back at me, blankly, rain streaming down her face.

Sykes had disappeared.

I beckoned to her and gestured toward the park gate, up the hill, frantically motioning for her to follow me. She looked at me, then back over her shoulder, nodded and, for once, obeyed. Big Boy barked and rushed ahead of her. It seemed to take forever to climb back up the rocky hillside. Halfway up, the dog bounded past me, nearly knocking me over. The sleeve of my parka snagged on an overgrown blackberry cane. I ripped the sleeve loose and made a mad dash up the last steep, brush-covered incline, onto the road. I looked back. Elyse was a few yards behind me. I glanced over to the left and saw Sykes headed our way. He could see me, but probably couldn't see Elyse.

I grabbed her arm and hauled her up onto the paved surface and over to the Volvo. I fumbled for the key, unlocked the car, and jerked the doors open.

"Get in the backseat with the dog and get down on the floor. Quick!"

She and the dog climbed in. I threw the Volvo into drive, expecting to hear the first bullet crashing through one of the windows. I made a tire-squealing run onto West Side Road, where I thought we'd have a better chance of losing Sykes than on the open road above the water. I figured we had maybe ten seconds before he'd be on our tail.

Ten seconds on a freeway is one thing; ten seconds uphill on West Side Road at dusk in a winter storm is another, but we made it in less than a minute to the Mt. Dallas intersection. I momentarily considered turning and making a run for Nick's place, then discarded the notion. It was all uphill and virtually unpopulated. If Sykes saw us turn, there would be an encore of Campbell Sawyer's accident. Or worse.

Seconds before we passed the Halcyon Hills development, I saw the glow of headlights climbing the hill behind us. I cursed the storm that had turned the night black as pitch, jammed my foot on the accelerator and handed the cell phone to Elyse.

"Call 4141. Tell the dispatcher where we are and that we're heading for the Port. We're going to make a run for *DragonSpray*. Have the sheriff or a deputy meet us there. Then call Rebecca and tell her where we'll be."

"Why not 911?" She peered over the back of the seat.

"Just do it, for God's sake! And *stay* on the floor." I had no time to explain that 911 doesn't work on cell phones on San Juan Island.

We were doing seventy in a forty-five zone, careening down the hill above the county park when I made a quick decision, doused the lights at the last minute and threw the wheel into a skidding turn onto the one-lane road that wound down to the park office. The only light to guide us was the night-light in the office. I skidded to a stop between the office and the water, saw a set of headlights fly down the hill and rush past the park entrance.

I inhaled deeply and tried to control my trembling hands. The red taillights climbed the next hill and disappeared. Our only escape would be to double back on West Side Road and hope Sykes didn't discover our ploy. I crawled back up to the road, put on the low beams and turned right.

I expected to see pursuing headlights around every hairpin curve above Haro Strait, but the rearview mirror reflected only blackness. Where the hell was the deputy? The hard rain on the windshield had become slush and Big Boy started whining. The long run downhill on Bailer Hill was far too open to attempt.

I made a sharp turn onto Wold Road, where I had to reduce my speed or risk ending up in a ditch.

"Did you reach the sheriff?" I asked.

"The dispatcher said the sheriff is still trying to get back from Waldron, but it's blowing forty-five knots over there. The deputy went out to Rebecca's, but nobody's heard from him since. She'll keep trying."

Waldron Island lies ten miles or so north of Friday Harbor. A return trip would require crossing President's Channel and San Juan Channel, both of which could become angry inland seas in a storm.

"What the hell were you doing out there, Elyse? I told you to stay out of sight!" I glanced over my shoulder. Big Boy was reclining on the seat, white face alert, huge pink tongue hanging from his mouth. Elyse had folded her thin frame into the small space behind the seat.

"I'm sorry. I had to look for my bracelet. It's all I had left of Gypsy's Legend." Her voice was that of a penitent child. My mind flashed on the antique gold-link charm bracelet she'd been wearing when she first came to my office.

"The horse your father sold?"

"Uh-huh."

I turned onto San Juan Valley Road and reduced my speed. My client's muffled voice had become tearful.

". . . had to find the bracelet . . . all I had left . . . my grandmother . . . when I won the Grand Championship."

I tried to listen to what she was saying and watched the headlights coming over the rise behind me. Pushing the Volvo up to seventy-five, I prayed the deer were smart enough to stay out of the road, braked momentarily at Douglas Road, noticed that the road was becoming icy, and barreled on up the hill, praying the Volvo wouldn't skid. The headlights behind us had turned off somewhere.

"The bracelet belonged to my grandmother. She

had it when she was a little girl. Every time I won a trophy, she added a charm. I thought I had lost it."

"It might have cost you your life." *And still might,* I thought grimly. *Mine, too.* I checked the rearview mirror. Anyone clever enough to have pulled off three murders must be smart enough to find us, a lone car on a deserted county road. Elyse's voice was rising from the floor behind me.

"My father is a total control freak, and I will never, ever go home with him. He's a complete racist and he hated Julio because he was Mexican. His family were immigrants and he married my mother because she was good Anglo-American stock, white, Christian and Episcopalian, and could trace her ancestors back to the *Mayflower.* When I married Julio, my father thought his whole house of cards would come tumbling down. He was furious when I got pregnant and he was happy when Julio was killed. He didn't care if we *never* found the killer."

Fortunately, she didn't know the half of it. Coming up the hill, I saw headlights about to pull out from the airport road and I lay on the horn. The lights came to a sudden halt. We flew past. I'd told Jared and Rebecca we were going down to the Port and it still seemed like the safest option.

The sheriff was probably still stranded over on Waldron and there was no word from the deputy. If Sykes had been trailing Elyse, it was conceivable he knew where my office was. I could head for the sheriff's office, but there would be no one there except for Angela. *'Spray* was the safest place, if we could make it down to the Port.

I turned right on Caines, left on Argyle. No headlights followed. The town lay quiet and deserted in the icy rain and wind. In the parking lot above the Port, I eased the Volvo into an empty space, cut the engine and headlights, and waited. No van had followed us into the lot. The only sounds were the rising wind and the sleet on the windshield.

"We've got to make a run for it. Can we leave the dog here?"

"He'll start barking."

"Okay," I said between clenched teeth. "We're going through the gate at the Yacht Club, down the steps and around toward the customs office. The new dock will take us right out onto 'F' and 'G.' Ready?" Without waiting for an answer, I hauled Elyse and the dog out of the Volvo. Bent almost double against the wind, the Beretta held low at my side, we virtually crawled through the gate and down the icy steps, the wind and sleet beating against our faces. No southwest wind this. The northern gales had arrived and the sleet was turning the docks into sheets of ice. I slowed my pace, thinking of the frigid water on either side of the narrow floating walkways, and kept carefully to the center of the docks, followed by Elyse and, I assumed, the big dog.

The wind was pushing *'Spray* hard against her fenders, which were creaking with every gust. A loose halyard flapped loudly in the rigging. With icy hands, I opened the lifelines, helped Elyse scramble on board the lunging boat and glanced behind me, looking for Big Boy, wondering how the hell I was going to get a giant dog on board. At the same instant that I spied the shadowy figure approaching on the icy dock, I smelled the pungent scent of musk aftershave, and froze.

43

It is impossible for me to recount exactly what occurred in the four or five seconds following Sykes's arrival on the icy dock.

While I had the Beretta ready, I did not use it, and probably would not have survived an attempt to use it. Some of what occurred remains crystal clear; some is forever frozen in slow motion. I can't say whether Sykes slipped and momentarily lost his footing, or whether Big Boy, lagging behind, had seen Sykes approach and sensed some menace.

I do know that one second I was standing in front of the dark figure whose face was dimly lighted by the lights on the dock, and asking, *Well, MacKinnon, how are you going to get out of this one? Is this how it's all going to end, you and the porcelain-blonde on the bottom of the harbor?* and the next second Big Boy rushed from out of the darkness, Elyse screamed, I heard a splash, then a barely audible cry.

". . . can't swim."

I will never understand why Big Boy didn't follow his target into the icy waves. He didn't, but stood on the end of the dock barking with fury at the struggling figure in the water. Without knowing whether I intended to shoot the drowning assassin or haul him back onto the dock, I wiped the icy rain off my face and scrambled onto *'Spray* in search of the spotlight I kept in the cockpit. As I switched it on and directed the light toward the unintelligible cries, *'Spray* heeled sharply to port and a tall figure climbed on board.

"Why don't you let me take care of this?" It was Wilhelm Muehler and the gun in his hands was aimed at the thrashing figure in the water.

"I don't think so, Mr. Muehler." I felt another strong gust of wind behind me and *'Spray* heeled sharply again. Almost by reflex, I reached and jerked the traveler line out of the jam cleat and let the wind slam the boom into Muehler's shoulder. He cried out, staggered backwards, and fell across the coaming. His weapon flew to the sole of the cockpit. I made a dive, grabbed the gun and threw it overboard. Muehler struggled to right himself, one hand holding his injured shoulder, his face contorted in pain, rage and frustration.

"You don't understand!" he screamed at me. He turned toward his daughter. "You ungrateful little girl! I did it for you! It was all for you!"

I looked at Elyse, her pale face and hair streaming with rain. She stared at her father, silent, trying to comprehend. She shook her head, either to get the rain out of her face or in an attempt to understand the significance of her father's words. Then her gaze jerked to the thrashing figure on the end of the floating dock. A look of horror came over her face.

Speechless, we watched as Sykes lunged out of the water and grabbed for Henry's old yellow power cord that lay along the dock. I stared at the gun in my hand, stared at the drenched figure. Only I understood Sykes's shriek of pain when his hands clamped over the frayed section of the cord. His face contorted, and with no further cry, dragging the yellow power cord with him, Julio Montenegro's murderer fell to his watery demise.

"Wilhelm Muehler, you are under arrest." I tore my gaze away from the choppy black waves and stared at the deputy, who was holding a gun on Elyse's father. Jared was standing immediately behind the deputy.

"For what?" Muehler spat out.

"For conspiracy to commit murder, to start with, and I'm sure we can go on from there. You have the right to remain silent. You have the right to an attorney. Anything you say can and will be used against you in a court of law."

Elyse stared at her father, final realization obliterating all bonds of filial affection. A long, long look of such pure abhorrence and icy valediction that I felt the hairs rise on the back of my neck. Without a word, she moved past her father, climbed stiffly down onto the dock, and began walking away into the black night, followed by the big wet dog.

44

The cold wind and sleet were gone, the ice on the docks had melted. On Wednesday morning I spied a rectangular window of blue in an otherwise gray sky, a sure forecast of more strong winds to come before the high-pressure area lying off the coast arrived just in time for Thanksgiving. Nick was coming up tonight. We'd spend the night at his place and head over to Victoria tomorrow on *DragonSpray,* sure to be a two-reef sail.

Last night at Angela and Matt's old house on Griffin Bay, after Muehler had been led away to the county jail to await the arrival of the FBI agents and we'd delivered Elyse back to the ranch—and after Cora Mae had been advised that the crisis was over— we'd tried to reconstruct the bizarre chain of events that had been set in motion when Wilhelm Muehler had hired Jamie Sykes to eliminate an undesirable son-in-law. Whether Muehler had also masterminded the subsequent assassinations, or whether it was a case of an assassin run amok, as Muehler had loudly insisted all the way up the lunging, icy dock last night, might never be ascertained. The files I'd copied from Muehler's hard disk in San Francisco were more than incriminating, and the one individual who could have verified or challenged Muehler's story was dead.

All seemed to be domestic bliss in the Petersen household, and Jared and I left about one a.m.

"Any pithy Holmesian quotes to close the case with, Dr. Watson?" I asked.

He was silent for a minute and then smiled. "The only one that seems relevant is terribly simple, I'm afraid. 'Dogs don't make mistakes.' " He gave me a hug and headed off for his car.

Sykes's body washed up on Turn Island the next morning. Deputy Fountain was successful in tracing the license plates on the dark-red van to a hot-car ring operating out of Spokane. Sykes's silenced Beeman Mini .380, as well as Muehler's 9-millimeter Luger that I had tossed overboard, were retrieved by a diver from the mud beneath *DragonSpray*. Based on my call to the Berkeley PD from Coeur d'Alene, the FBI had searched Sykes's cabin in Idaho while he returned to the island to tie up loose ends. It hadn't been hard to get warrants for his and Muehler's arrests. As it turned out, only one was needed.

The anonymous half-million-dollar insurance policy on Julio had finally been explained when I'd emptied my briefcase that morning and the other floppy disk I'd stolen from Muehler—the Quicken 2000 backup— fell out. It contained his accounting data files for the current year. With the assistance of the "adolf" password, Zelda was able to print out the check register that contained the incriminating entries: a payment to a New York insurance broker for the premium on the policy and an earlier entry to a San Francisco doctor for $5,000. Both entries included the same memo: "j.m. policy."

A message had arrived from Sergeant Wineheart: Felipe De los Santos was hiding somewhere in the Andes Mountains of Colombia. The IRS was most unhappy with him. Ditto the Drug Enforcement Agency. Ditto girlfriend Nancy, who had invested fifty G's in Felipe's import business.

There had also been an e-mail from Melissa: *We got to Mendocino last night. Gilberto loves it here. He's helping Grandma make pecan tarts. It's okay that you didn't come down. Have a great Thanksgiving. Love, Melissa.*

I leaned back in my chair, put my feet up on the old desk. The last of the golden leaves from the big-leaf maple outside my window were drifting down. I watched them blowing along the street and thought about Elyse. She had stopped by to say thank you; she was going to stay on at the ranch and help Gregg, so Rebecca could leave after Christmas with Lars, destination New Zealand. Which reminded me that my only investigative loose end was the still-missing heir, Harrison Petrovsky, last reported leaving New Zealand aboard *Ocean Dancer* with his Tongon soulmate. I fired off an e-mail to the Kiwi P.I. requesting an update.

A soaring soprano voice drifted up the stairs accompanied by the buttery scent of fresh popcorn. I descended to find Zelda, her hair the color of a raven's wing, scowling at her monitor. I filled a bowl with white kernels and went to sit on the corner of her desk, which was covered with culinary magazines. She was finishing a phone conversation.

"That was Doris," she said.

"Sykes's neighbor? "

"Yeah. She's going to adopt Snowy, Sykes's cat. She says the cat was practically living with her anyway."

"Are you and Sheldon doing turkey for Thanksgiving?"

"Sheldon and I had a fight. He thinks I'm unstable." She frowned and scratched her knee above the cast. "Boris is coming over to help me do the turkey."

"Who's Boris?"

"I met him while I was waiting for Sykes at the Silver Ass. He lives in Vancouver and he's ex-KGB. He doesn't know much English. Is Russian hard to learn?"

The Second Law of Thermodynamics is that everything tends toward disorder, and chaos theorists have
posited that the flap of a butterfly's wings in Brazil
may precipitate a tornado in Texas.

It may be so.

With the clarity of hindsight, I admit that the angle
of breaking waves on the Bering Sea in December or
the strength of the bar brandy in Henley's Bar on Ko-
diak Island may have precipitated the lamentable
events that transpired on a windy and overcast March
night in the San Juan Archipelago of Washington
State two decades later.

It's not impossible.

Twenty years in law enforcement and private investigation have convinced me that life is nothing if not
disorderly and chaotic.

Chaos theory and butterfly wings were not, however, the focus of my thoughts as I climbed the wide
stairs and trudged down the second-floor corridor of
the old brick San Juan County Courthouse around
9:00 A.M. on the first Tuesday in May.

Nor was I pondering the ugly results of my investigation of the parents of an abused child currently in
protective custody in Friday Harbor.

I was, in fact, petulantly dwelling on the abrupt ending
to the bucolic weekend I'd spent with my lover, Nicholas
Anastazi, sailing the waters of Trincomali Channel and
rocking at anchor in Montague Harbor on Galiano Island. And as I dwelt—for the fiftieth time—on the fact
that Nick had deserted me at Montague to fly back to

Seattle to the aid and comfort of his ex-wife, who had been arrested for reckless endangerment and Driving Under the Influence on Saturday night, I was nearly knocked on my fanny by a body that came hurtling backward out of the County Commissioners Office.

"This island is not a whore! And it's bloody well time you pimps stopped trying to rent it to the highest bidder! Over my dead body are a bunch of jerks in Gore-Tex jumpsuits going to take over American Camp. There are eaglets in the nests and probably a hundred newborn kit foxes on the prairie. Are you all a bunch of *dunderheads*?"

It was the very angry figure of Abigail Leedle. A thick plait of white hair hung down her back and her tall, sinewy body was clad in faded blue denim overalls. Abigail was a wildlife photographer, an octogenarian who'd spent her life among these rocky, forested islands. I clutched at the wall for support, regained my balance and recovered my worn leather portfolio from the floor. Abigail threw a rucksack over one sloping shoulder, clenched her jaw and nodded at me with narrowed blue eyes.

"Sorry, Scotia, I didn't mean to knock you over."

"Not a problem, Abby."

"Mrs. Leedle, please come back so we can talk about this." James Melbourne, the dark-haired, bearded commissioner from Orcas Island, stepped into the hallway, his voice pleading. "They won't disturb the foxes or the eagles. And they've promised to restore the prairie and the beach when they're done filming."

"Horse puckey." Abby snorted and struggled into a brown canvas barn jacket. Shoulders hunched, she stalked down the hall toward the stairway. "I'll see you in court, James," she threw over her shoulder. "Your daddy would roll in his grave if he knew what you've agreed to."

She shook her head in disgust. Slapping her sandals along the corridor, she disappeared down the stairs.

Melbourne gave me a what're-you-going-to-do look, shrugged, retreated inside the commissioners' office and closed the door.

Abby wasn't alone in her outrage and I replayed

her histrionic outburst while I turned the surveillance report over to the Prosecuting Attorney's assistant and headed back down to the lower level.

The BOCC's decision to allow On The Edge, a manufacturer of upscale outdoor wear, to do a catalog photo shoot on the pristine prairies above Haro Straight was not a popular one. Last week's *Letters to the Editor* in the three island weeklies bore vociferous testimony to the unanimity of feeling that the commissioners' decision was a capitulation to the tourism interests on the island.

American Camp, the area that On The Edge had staked out for their photo shoot, is located within the island's national historic park, where, in 1859, the U.S. and Great Britain narrowly avoided an all-out war. The provocation for the conflict concerned the shooting of an English pig by an American farmer who was attempting to cultivate potatoes in the midst of the British-owned Hudson's Bay sheep pasture. When the American farmer refused to make fair restitution for the pig, he was threatened with arrest and the 9th U.S. Infantry was dispatched to San Juan Island. The Brits responded by sending three Royal Navy warships and the two sides ended up in a twelve-year joint occupation of the island—the Americans on the open prairies above the strait, the Brits in an encampment on the edge of Garrison Bay, ten miles to the north.

The porcine dispute was ultimately arbitrated by Kaiser Wilhelm of Germany, who, in 1872, awarded the San Juan Islands to the United States. On which date the population of the islands—not including the garrisons—was 184. The conflict and its resolution are celebrated annually in a Pig War Barbecue at the San Juan County Fairgrounds.

Two restored white frame buildings remain from the long-ago American encampment, situated above the windblown prairie grasses that are home to the dens of small recently restored, red San Juan foxes.

I hurried across the courthouse parking lot, shivering in the cold wind blowing up off the harbor. Large, ominous gray clouds scudded overhead. It was a day halfway between winter and spring. Rain was predicted for tonight. I wondered why On The Edge hadn't waited until summer for the photo shoot. Or perhaps they assumed that spring arrived in April, as it did two thousand miles to the south. In the San Juans, we were lucky if the cold rain stopped long enough for the 4th of July parade.

I have a small second-story office in the historic, brown-shingled Olde Gazette Building on Guard Street, where I do mostly routine investigations for lawyers and insurance companies. The first floor of the building is occupied by Soraya Brown, a naturopathic physician, and Zelda Jones, who runs New Millennium Communications and provides me with computer research in connection with my investigations.

When I stepped into New Millennium, I was greeted by the scent of freshly brewed coffee and an operatic aria—Puccini, I think—neither of which was unusual. Nor was it uncommon to find a handsome man lounging in the upholstered chair beside Zelda's scarred walnut desk. In the years that I've had an office in the building, there have been a number of men lounging beside her desk, some more smitten by my carrot-haired assistant than others. What *was* extraordinary was that Zelda was gazing into the eyes of this particular bearded, dark-haired man and simpering. When this carrot-haired feminist par excellence simpers, something curious is in the wind.

"The crew party is scheduled for a week from Saturday," the man said. "I know Edie needs help." The object of Zelda's simper reached for a Post-it pad on her desk and scribbled a number. "Call her. She likes to do exotic parties. She'll be delighted to hear from you."

The man unfolded his six-foot-something frame from the chair and extended his hand to me. I took in the lightly tanned face, the windblown hair, the thick creamy turtleneck sweater under the elegant black leather jacket. Not exactly local attire, even if he was wearing wrinkled and less-than-clean blue jeans. I returned his handshake and gazed into the brown eyes fringed with long lashes.

And resisted the inclination to simper.

"Ms. MacKinnon? I'm M. J. Carlyle. I called last week about an appointment. I believe it was for nine o'clock?" His smile was warm and full of charm and he looked astonishingly like a model in a recent Got Milk ad, sans the mustache.

M. J. Carlyle. The man who'd called last Thursday as I was rushing out to get ready for the weekend. I glanced at the clock. *Merde*! Forty-five minutes late.

"My apologies, Mr. Carlyle. I got held up at the courthouse." More accurately, knocked down at the courthouse. "Please come upstairs." I ignored the mail in my cubby and my need for a cup of coffee and led the way up to my office.

He followed me up the narrow stairs and stood while I unlocked the door that said *S. J. MacKinnon Investigations and Research*. I switched on the overhead light, draped my polar fleece shirt on the coat rack, and motioned him to one of the white wicker chairs beside the desk. I'd forgotten to turn off the small radiator on Thursday, and the warmth provided a pleasant counterpoint to the wind-tossed maple tree outside the old casement window.

Carlyle declined my offer to hang up his jacket, placed his attaché case beside his left leg, and glanced around the office. My office is modest in the extreme. I've never replaced the old oak desk abandoned by the last tenant and the wicker chairs would never make it into the pages of *Architectural Digest*. I was also chagrined to see that the leaves of the tall ficus in the corner were turning yellow. When plants do that, I can never figure out if it's because of too much water or not enough water. I stole a glance at M. J. Carlyle's three-hundred-dollar leather jacket and wondered if he wished he'd called a more upscale P.I.

I reached for a yellow-lined pad and pen. "What can I do for you, Mr. Carlyle?"

"M. J., please. I grew up here. It makes me feel old to be called Mister." The smile had disappeared from his handsome face and he took a deep breath. "As you probably know, I'm with the crew from On The

Edge. But the matter I wanted to see you about is my sister Tina. Tina Breckenridge. I don't know if you knew her. She disappeared in March."

I stared at him, trying to remember the details I'd read in one of the papers: the unexplained disappearance of a local woman. What I did remember was that M. J. Carlyle was the creative director for On The Edge, the group that had sent Abigail Leedle into a temperamental tailspin. His name had been in several editions of the *Gazette* while the question of whether or not to give the permit had been bitterly debated. I didn't know that Tina Breckenridge was his sister.

"An accident with her sailboat, wasn't it? The boat was found but she wasn't?"

He nodded. "The boat was found drifting over near Sucia, but they never found her body. And it was no accident, never mind what the official record says!"

"How do you know?"

"Tina was an incredible sailor and an excellent swimmer. She knew boats inside and out and she didn't take risks. We both grew up on a sailboat. She's built boats, she's raced boats, and she did the single-handed Trans-Pac twice. There wasn't even a storm the night she disappeared."

"If she didn't fall overboard, what do you think happened?"

He reached for his attaché case, placed it on his lap, unsnapped the latch, extracted two pieces of paper, and handed them to me.

The first was a photocopy of the *Friday Gazette* article on the details of Tina Breckenridge's disappearance and the offical abandonment of the search for her body. The second was an e-mail message from *pleiades@island.net* to *carlyle@ontheedge.com.*

> *Big brother: Could we get together when you come up for the hearing? My little problem has become a big problem. Love, T.*

I glanced at the *Gazette* piece. The e-mail was dated March 1, two days before the *Alcyone* had been found.